a little help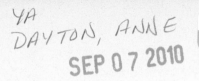
from my friends

a little help from my friends

a miracle girls novel

Anne Dayton and May Vanderbilt

FaithWords

NEW YORK BOSTON NASHVILLE

FaithWords
Hachette Book Group
237 Park Avenue
New York, NY 10017

Visit our Web site at www. faithwords.com.

Printed in the United States of America

First Edition: October 2009
10 9 8 7 6 5 4 3 2 1

FaithWords is a division of Hachette Book Group, Inc.
The FaithWords name and logo are trademarks of Hachette Book Group, Inc.

Library of Congress Cataloging-in-Publication Data

Dayton, Anne.
  A little help from my friends / Anne Dayton & May Vanderbilt.—1st ed.
     p. cm.
  Summary: Returning for their junior year of high school in Half Moon Bay, the Miracle Girls—four friends who share a bond of faith—protest the firing of a beloved teacher, while Miracle Girl Zoe struggles with family, boyfriend, and financial issues.
  ISBN 978-0-446-40757-1
  [1. Friendship—Fiction.   2. High schools—Fiction.   3. Schools—Fiction.
4. Family problems—Fiction.   5. Christian life—Fiction.   6. Half Moon Bay (Calif.)—Fiction.]   I. Vanderbilt, May.   II. Title.
  PZ7.D33847Li 2009
  [Fic]—dc22
                              2009001242

acknowledgments

Anne: A special thanks to the real Mrs. Narveson, for teaching American History like no one else could.

May: Thanks to both of my families for being patient when I don't call as often as I'd like, show up with wet hair, and wear out-of-date clothes. Your understanding helps me stay sane; your support means everything.

We also owe a huge debt of gratitude to Claudia Cross, our heaven-sent agent, and Anne Horch, our brilliant editor. And to Seth Fishman and Katie Schaber, the indispensable masterminds behind the scenes. And to the rest of the devoted people at FaithWords who make our books a success: Rolf Zettersten, Harry Helm, Jody Waldrup, Jamie Slover, Dylan Hoke, Grace Hernandez, Pamela Clements, Amy Biter, Jana Burson, Laini Brown, Preston Cannon, Miriam Parker, and April Frazier.

a little help
from my friends

I *t's seriously messed up to live next door to your boyfriend.* This summer Christine pointed this out at least a dozen times, and now as Marcus's panicked voice comes through my cell phone, it's her voice that rings in my mind.

"Zoe, there's a strange trailer in your backyard!" Marcus says. He's breathless, as if he just ran inside to call me—and it wouldn't be the first time. When you live next door to the Farcuses, you come to expect these calls.

I am dating Marcus Farcus: lover of board games, player of shiny brass instruments, collector of insects, and monitor of neighborhood goings-on.

"I was taking a swim, and I saw a trailer go by on the dirt road." Marcus is very dutiful about getting in his laps in his backyard pool, though you'd never tell by looking at him that he exercises or spends any time in the sun. His entire family has huge heads and pale, thin bodies, kind of like a family of vanilla lollipops. "Maybe you should check with your parents to make sure everything is okay?"

"I'll look into it and then come say hi. Does that work?"

"Excellent." He lets out a breath. "I'll see you soon."

I smile and snap my phone shut. A lot of the kids at school don't understand Marcus, but I'm pretty shy myself, so I know that when he calls about a strange trailer, he's partly just looking for an excuse to pick up the phone.

"Dreamy?" I call out to my mom, but she's not in the kitchen. My parents are total ex-hippies who insist I call them by their first names. "Ed?" A silence echoes back. They must be working in the garden or something. I shrug, tug the sliding glass door open, and step out onto the deck. I scan the area around the patio, but I don't see anything, so I start down the path that leads through the woods.

When I was little, I always felt a sense of excitement when I walked down this path. Winding under the tall trees, through the woods, it seemed like I was stepping onto another planet. Once you get a little ways into the forest, the house disappears from sight, and it feels like your own private world. I used to search for fairies as I walked along this path, certain I would see them if I looked hard enough.

Of course, things are different now. There was a time when we owned thirty acres out here, but bit by bit, my parents have sold off sections of land. Last year they sold the lot next to us to the Farcuses, then watched in horror as they bulldozed the ancient redwoods to build their new house. It's worked out all right for me having Marcus next door, but I miss having a whole forest to explore.

As I wind my way down the dirt road, I see the spot where the pond usually is. It's dried up now, no more than a puddle, thanks to a couple of scorching months. It doesn't rain a lot here even in good years, but this summer our town has gone from a mellow golden color to parched, depressing brown. Not great if you're in the landscaping business, like Ed.

"Dreamy?" My voice echoes, bouncing off the trees, but

I don't hear any response. The hair on my arms raises, and I walk faster. The only other place they could be is the horse stable. What if something happened? I know better than anyone how dangerous those horses are. What if what Marcus saw wasn't a trailer but an ambulance?

"Ed?" I try to remain calm but can't stop myself from breaking into a jog, dodging tree branches and jumping over roots. There, in the distance, I can just make out the top of the stable, and I run toward it, but as I get closer, I hear a low wailing sound. I sprint down the path. "Dreamy! Ed!" *Please, God, let them be okay.*

The stable comes fully into view, and my breath catches in my throat. There's the trailer Marcus saw, glinting in the sunlight in front of the open stable door. Strange noises sound from inside, so I run to the back door and freeze.

"Dreamy, please," Ed says, pleading. His face is red, and his eyes are glassy with tears. I step out of their line of sight and peek around the door frame. What's going on? It's dark inside the small stable, but the light streaming through the roof's irregular and warped planks casts a thatched pattern on the scattered hay.

"I'm sorry," Dreamy says, leading Mama Cass, her golden palomino, out of the stall into the main aisle of the stable. "I really am. But it's either her or us, Ed. Please try to understand." She pats Mama Cass's mane. Dreamy's voice is low and calm, but I can see from here that she's upset. She walks toward the open stable door, and I step back. "She's my horse. I'm not selling Dox yet." Dox is Ed's horse, and he unabashedly loves him more than the others—almost more than anything.

"We'll sell some more land." Ed runs his hand across his eyes and wipes the moisture on his dirty jeans. "We don't have to do this."

"Yes." Dreamy stops, turns to face Ed. "We do." There's an edge to her voice. "We have to sell the land anyway. It's not enough. Will you stop acting like a child and face the facts?" Mama Cass yanks her head away, and Dreamy rubs her soft muzzle to comfort her. "Horses are expensive. We're broke. We have to sell them, or we'll lose everything."

Ed makes a noise, but it sounds more like a wail than words.

They walk toward the front door, and I duck around behind the side of the building, trying to get air into my lungs. Since when are we that close to the poorhouse?

I sneak to the edge of the stable and peer down the long wall to watch as Dreamy leads her faithful horse into the bright sunlight. Mama Cass blinks and follows dutifully as she pulls her toward the trailer. A young woman jumps out of the cab of the truck and takes the lead line, and Dreamy lets go of the rope and rubs her hand over Mama Cass's smooth coat.

Part of me wants to run out and stop her. She can't sell our horses. Sure, I haven't ridden Alfalfa since the accident, but they're part of our family. Those horses mean the world to Ed.

"Wait!" Ed runs out of the stable, his eyes red, and I have to run to his side.

But I don't move. I can't make my feet go. Maybe it's because I know it's useless. Once Dreamy makes up her mind, it's not worth trying to change it. Maybe because I can see that even though she's trying to be rational, this is killing her too. She loves that horse more than anything, and we must be in dire straits if she's willing to part with her. And part of me stays here, out of the way, because somewhere deep down, I know the horse isn't really what's at stake.

"Now you be good." Dreamy bites her lip and runs her hand along Mama Cass's back as the handler leads her away.

"What about Nick?" Ed says, clenching his fists at his sides. "We're a family of four. We need four horses. Dreamy, please?"

Dreamy crosses her arms over her chest as Mama Cass steps onto the metal ramp that leads into the trailer.

"News flash, Ed. Your son lives halfway across the country, and your daughter hasn't been near a horse in two years." My cheeks flush. "She says she'll never ride again. You're not going to change her mind."

With each step up the ramp, a metallic clang rings out.

"It's time to accept it."

Ed watches, opening and closing his fists, as the handler secures the horse and closes the back door of the trailer. She climbs into the cab, and the engine roars to life. A moment later, the truck is driving up the rutted dirt road.

"We're not going to be riding as a family anymore."

I bite my lip so I won't dare say anything. I heard exactly what Dreamy said, didn't miss a single syllable, but somehow once it left her mouth it hung in the air as something different entirely. It sounded like what she really said was we're not a family anymore.

Ed kicks the stable door with his worn work boot and storms off toward the last bit of thick woods we own, muttering under his breath.

I stay frozen for a while, training my eyes on Ed's back as it disappears out of sight. I turn and notice the sun falling on Dreamy, illuminating her tense shoulders. This long, hot summer has taken a toll on all of us, drying up the land, my dad's business, our money . . . and us. Our family is falling apart.

I watch, rooted in place, as Dreamy starts to walk back up the road. Even from here I can see the tears on her cheeks as she heads toward the house, and I know I have to do whatever I can to make us whole again.

2

The first day of junior year is hardly off to a rousing start. I was late to the kickoff assembly because Ed's car wouldn't start this morning. I hardly got any sleep because Dreamy and Ed were fighting in hushed, angry whispers late into the night, which is stupid because, hello, I can hear them. Never mind that my locker is in a dusty corner of the crumbling J-wing, near exactly none of my classes. And this morning I met the new English teacher, Mrs. Dietrich, who wore her hair in a tight bun, announced that she wouldn't put up with any "roughhousing," and promptly assigned us a paper on Homer's *The Odyssey*, which, by the way, is not even written in real English.

I make it to third period with several minutes to spare. Tragically, this is the best thing to happen to me today.

"Red."

I turn to the left and start. "Christine!" The desks in this classroom are arranged in a giant U shape several desks thick, and Christine is sitting at a desk at the bottom of the U, farthest from the teacher's podium. She waves me over, and I plop down in a blue plastic chair on her right. "I didn't know you were in this class." This year is already looking better.

"They forgot to put me in art, so I had to go to the office and get my classes rearranged this morning." Christine shrugs. "American history, here we come." Seats begin to fill up, and I recognize most of the faces around me. I've been in school with the same people since kindergarten.

She leans in and whispers to me. "Can you believe who sat next to me?"

To her left, I spot Kayleen, the blonde princess who stole Andrew Cutchins away from Christine last year. In her back-to-school outfit, Kayleen could be mistaken for a Hollywood starlet.

"I'm not moving." Christine crosses her arms on her chest. "She can move. I was here first." Kayleen yawns dramatically.

The teacher, Mrs. Narveson, according to the printout of my class schedule, is standing at the front podium, reading a book as if she doesn't notice her classroom filling up. She's short and a little plump with kinky blonde hair.

"Did Riley bug you about that Full Moon Party yet?" Christine asks, her voice returning to a normal volume. "I saw her in the parking lot before school, and she told me to convince you to go."

A few students shuffle and take the last of the open seats, but I can't help but notice that no one is willing to sit by me. Typical.

"Yeah." I inspect my nails for a second. "We'll see." The Full Moon Party is a beach bonfire held during the first full moon of football season. It's a tradition for the students of Marina Vista. Correction: it's a tradition for the *popular* students of Marina Vista. Riley is one of the anointed at this school. She could hang with the in crowd if she wanted, and sometimes she does, but for some reason she spends most of her time with us.

"It's not for a few weeks anyway. Tyler said it might be cool."
Christine doodles a quick picture of the moon on her paper.
"I might check it out, but I—"

The bell rings, cutting her off.

"WE ARE ALL PRODUCTS OF OUR HISTORIES,"
Mrs. Narveson booms, raising her pointer finger in the air.
We stop talking and snap our eyes to the front. "You can't
understand a person without understanding their past."

What is wrong with this teacher? Isn't she going to intro-
duce herself? What about roll? Doesn't she, like, have to take
roll? People sit up straight and turn to the podium—if just to
watch the spectacle going on.

"Who you are today and who you will become are in large
part due to your history. Likewise, you can't understand our
fine nation without understanding how we got here."

A noise interrupts Mrs. Narveson's bizarre performance.
The door opens, and the whole class turns their heads quickly,
on high alert. What now? There, standing in the doorway, is a
tall guy I've never seen before.

"Another hapless victim of history." Mrs. Narveson shakes
her head sadly and motions for him to come in.

He steps inside the room with a bored look in his eyes and
intentionally lets the heavy door bang closed behind him.

"You must be Dean." She grabs a thin, black notebook
from her podium and makes a little mark in it. "From New
York, right? I was warned about you."

My eyes widen, but this new guy, this Dean, doesn't even
flinch. He looks around the room with a sly grin on his face.

"Welcome to the story of humankind. Take a seat." Mrs.
Narveson points at the desk next to me, the last link in the U.

He threads his way through the desks, head held high, and I notice he carries a black messenger bag, not a giant backpack like the rest of the guys around here. I sit up a little straighter, suddenly conscious that I was slouching. He tosses a look my way that I can't read, then drops into the empty seat next to me. I hear whispering behind me. He crosses his arms over his chest, stretches his legs out in front of him, and immediately goes back to looking painfully bored.

Mrs. Narveson gives her head a little shake and then presses on. "The first thing you have to understand is that where you end up is primarily determined by where you begin." Mrs. Narveson nods as if this statement is an obvious fact, though my head is spinning a little. "As of this moment, you begin your journey with the person next to you. That's your partner for the first semester. You'll collaborate on several projects over the course of the semester, and they'll comprise 50 percent of your final grade. Together you will make history." She laughs, a little maniacally, then begins pointing to people to assign groups.

"You and you," she says, using her index and middle finger to indicate two kids in the front. "You and you." I flash Christine a thumbs-up, and she gives me the rock-n-roll sign. "You and you." History is my favorite subject, and Christine and I already know we make a great team. "You," she points at Christine, and I nod to show her I understand, "and you." But she's not pointing at me, she's pointing at Kayleen, on the other side of Christine. She's being paired with her ex-crush's new blonde girlfriend?

I gape at her, then count the chairs in the row. Christine raises her hand to protest, but Mrs. Narveson ignores her.

One and two go together, three and four, five and . . . oh no. Christine is six. I'm seven and that makes—"you and you"— me and Dean a team.

Dean smirks at me. I glare down at my desk, boring my eyes into the table. What kind of cracked system is this? This guy's attitude is already wearing on me, and we're only five minutes into the first class.

"Wait." Mrs. Narveson steps back and puts her hand to her chin. "Did I do that right?" She starts pointing at groups again, silently recalculating, and I watch her, hoping. Maybe she counted wrong, and I can be with Christine after all. But when she goes through the class again, nothing changes. She nods, mumbles about losing her mind, and finishes counting off pairs, then walks back to the front of the room.

"That's it. Your lot in life has been cast." Everybody groans, and a sinking feeling creeps over me. This deadbeat is going to make me do all the work. "If you don't like it, maybe next time you'll have the good fortune to be born into another time, or into a better family, or on a different continent. For better or for worse, most of your life—who your parents are, when you live, where you live, what kind of cultural restrictions affect you—is determined by things you have no control over. It's been this way throughout the history of the world, and our nation in particular. Welcome to history, people."

She walks to the blackboard and begins to write in big, broad, uneven letters: HISTORY IS ABOUT PEOPLE. FAIL TO UNDERSTAND THEM AT YOUR OWN PERIL.

This brings a few chuckles from around the room, but Mrs. Narveson turns and smiles at us knowingly, then continues writing. She's a little wacky. I mean, *peril*? I glance at Dean, who is drumming his fingers on his desk. A sense of dread fills my stomach. My history project partner is some kind of burnout.

"Pencils out. It's time to hit the books. Summer is officially over." Mrs. Narveson begins to scratch out the words, "Build-a-Nation Project—20% of Your Grade."

I furiously take notes about the assignment. The first project is to make our own country from the ground up, meaning we'll have to dream up a flag, formulate a type of government, and even draft a constitution. With each new element Mrs. Narveson adds to the list, my spirits sink a little further.

Christine stops pretending to take notes and scratches a message to me at the top of her paper instead. "Your new partner," I read slowly, squinting my eyes to make out the lettering as she prints neatly, "looks like a snob. Must rethink my plan to move to Manhattan."

I sneak a quick peek at Dean, who's now leaning back in his chair watching me, arms crossed over his chest, a knowing smile on his face. I can already see what he's thinking. He's glad he got paired with the shy girl. He knows he can get me to do all the work for both of us, and I'll never tell.

Just great. Exactly what I need.

3

So, how does it feel to be back?" I flop onto the hood of Christine's silver beater and Riley scoots over a little to make room for me. The heat from the metal feels good on my back, and I close my eyes and let the sun warm my face.

After my rocky start to the day, things have started looking up quite a bit. I'm now first chair in the flute and piccolo section in band, and today was my first chance to enjoy that honor. At lunch no one even dared take our little broken picnic table because people know it belongs to the Miracle Girls. And the rest of my classes seem doable, no crazy teachers or weird partners. All in all, being a junior feels kind of . . . good.

"Junior year. Woo." Christine turns up her stereo, and an old rock song plays out over our little corner of the parking lot.

"It *is* nice being an upperclassman," Ana says, leaning against the cherry red frame of her Audi. She got it for her birthday in June and hasn't let one speck of food, one drop of liquid, or one muddy shoe enter its hallowed interior. My birthday is in a few days, but there's no way I'm getting a car. Ana holds her phone in front of her, texting furiously. "You have to admit it felt pretty awesome to sit on the other side of the gym at the rally this morning."

"Beats slumming it with the frosh." Christine pulls a pair of sunglasses out of her bag and slips them on.

"It's weird to have Michael at Marina Vista," Riley laughs. Her brother is a freshman this year, which is just crazy. He seems way too young to be in high school.

Ana pokes at the keypad again, her thumbs moving so fast that they're practically a blur.

"You're going to break that thing, Ana," Riley says.

"Dave is trying to cancel our date on Friday night," Ana says, typing again. After more than a year of pseudodating, Ana and Dave were finally allowed to go on actual dates after she turned sixteen. "For band practice or something. We're, uh, discussing." She slams her phone shut.

The sun glints off the windshield of cars scattered around the lot. This whole place looked so much bigger, more frightening, when we were freshmen. Now that we're older, it doesn't seem so scary at all. Perhaps we've gotten used to the pace of it, and the size, or maybe we know our way around and how it all works. Maybe we've been around long enough to know that everyone else is as confused as we are. Plus, we have each other.

A white Hummer slows next to our group, and the window rolls down. A sense of dread fills my stomach.

"My, my, my," Ashley Anderson, cheerleader and Riley's ex-best friend, leans out the driver's side window of her ridiculous vehicle. "Look at the Troll Patrol. Ana has an Audi." Ana rolls her eyes at Ashley. "Christine's hair doesn't look like puke"—to be fair, Christine's hair did sort of look like puke when it was green—"and Zoe shot up like a *weed*. You're really not even *fa*—"

I brace myself. *Don't say the* f *word. Don't say the* f *word.*

"I see you haven't lost that peppy spirit." Christine cuts her off and crosses her arms over her chest. Her smooth black hair gleams like vinyl in the sunlight.

I used to be a little overweight, but this summer I shot up almost overnight. All my jeans became high waters, my baby fat melted away, and I went from being the shortest Miracle Girl to the tallest.

"Looks like a lot has changed this summer." Ashley snaps her gum. "But what's going on with your head Mouseketeer? I thought you guys were going to wage some campaign to get her back?"

I see Ana tense up. Ashley is talking about Ms. Moore, who was just an English teacher at Marina Vista, but she came to mean so much more to us. At the end of last year the school board suspended her under very mysterious circumstances. She angered a well-connected parent, but no one knows how. This summer we tried to get people from our school to sign a petition to reinstate her, but everyone has been pretty apathetic about the whole thing.

"Don't you have some jock to drool over?" Christine smiles at Ashley.

Ashley watches us for a minute, but when no one else responds, she turns up the thumping bass on her stereo and drives away without another word.

"Why does Ashley hate us so much?!" Ana glares at her car.

"She's unhappy," Riley says quietly. Ashley makes a left turn out of the parking lot just ahead of oncoming traffic and races away, ignoring the school zone speed limit. "But she kind of has a point." Christine chokes on her gum and gives Riley a horrified look. "I mean, about Ms. Moore. We wanted to get her back, and we didn't really do that this summer."

"We tried, though," Ana says.

"Yeah." Riley lets her breath out slowly. "But did we try hard enough?"

Ms. Moore got a job at Bayside Books to pay the bills while she's waiting for the school board to reinstate her. We've all stopped in to strategize how to help get her back, but we never really got as far as we were hoping to. Maybe we could have done more.

"I had to meet with Mrs. Canning today," Christine says quietly. When her mom died, Christine started meeting with Ms. Moore for counseling sessions once a week, and I don't know how she would have survived without Ms. Moore's guidance, especially last year when her dad was planning his wedding to The Bimbo. I mean Candace. I have to start calling her Candace. "She doesn't get me at all. She tried to hypnotize me. She didn't even laugh when I said it was all coming back to me and that in a former life I was a chicken."

"We need Ms. Moore for Earth First too." I push myself up to sitting. "Without an advisor, the club will have to fold."

"But what are we going to do?" Ana sighs. "We tried the petition thing. We're not lawyers, and we certainly don't have any pull with the school board. We don't even know who filed the suit in the first place. How would we figure out who it was and prove it, let alone do something about it?"

I look out across the parking lot, toward the school. Its high gray walls don't seem as intimidating as they did even a few months ago.

"Hmm." Christine bites her lip and twists the little gold

stud in her nose. "There has to be a way. Don't you want to bring Ms. Moore back?"

"More than anything." Ana peeks at her phone, then snaps it shut. "But do you really think we can?"

"Maybe not by ourselves. But with all of us working together? We definitely could." I dust the black gunk from Christine's car off my hands. "We're not like the other kids at this school," I say slowly, watching as two wiry guys shake up cans of soda and spray each other by the bus loading area. "Remember how Ms. Moore saw that?"

The four of us met in detention one day early in our freshman year. Somehow Ms. Moore, who was the detention monitor that day, knew we were destined to be together. She assigned the four of us to a group and made us each write about the day our lives changed. That's how we discovered we've all come back from the grave, that we're all honest-to-goodness miracles.

"We're the Miracle Girls." Riley stretches her legs out in front of her, long and tan under her cheerleading skirt. "That's got to count for something."

"If you guys are in, I'm in." Christine nods as the song changes again. "I'll do whatever it takes to bring Ms. Moore back."

I glance at Ana, who nods. "Okay, then," I say, sounding for all the world as if I know what I'm doing. "That's decided. The Miracle Girls are going to save Ms. Moore."

4

It's a gorgeous evening. The moody sky has cleared up, and the sun is now shining through the trees that encircle the deck. It drizzled a little this morning, not enough to matter, but it seemed like a lucky sign. The Miracle Girls are here, Ed's got his favorite Beatles album blaring in the backyard, and Marcus has been dutifully by my side all afternoon. I even went to the DMV and got my license on the first try. On the surface, it looks like the perfect sixteenth birthday.

But something still doesn't feel right. Dreamy and Ed spent the morning getting in one little spat after another while they prepared for the party. At noon they stopped talking to each other entirely, and since then Dreamy has been keeping herself busy with preparations, bringing out trays of veggies and bowls of chips all afternoon, and Ed has been manning the grill. I haven't even seen them look at each other.

"Hey, Zoe, you want another veggie burger?" Marcus calls, loading up a plate for himself. His polo shirt hangs loose on his arms.

"I'm good." I shake my head and lean back against the picnic table.

"I wonder if he ever gets tired of being nice." Christine takes off her sunglasses and wipes them on the edge of her shirt.

"Marcus?" I watch him now, helping Ed with the grill. "Nah. I don't think so."

Ana smiles at Marcus. "We should go on a double date. Maybe Marcus could rub off on Dave."

"Yeah, where is your other half tonight?" Riley pulls her sweater over her head. The evening is already starting to cool off.

"Band practice." Ana rolls her eyes and looks out at the dried-up grass. "Let's not talk about that." She puts her sunglasses back on and turns to Riley. "How's Tom?"

"He's good." Riley can't help but smile at the sound of her boyfriend's name.

"When will you see him next?" Ana asks.

Riley's shoulders fall. "Two days from forever, at the rate we're going." Tom's a freshman at UC Santa Barbara, five long hours south of here. I give her a side hug, and she smiles. "We knew it would be hard. But he says he likes his classes, so that's good."

As Riley tells a story about Tom's first week in college, a happy honking sounds in the backyard. I freeze. Ed picks up a glass and a knife from the wooden picnic table.

"What's going on, Zo?" Riley asks, her brow creasing.

Ed clinks the knife against the glass a few times. "Could I have your attention, everyone?" He clears his throat. "We've got a big surprise for Zoe's birthday."

Could he possibly mean—? No, he couldn't. But then . . . he does have a college friend who restores old cars, and he has been scrimping and saving a lot these days. "Can we all go to the front of the house?"

I turn to him, my heart racing in my chest. "A surprise?"

Dreamy smiles, lopsided and mischievous. "It sounds like it's in the driveway right now."

I take off at a sprint, and Marcus and the Miracle Girls are right behind me. It has to be a car. What other big surprise do you give a sixteen-year-old on her birthday that you can park in a driveway? Which also honks loud enough for the whole neighborhood to hear?

"Ohmigosh!" Riley shrieks. "A car!"

"What kind do you think it is?" Christine asks as we push open the wooden gate that separates the front and back yards.

"I hope it's safe," Marcus says.

"This is so exciting, Zo!" Ana says. "Did you even know they were shopping for a car?"

We round the dried-up rose-tip shrubs, and I stop in my tracks. I scream.

It's beautiful. It's shiny and black, and much newer than I would have guessed. The windows are tinted, and it looks sleek and fast. How did they—

"I told you!" Ed says, following right behind me with Dreamy on his heels. I rush toward it, and I think a high-pitched noise might be coming out of my throat, but I'm too excited to tell for sure. Just as I get close enough to touch it, the back door opens, and a tall, brown-haired guy steps out. I screech to a halt.

"Surprise!" Dreamy and Ed scream together.

"NICK?!" I suck in my breath. It's—how did he—when did they—

What is my brother doing here?

He leans back into the car, says something to the driver,

grabs a duffle bag, and raps on the roof twice. Before I can even process what's happening, the car drives away.

"What are you doing here?" I think my mouth might be hanging open. Is this my surprise?

"Happy birthday, kiddo." Nick walks toward me and drops his bag on the ground, then wraps me in a hug. He smells like grease and sweat. "When did you get to be so tall?"

I try not to pull away too quickly. What's going on? It's not like Nick and I are super close. He was almost out of the house by the time I was born. He's more like a fun uncle than a brother.

"Zoe?" Ana says softly. I turn back toward my friends, frozen in place. They look stricken. Marcus reaches his hand out to me and I ignore it.

"This is my brother, Nick," I say, pasting a smile on my face. "He lives in Colorado." I lean over and pick up the strap of his bag. "On a ranch. I guess he's here for a visit."

"Not anymore," Nick says, leaning over to give me a noogie. I pull away. What is he talking about? Nick surveys the crowd in front of him and gives a small wave.

"What?"

"Nick's come home to live with us for a while." Ed gazes at him, then smiles at me while Dreamy runs over and grabs Nick in a hug.

I swallow back a lump in my throat and catch Marcus giving me a sad, sympathetic look.

I'm a horrible, selfish person. I love Nick. My parents can't afford to buy me a car, and I, of all people, know that, and yet as the tears sting my eyes, I have to admit that I'm kind of disappointed.

"Told you it was a good surprise!" Ed says, taking Nick's bag from me and ushering us all to the backyard. "What could be better than having all the Fairchilds together again?" The girls are already heading back around the side of the house, silently. Marcus jogs quickly over to my side and takes my hand in his. He gives it a little squeeze, puts his arm around my shoulder, and pulls me close.

5

I look at my watch, glance around the library one last time, and finally admit to myself that Dean is not coming. He's now a full fifteen minutes late, and really, I don't blame him. I blame the red-headed band geek sitting in the library all by herself. I should have known better than to believe this guy.

Something about him makes my skin itch. Not that he's done anything to me. Well, not that he's done anything at all, actually. Most days he just sits in Mrs. Narveson's class with his arms crossed over his chest, sneering at her. He doesn't take notes, he doesn't ask questions—I don't think he even listens.

I sigh and crack my textbook to the section called "Don't Tread on Me: A Country Is Born." The point of Mrs. Narveson's Build-a-Nation project is to show us the challenge our fore-fathers faced, and she wants to make it as realistic as possible, so we have a huge checklist of things we have to decide with our partners. That is, of course, if I *had* a partner.

I scan the stacks of books and even crane my neck to check the computer lab, but still see no sign of him.

"Looking for something?"

I jump. How did he sneak up on me like that? I gesture toward the empty chair across the table, and for a second, I'm relieved to see him. I haven't been stood up after all. But when he flops into the chair next to me, crowding my personal space, and tosses his bag on the ground, the relief turns into dread. Why did I force this guy to come? I should just accept my fate and get started on this project by myself. He's only going to slow down my progress. I roll my eyes and move my backpack across the table.

"Get held up?" I force myself to smile.

"Yeah. Sorry." He shrugs and doesn't offer anything else. He leans back in his chair, locks his fingers behind his head, and smiles. "You got the assignment? I forgot my history notebook."

"Sure." We're off to a great start. I shove my folder over to him. "Here's the list of things we need to do. I went ahead and drew up a schedule while I was waiting for you." I shoot him a look, but he doesn't seem to notice. "I figure first we need to nail down the really basic stuff, then we can start drafting our constitution, and finally write the twenty-page paper. If we can stay on the schedule I laid out—"

Dean starts laughing.

"What?" I grit my teeth. I can tolerate being ignored or even picked on by popular people, but I can't stand being laughed at.

"I'm sorry." Dean shakes his head at me, snickering into his hands. "I can't help it. You're kind of killing me with this schedule."

I snatch my folder back. "We need a schedule. Everybody else already got started." Even Christine and Kayleen are working on their flag, and they're practically sworn enemies. I grab a pen from my backpack and put it in front of him. "We're behind, and I can't afford to fail."

"Okay, okay." He puts his hands in the air. "Calm down. I'm

on your schedule." He leans over, pulls a red spiral notebook out of his messenger bag, and flips to a blank page. "But I'm not worried about all those other teams, and you shouldn't be either. We've got something they don't."

"What?" Please tell me we have a secret weapon I haven't thought of. Maybe he's done this project before at his old school?

"Brains." Dean stretches in a dramatic way and puts an arm behind my shoulder. I stare at it, horrified. "I'm not just a pretty face, Zoe."

"Let's try to stay focused." I scoot my chair away from Dean, hopping it across the floor. It's true that Dean is very handsome, like an actor or something, but it's still pretty rude to brag about it. Popular people, I swear. They are a separate race from the rest of us. "Why don't we start with something basic?" I scan the list of things we need to invent for our country. A constitution? No, that's like jumping in in the middle. A flag? A name? No, no. "Let's decide what type of government we want, and then we'll theme everything around that."

"Is that what the schedule says?" Dean has a smile I can't quite read, but I ignore him. "I want to stay on the schedule. That's how it works when you invent an entire country. You should have seen John Adams's schedule."

I pretend I can't hear him. "I was thinking we should right the wrongs of America with our new country." I flip quickly through the section in our textbook explaining different government types. "We could do something where we all share the work and the profits. Eliminate poverty."

"No way." Dean leans forward, suddenly taking an interest. "I want to be king."

I raise an eyebrow.

"What?" He takes the textbook from me and flips a few pages forward. "You can be queen if you want." He stares at me, mischief twinkling in his cobalt-blue eyes. "I'll even share my power fifty-fifty."

I prop my head in my hands and cover my face. I think I liked it better when Dean wasn't here *helping*. How do I tell him I don't mind doing this all by myself? He can kick back and depend on me to bring home the A for our team.

"What?" I can hear the mocking in his tone. "What did I do?"

"You are impossible," I say through my fingers. He doesn't laugh or snort or say anything. I peek at him through my left hand, and he winks at me.

"You're the one who wants to found a communist state." He shoves the book toward me. I stay still for a second, trying not to give in to his blatant attempt to get under my skin again, but eventually I realize I can't spend our entire study group with my head in my hands.

I sit up and look at the book, and he reaches across the table and points at the definition of a communist state: a type of government where all goods are owned in common and available to individuals as needed. I gulp.

"Mao? Lenin? Trotsky?" Dean raises an eyebrow at me. "I don't think following the advice of those guys is going to get us an A."

I search my brain for those names. I know I've heard of Mao, but unless he means John Lennon, one of the Beatles, the other two don't sound familiar.

"Fine," I say, trying to recover a single shred of my dignity. "No communism. Obviously that's not what I meant." I make a mental note to pay better attention in Mrs. Narveson's class. "But no monarchy either. I don't want a bunch of impoverished serfs on my conscience." I raise my eyebrow back at him. I may not have Riley's big brain or Ana's devotion to studying, but I'm not stupid either. I make my fair share of A's and B's.

Dean sighs and bows his head. "As you wish, milady."

It takes us a good hour to argue over every type of government in the book, plus two I'd never even heard of. Dean looked those up on his iPhone to prove they exist. Somewhere between meritocracy and constitutional monarchy, I began to relax. I didn't notice it right away, but now my shoulders feel loose, and in my mind I begin to picture the beautiful red A that will be staring back at us at the end of the project.

Finally we settle on a social democracy. I like its emphasis on compassion for the poor, and Dean likes that it promises freedom for the individual. "Here's what I think our flag should be." Dean holds up his iPhone and shows me a picture of a black pirate flag.

"Ohmigosh, is that the time?" The top banner of his iPhone flashes 4:55.

"Turning into a pumpkin?" He leans back and beams at me.

"Yes." I snap my textbook shut and shove it into my bag. "I can't believe we lost track of time. It took us an hour just to decide on a type of government."

"Don't worry. I don't blame you." Dean holds up my history folder with my timeline. "Your preoccupation with the schedule delayed us a little, but I can overlook it."

"Whatever." I take my history folder from his hands and give him a mock scolding look, which is progress because a few hours ago there would have been no mocking about it.

"Just be on time next time and try to be"—he grins from ear to ear—"less of a pain in the butt."

He laughs like it's the best joke he's heard in a long time. "Let me walk you to your car."

"No." A blush creeps into my cheeks. "I'm getting a ride with my friend. I have to run to catch her." Dean stands up and seems to be contemplating escorting me by force. "Like, literally. I'm going to run."

"Bye, then." Dean pulls the strap of his messenger bag over his head and steps to the side. "Don't mow anyone down."

"Yeah, okay." I hesitate, trying to read his face. Is he laughing at me because I'm going to run across the campus? Is he sad I'm ditching him? Does he not care? I glance at my watch. No time to figure him out. "See you in class."

I push open the library door and take off at a sprint. Marcus stayed late to work on an extra credit project in science, and his mom is going to give us a ride home.

As I run, my books bounce up and down, banging into my back, but I keep going. Hopefully Mrs. Farcus will wait. Getting a ride with your boyfriend's mom is kind of lame, but anything is better than having to call Dreamy to come pick me up. She drives an old van with a spray-painted scene of horses running through a desert by moonlight on the side. I round the corner of the B-wing and finally make it into the parking lot—and screech to a halt.

There's the Farcuses' Camry and Christine's car. And is that . . . a guy with Christine?

"You are such a liar!" Christine's voice drifts out her open window. Something in her tone makes me stare. Tyler grabs Christine in a headlock and gives her a noogie. She comes up laughing and gasping, then starts slapping him on the shoulder. Tyler grabs her hands and holds them in his.

I force myself to turn away and head toward the Camry.

Tyler. Christine had a huge crush on him freshman year, and they even went out one time, but things fizzled. They've been hanging out at youth group this summer, but I didn't realize how, um, personal things were getting between them. I glance again and see them comparing the size of their hands, palm to palm. It's clear, even from this distance, that they're lost in their own world.

I give my head a shake, then smile at Marcus and his mom like I never even saw it.

6

Ms. Lovchuck stares at us over the rim of her hot pink reading glasses, a plastic smile pasted on her face. She must have at least ten pairs of glasses. I think she gets them from the revolving display at the grocery store on Main Street. A gold chain dangles from the sides of the frames and loops around her neck.

"What can I do for you ladies?" Her words are kind enough, but her voice is cold. I've never understood why someone who hates teenagers this much is the principal of a high school. The fish tank in the corner of the room gurgles.

Ms. Lovchuck had to borrow two extra chairs from the vice principal's office to fit us, and we're a little squished, but I don't care. It makes me feel stronger to have all the Miracle Girls gathered around me.

"We'd like to talk to you about Ms. Moore," Ana says, pulling a manila folder out of her bag. Thank goodness for Ana. She's so organized and self-confident. If it were me, I'd stammer and stumble over my words and walk out of here feeling like an idiot. "We would like to petition to bring her back." Ana lays the folder on the table.

Ms. Lovchuk doesn't flinch. "I'm afraid I can't discuss any details of Ms. Moore's situation at this time."

A purplish light shines out of the fish tank, casting a weird glow on Christine's shoes. Silvery fish dart around nervously, and there's some grayish algae growing on the side of the tank.

"We know she was fired unfairly," Riley jumps in, leaning forward in her creaky metal chair. "And we want to know what we can do to get her reinstated."

"I'm sure Ms. Moore appreciates your concern." Ms. Lovchuck writes something on the legal pad in front of her. "And I will make a note of it."

A fat, slow fish slides along the bottom edge of the tank, feeding off the scum on the bottom. It's disgusting, but I can't make myself look away.

"We really want Ms. Moore back." I feel my cheeks turn pink as the words leave my mouth. Oh no. We were supposed to come in here and argue our case rationally. Dreamy gave me a crash course in protesting this morning and told me that to convince people in power to change their minds, you can't be too emotional. You have to appeal to their reason, but the words are already out, so I press on. "She's the best teacher this school ever had."

Ms. Lovchuck clears her throat. Uh-oh. I ruined it. She's not taking us seriously at all.

The stupid bottom-feeder glugs its way along, scooting his disgusting fish face along the edge of the glass, going nowhere.

"As I said," she says, enunciating each syllable clearly, "I will make a note of it, and I'll see what I can do. But I cannot discuss the situation further."

She takes her glasses off and lets them fall on their little chain. She watches, waiting for us to respond, and eventually Ana takes the folder off the desk and shoves it into her bag.

"This isn't fair." Ana's voice rises. "This is a public school. Our parents pay taxes. We have rights." She zips her bag, creating a strangely angry sound. "We just want to know who filed the case against Ms. Moore."

Ms. Lovchuck smiles too widely and gestures toward the door. "Have a nice afternoon, girls." There's a note of false cheerfulness in her voice. "Thank you for stopping by."

7

As I walk away from the noise and chaos of the party, the light from the bonfire casts a soft orange glow over the sand. We came to the Full Moon Party, as promised, but now I'm sort of regretting it. Ana and Dave are having a "discussion," as she calls it, by the water's edge. From what I could gather, Dave didn't really want to come tonight. Christine and Tyler are taking a moonlit stroll, and Riley is talking to some girls from the squad. We're all here, but it doesn't change the fact that this feels weird. Even if I am an upperclassman now, this is Riley's world, not mine.

I take a few more steps toward the water. It's peaceful here in the darkness just beyond the light from the fire. The crash of the waves washing up on the shore is soothing. I take off my flip-flops and enjoy the cool sand under my feet.

My phone buzzes. I pull it out of my pocket and glance at the screen. Marcus.

You home? Want to talk? I miss you! I won using only Development Cards tonight!!!

I smile. This summer we fell into a nice routine of pedaling our bikes down to Bayside Books on Saturday nights. As long as you buy coffee they don't care how long you sit in the café and read. Plus, I always got to catch up with Ms. Moore while I was there because business at the bookstore is slow at night. I was nervous about asking him to reschedule our date night, but he was really sweet about it. He played Settlers of Catan, this weird German board game, with some friends instead. Parties aren't his thing.

> Awesome! This party is making me uncomfortable. ☹ Shouldn't have come.

Behind me the sound of the party swells as a few football players pick one of the cheerleaders up in the air. I know I should go back, but it's kind of nice to be here in the shadows for a little while. I flip my phone shut.

"Enjoying the view?"

I look up and see a tall guy in a black hoodie silhouetted by the glare of the fire. I squint into the light, trying to make out the face hidden in the shadows.

"Um, yeah. I guess."

The figure steps into the light, and I recognize the cool, blue eyes, the square jaw and smooth face.

"Dean." I laugh a little, but it comes out forced. What is he doing here? "Sorry, I couldn't tell who you were." I take a step back.

Dean shrugs.

"I didn't know you were going to be here."

He crosses his arms over his chest. "*Some* people at this school have been very welcoming." His tone is teasing.

"Maybe they've never been your history partner." I flip my

phone around in my hand. An awkward silence hangs in the air. "I was texting my boyfriend."

"That's cool." Dean nods like it doesn't matter to him one way or the other. He takes a seat on the sand next to me. "Why aren't you joining in the jamboree?" He jerks his head toward the party going on behind us.

"I needed a break." I dig my hands into the pockets of my sweatshirt.

"Me too," he says simply. He pats the sand next to him.

"Fine." I lower myself down. The sand is soft and cool. My phone chimes in my hand, telling me Marcus has responded to my message. I glance at the phone, turning it over in my hands.

"Gonna get that?" Dean motions at my phone.

I shake my head. "I don't think so. Later, maybe." I quickly switch it to vibrate.

"Interesting," he says, which kind of bothers me. He studies my face for a moment, but I'm careful to keep it blank and not give anything away.

"So, is it true that you're from New York?"

Dean stares at the ocean and stays silent for a long while. I can hear the bonfire crack and pop in the distance, and in the quiet I slowly become aware of the cool of the sand seeping through my jeans. "Yeah. It's not like here." I wait for him to go on, but he doesn't say anything more.

"Well, how was it different?" I'm not sure I really care, but it's better than awkward silence.

"You ever been to Brooklyn?" Dean looks at me skeptically, a touch of the arrogance I detected that first day in his voice.

I shake my head. "The streets are alive," he says simply. "More people, more excitement, more interesting things going on."

Oh. Is that all? So, apparently *everything* is better in New York. I roll my eyes.

"But my mom got a job with a dot-com start-up in Silicon Valley, so here we are, whether I like it or not." He digs his feet into the sand. His hair is dark and short and slightly messy. It looks like it's actually a real style of some kind, not the sun-streaked, dried-out-from-the-ocean frizz most of the guys here have.

"Some of us like it here."

For a while, we're both lost in our thoughts. I shut my eyes and try to enjoy the calming sound of the surf. I swear living with my parents is giving me the early signs of post-traumatic stress disorder. I'm walking on eggshells all the time, hoping that nothing sets them off. Meanwhile my brother is a shadow, always holed up in his room, wasting hours and hours on his stupid laptop.

"I hear you're a musician." Dean's voice is deep.

"Not really." I flush, grateful that it's too dark for him to see. How did he hear that? "I'm not in a band or anything. I'm only in the marching band, which is hardly"—I get another text from Marcus when I'm midsentence, so I press the button to stop the vibrating—"like being in a real band. No leather, no lead singer with a criminal record. It's just a bunch of geeks playing the fight song, really." Dean watches as I babble on, his eyebrow cocked. "Why do you ask? Do you play an instrument?"

"My dad's a professional musician. He plays the sax." Dean keeps his eyes focused on the ocean. "Moving here was a compromise for him. At least he's pretty close to San Francisco. He played all the jazz clubs in New York."

My phone buzzes again, and I contemplate quickly checking to make sure everything is okay.

"Well, that and my mom loves to sail. She wanted to live by the water, so here we are."

There might be a crisis or something. Maybe one of the horses is out. I flip my phone open secretly and see that I have three text messages from Marcus.

"Granted no one asked *me* where I wanted to live." Dean pushes himself to his feet and takes a few steps toward the huge Pacific Ocean, stretched out before us. My eyes rest on his back, but I quickly skip beyond him, to the vast moving abyss on the other side of his dark figure. There is incredible power in the waves, constantly pounding away at the shore, slowly breaking down the vast cliffs into smaller and smaller pieces. I don't understand how you can look at the ocean and not see God. I whisper a quick prayer for my family, hoping that a creator big and powerful enough to fill the oceans can fix us.

I watch Dean staring at the sea, then steal a glance at my phone and scan Marcus's messages. Oh, I get it. My stupid text to him made him worried that people were drinking or doing dangerous stuff. The first two are panicked one- and two-word messages wondering where I am and why I haven't called. The last one says:

Call me. Please. I'm worried.

Dean turns around, the moonlight casting his dark shadow up the beach.

"What did your messages say?" I feel like he's daring me to say or do something, but I don't know what.

"My boyfriend is worried. I need to call him."

Dean doesn't move, seems not to even breathe for a few seconds, then he walks over to me and puts out his hand. I stare at it, trying to figure out what to do. I glance up at him. He has a cocky grin on his face.

"You know," I say as I reach out for his hand. "I think you should give it some time. It's not really so bad here."

Dean pulls my arm gently, and I'm slowly lifted back to a standing position. He lets go of my hand, and I dust my palms off.

"I never said it was."

8

When I wake up Sunday morning, the forest is shrouded in fog. It even drizzles lightly for a minute, little drops decorating my window, but then it stops. You can't grow up in Half Moon Bay without learning to love the fog. Our little town is nestled between the ocean and the mountains, and the moisture blows in off the water and settles over the town most days, thick and damp and comforting. Unfortunately, it's not the same as rain, which soaks into the earth and feeds the thirsty soil, so it doesn't help much with the drought.

My stomach is rumbling, and my eyes feel sticky as I make my way down the stairs. I need some tea, and hopefully there's something in this house to eat. We usually leave for church at nine thirty, which gives me an hour to get ready. I pad across the carpet and into the kitchen, my socks slipping a little on the linoleum as I turn the corner.

"Oh." Dreamy blinks and takes a step back as I enter the room. She's slicing green onions at the counter, and Ed is standing next to her, leaning his backside against the fridge, arms crossed over his chest. "Zoe."

Ed flushes. "I hope we didn't wake you, Butterbean." He flashes a small smile, revealing his crooked front tooth. "Your mom and I were just talking."

"Hey." Part of me wants to hug them both good morning, but something holds me back, some unseen tension. Maybe it's that neither of them makes a move to hug me first. "I guess everybody's up early today."

"Yep." Ed scratches at the stubble on his chin. The syllable hangs awkwardly in the air.

"You got in late last night," Dreamy says quickly and pastes a grin on her face, but the lines around her mouth show that she's clenching her teeth.

"I was out with the girls."

They both stare at me, as if waiting for something to happen.

"I think I'm going to make some tea." I move toward the cabinet above the sink, and Dreamy ducks out of the way. "Have you guys had breakfast?"

They look at each other as if they're not sure of the answer.

"Not yet," Dreamy says at last. "Look, Zoe, why don't you go on upstairs and get dressed? I'm making that potato and green onion frittata." It's not really a frittata because it's held together with tofu, not eggs. Dreamy and Ed are vegans, but it's one of their better dishes. "By the time you're ready, it'll be on the table."

I'm not a child. I can see what's happening here. She wants me to go away so they can finish whatever tense discussion I interrupted, but because she's my mom, and because I don't know what else to do, I obey. I lay the box of tea bags down on the peeling Formica counter and turn to go just as the glass door slides open.

"What's going on?" Nick brushes the back of his hand across his forehead and steps inside. He pulls off his work gloves and looks around. He catches my eye, and I shake my head. He smells like manure.

Dreamy lets out a long breath. "Okay, this wasn't really how I wanted this to happen, but I guess we might as well do this now." She gestures to the table. "Why don't we all take a seat?"

I follow her to the dining nook, pull out a chair, and sit at the scarred kitchen table. Ed lowers himself down across from me and leans his elbows on the table. Nick sighs and takes off his work boots, then finally joins us, tossing his gloves in front of him. I don't know what his problem is. Maybe he's really tired or something.

"I guess this won't come as much of a surprise, really. You know we've been having problems recently." Dreamy speaks slowly and carefully, enunciating a little too much, like she's rehearsing her lines for community theater.

Ed slides his big weathered palm across the table and grabs my hand. I used to find the calluses on his hands comforting, the knotty bumps familiar. Even as a child I could shut my eyes and trace our shared history in them, but right now they sort of sicken me. They're only more evidence of how rough and uneven life is.

"Dreamy and I still love each other very much," he says as my stomach turns over.

"But we've decided to get a divorce." She rubs her fingernails across the scarred wooden tabletop. "It's not something we're happy about, it's just . . ." She turns her palms up. "It seems like it's the best thing, considering, well, you know, everything."

The room is silent except for the soft ticking of the clock above the sink.

Ed clears his throat. "You have to understand that this has nothing to do with you."

I pretend I don't hear him. This has everything to do with me.

"We thought . . ." Dreamy falters. "We wanted you to know that you can talk to us, either of us, any time, about this. About anything really. We don't want this to change . . . anything."

The ridiculousness of this statement is so astounding I don't know what to say. This changes everything. It can't not.

Nick runs his fingers through his sweaty hair. "If that's what you have to do, I support you." He stands up and slides across the linoleum in his stained socks. No one says anything as he walks across the kitchen, into the living room, and up the stairs. The railing shakes as he grasps it and pulls himself up to the second floor. A moment later he enters his bedroom and slams the door.

"Zo?" Ed bites his lip and rubs his gnarled palm over the back of my hand. He waits, watching me, his eyebrows raised. His face, so full of expectation, is the last thing I see before I burst into tears.

♡

Ed is filling cardboard boxes when I decide the walls of my room are pressing in on me. I've been lying completely still on my bed, listening to them unload Ed's closet through the paper-thin walls, since the big announcement. I'm in total shock. He's moving to one of the tourist motels on the beach. I have so many questions—when will I see him again? What about the horses? What about holidays? Do I have to go to the motel on the weekends?—but I can't bring myself to ask any of them. Instead I've been lying here, praying my heart out, begging God for help, for healing, for a miracle. Dreamy and Ed are just going through a rough patch. God needs to work on their hearts, show them what they're risking.

After I've begged and pleaded for a half hour straight, I slip my feet into sneakers and creep downstairs, avoiding touching the rickety metal banister that always squeaks. I tiptoe across the living room and make it to the door before I realize that no one is even paying attention. Nick is playing on his computer, and Dreamy and Ed are too wrapped up in their own drama to notice me avoiding them. With a sigh, I slide open the glass door, step out into the cool, moist air, and head toward Marcus's house.

The path to his house is familiar, and somehow that's comforting right now. My foot catches on a root, but I regain my balance quickly and start to walk faster, moving my legs quicker and quicker, and before I know what I'm doing, I start to run.

I take deep breaths as I go, filling my lungs and exhaling slowly, over and over, trying to focus on the rhythm of my breaths and the feel of my feet slapping against the hard earth. The more my lungs scream, the lighter my heart feels, and I pray, asking God to help me, to fix this whole thing, to make my parents love each other again. The only answer is the soft whisper of the wind sighing through the tops of the trees.

I slow down when I see Marcus's house. I take a few steps, then bend over and clutch my waist, trying to gather big lungfuls of air. I walk up the steps to his front door and peer in the window over his kitchen sink.

The entire Farcus family is gathered around the kitchen table, hunched over a game of Monopoly. Marcus and his dad are exchanging pastel-colored money, and his mom is throwing her head back, laughing. There's something sweet about the scene, too sweet. A little too perfect.

Marcus is who I should talk to. He'll tell me everything is going to be all right. But I stay still, watching them, and I can't bring myself to ring the bell.

I turn and walk back down the stairs, my shoulders sagging.

It only takes me a few minutes to get back to the house, grab my bag, sneak the set of keys out of the bowl by the door, and head to the car. No one notices.

9

Naturally, the parking spaces along Main Street are all taken on a Sunday afternoon, but I'm not in any state to drive around town for hours looking for one. I'm shaking, and my eyes keep filling with tears, and I know I'm not thinking rationally. I park next to a yellow-painted curb reserved for commercial deliveries and quiet the engine. I grab a scrap of paper from the dash and a pen from under the passenger side mat and scrawl, "Please don't tow. Life falling apart." I swing my bag over my shoulder, open the door, and put my note under the windshield wiper. I barrel over to the bookstore and don't glance back.

I can feel people staring at me as I walk down the sidewalk. My hair is greasy and matted to one side of my head. I'm wearing old jeans, cinched tight around my waist with a belt, and scuffed gray sneakers. My eyes are puffy, and I'm sure they're bloodshot. But though I look like a zombie, I feel a strange sense of calm. Ms. Moore will know what to do.

My phone rings, and I see it's Dreamy calling. I silence it, push open the heavy glass door of Bayside Books, and step into the cool air, then take a deep breath. The rich, earthy aroma of coffee wafts over the half wall that separates the café from the rest of the store. Bayside is not the only bookstore in town, but it is one of the largest, with high ceilings and dark, painted walls. The tall rows of shelves, lined with books, usually give me a thrill.

I spot Ms. Moore at the information desk, leaning her elbows on the counter, staring at a newspaper and chewing on the end of a pencil.

My breaths begin to catch in my throat. "Ms. Moore." I rake my fingers through my hair, trying to smooth it down.

She studies me for a moment, then drops the pencil she's been using to—I can see now—work on the *New York Times* crossword puzzle. Without a word, she nods, folds the paper in half, and puts the Back in Five Minutes sign up.

"Let's go," she says, gesturing for me to follow her. It takes me a second to make my feet move, but I skip a little and catch up to her as she walks out onto Main Street.

"You're just leaving?"

She nods.

"Are you going to get in trouble with the manager?" The last thing Ms. Moore needs is to get fired from another job.

"Maybe." She looks to the right, then turns and starts walking toward the main part of downtown. Great. More people.

I step off the curb to dodge a woman with a double stroller. Within moments we're crossing the historic bridge, and then Ms. Moore veers to the left and begins to carefully pick her way down the steep banks of Pilarcitos Creek.

I hesitate for a moment, thinking about how uncoordinated I am and wondering if there are snakes down there, but when she reaches the bottom I realize I have no choice. At least no one will hear us down by the creek. Carefully, with my arms out from my sides, I make my way down to the rocky bank.

"Now, what's going on?" She pulls her short hair back into a tuft of a ponytail and turns to me.

The water burbles over the occasional rock and twig. Dreamy and Ed once launched a huge campaign to enact stricter legislation to protect this creek.

Where do I even start? I take a deep breath. "Do you believe in love?"

She tucks her hands into the pockets of her jeans and sighs. "Yes. Very much so."

I consider her answer. She didn't even hesitate. "Even though . . ." Ms. Moore hasn't made a secret of the fact that she moved to Half Moon Bay after she broke off her engagement. "You didn't . . ."

"It's not that I didn't love him, Zoe." She's always had this eerie way of knowing what people are thinking even before they say it. "That wasn't it at all."

"Oh." I bite my lip. "Do you believe it's possible to love somebody forever? To like . . . stay together and stuff, through all the bad stuff?" I'm tripping over my words because I'm not really sure what I'm asking here, but she seems to understand anyway.

"Absolutely." A lock of hair falls down over her eyes, and she brushes it back. "Sometimes."

I wait for her to go on, but she doesn't. Tiny, almost microscopic bugs dance and skip on the creek's surface.

"But shouldn't people stay together?" I try again. "Even when things get hard and you're not sure you love the other person anymore and stuff?" I find a large broad rock a little ways up the creek and plop down on it. "Don't you stay with what you have? You don't go off just because something better comes along or you don't feel like being together anymore, right?"

Ms. Moore joins me on the boulder and lets out a long breath. "You're asking some tough questions, Zoe."

I nod.

"The thing about love is, the first rush is glorious." I used to play down here as a child. Is the creek lower now because of the drought? Or have I just gotten bigger, and my perspective has changed? "You know that." I flush, but she doesn't seem to notice. "But after a while that feeling fades. You can't sustain it forever. Love becomes something different, something deeper, more fulfilling, and that's what makes relationships work for the long term."

"You think people should stay together?"

Ms. Moore shrugs. "It's pretty dangerous to make judgments about what other people *should* do, Zoe."

We both fall silent, and I listen to the distinctive screech of a blue jay in the distance.

"So are you going to tell me what happened?" She says it so quietly I almost don't hear her over the burbling of the water.

High above our heads, the Sunday shoppers and strollers are going about their leisurely day downtown, greeting one another, chatting about ordinary things. But down at the creek, it's quiet and feels like our own secret world. The tall trees shade us from the afternoon sun, and the longer I sit here, the more in tune I am with the subdued chirps and twitters of the birds and bugs.

"Dreamy and Ed are getting a divorce."

She nods, keeping her eyes trained on the stream.

"That doesn't mean they don't love each other." She starts to say something more, then stops herself. I wait. "Sometimes marriages don't work out, and sometimes there are good reasons for that," she says at last. "But couples don't stay together for as long as your parents have without love."

"But then how can they just throw it all away?" I shake my head. "They're tearing our family apart. How can they decide that it's all over, that they're done trying?" My voice rises a little, and I can feel tears begin to sting my eyes. I didn't realize I had any more tears left in me.

"I don't know, Zoe." She picks up a small rock and turns it over in her hands. "I don't know what happened with your parents. But I do think love doesn't always look like we expect." The blue jay pipes up again, squawking out an almost pained sound. "Sometimes it means loving the other person enough to let them go."

I think about how much they've been fighting recently, about the sad stoop of Ed's shoulders and the defeated look in Dreamy's eyes. I think about Nick, and the matter-of-fact way he accepted the news this morning. Maybe they're not tearing the family apart. Maybe it's been crumbling, bit by bit, for a long time, and I never noticed.

I zip up my hoodie as a cool breeze blows past us. Ms. Moore crosses her arms over her chest.

"You're saying there's nothing I can do?"

Ms. Moore turns her head. "I never said that." She unleashes the rock in her hand, trying to skip it, but it sinks with a satisfying plunk. "I never said anything like that."

"But you said . . ."

"I said sometimes love means letting go." She laughs and shakes her head. "But that's not the only thing it means. Sometimes love means fighting for a relationship."

I run my hands over the rough stone under us, and my finger finds a small indentation to trace. Talking to Ms. Moore makes my brain hurt.

"They may have given up on their marriage, Zoe, but that doesn't mean you have to. If you want this badly enough, you have to fight for it."

"I don't know how."

"I think you do." She gives me a sly smile. "I think if you try, you can come up with some ways. Make them spend time together. Force them to come together. Give them something to care about outside of themselves. If you really want to do this, you have to help them see that they don't want to live without each other."

I try to follow a stray leaf as it makes a circuitous journey over the tiny rapids. It gets stuck briefly on a log, then breaks free and ambles past us and under the old bridge.

"You seem to know a lot about this whole fighting thing."

"What do you think I spend my time doing?" She smiles slyly. "Every minute I'm not working at that bookstore, I'm working on my case, Zoe—talking to people, looking for legal loopholes, researching similar cases. I know I was suspended unfairly, and I want nothing more than to get back into that classroom." She turns to face me. "I'm not giving up, and neither should you."

♡

I walk back to the car slowly. My muscles feel heavy and sluggish, and my mind is spinning in circles. I'm more confused than ever.

The crowds are thinning out, and the sidewalks are less packed now, but as I thread my way toward the car, I decide what I have to do next. I pull out my phone.

If I'm going to fight for my parents, I'll need serious backup.

I scroll through my contacts and stop on Riley. I'll try her first. She answers on the third ring.

"Riley, Dreamy and Ed are getting a divorce." I take a deep breath. "I need your help."

10

The bleachers shake as our quarterback throws a perfect spiral and a brawny senior catches the ball and rushes toward the end zone. He gets creamed at the forty-yard line, but all around us people are stomping their feet and yelling. That's a second down. I've been to every home game since freshman year, and most of the away games too, so I've managed to pick up the rules.

The players line up behind the ball, and at the drum major's lead, we stand up and launch into a quick little number we call "Go, Team, Go." It probably has a real name, but we call it that because during this one part, the cheerleaders scream "Go, team! Go!" to our beat. This is why I love the games—because it feels like we're a part of the action. Some of the trumpet players start dancing, and the cheerleaders on the track clap their pom-poms together. Riley catches my eye and winks as she screams with the rest of the squad.

Tonight's game is especially exciting because, for once, it looks like we might actually win. We're playing our rivals, Seaside High. A bunch of the kids from church go there, including Dave, who plays in their marching band. But mostly, it's exciting because being here means I'm not stuck at home moping. It's a nice change.

We finish the final notes of the song just as the quarterback snaps the ball, and we settle back into the bleachers. I scan the rest of the student section, where everyone is goofing around and decked out in our official Fighting Starfish colors. There are some kids I recognize from my classes, and all of Riley's popular friends are down by the front. Even Christine and Ana are here, huddled together in the student section, trying to fight off the sharp October cold. I crane my neck, searching for one more person. I guess I didn't really think he would be here, but I check out the top rows of the bleachers for his dark hair anyway.

"Looking for me?" I yank my head around. Marcus is grinning at me from two rows up.

"Totally." I try to smile. I haven't told Marcus about Dreamy and Ed. I will tell him, I guess. I just need . . .

Marcus gives me a thumbs-up, and I look away.

♡

After the marching band performs the half-time show, we have a few minutes to hit the bathroom and get food before the next quarter starts. The girls are waiting for me when I get off the field.

"Nice job, Red." Christine claps me on the back as we walk out of the bleachers area and onto the uneven cement by the bathrooms. "I especially loved the part where the girl dropped her flag."

I smother a laugh. Our color guard is a bit clumsy this year, and it was a pretty spectacular flop. The giant garnet flag practically landed in Seaside's stands.

"And you make that uniform look as good as it possibly

can." Christine eyes my hat with the little white feather coming out of the top.

Ana elbows Christine and glares at her.

"What? You said to be supportive. I'm pointing out my favorite parts." Christine smirks at me, and I smile. She pretends to have this hard exterior, but she's trying to help in her own way. And it's kind of sweet they talked about supporting me tonight.

"Oh, and you guys are doing great too," Christine says to Riley. "Don't want to leave the cheerleaders out. Way to . . . cheer. You guys are really . . . cheerful."

Riley rolls her eyes and gets in the snack bar line.

"How're you doing, Zo?" Riley slings her arm around my shoulder, and I rest my head against hers.

"Okay." I sigh and dig in my polyester pocket for some cash. "Neither of them are here, so that feels a little weird." Dreamy and Ed used to come watch every game. They'd sit up at the top of the bleachers with the other band parents. "And I talked to Ed for hours last night. I couldn't convince him to move back in."

"We're going to be here for you, no matter what happens," Ana says, coming up on my other side.

"And MarFar. Don't forget MarFar. He'll be there for you too." Christine makes a kissing noise with her mouth, and I swat at her.

"Hey, Ana, is that—" Riley asks and we all turn. Tyler is standing with two people in blue-and-white Seaside band uniforms. Oh, it's Dave, but he's got his arm thrown around . . . is that . . . Jamie?

I squint across the crowded space. It looks like Jamie. She

goes to youth group with us, and she sometimes sings with Three Car Garage, the band Tyler and Dave started. But why does he have his arm around—

Dave throws his head back to laugh, and his arm slips off Jamie's shoulder, but it's too late. Ana is frozen in place, her eyes wide. Just then, Dave looks up and sees Ana. He motions for her to come over, grinning from ear to ear, but Ana doesn't move. Her cheeks are turning red.

"Who wants some popcorn?" Riley says, but her voice sounds high and strained. "*Ana*, didn't you want some popcorn?"

Ana doesn't answer.

♡

After the game, Marcus and I head to the band room to change out of our dorky uniforms, then start back toward the cars. The air in the parking lot is jubilant. It's a clear, beautiful night, it's the beginning of the weekend, and Marina Vista has just won its first game against Seaside in ten years. All around us people are whooping and screaming as they make their way to their cars. I clutch my piccolo case close as I walk through the crowds to the dark lot toward the cars. All of us—boyfriends and, uh, Tyler, included—are supposed to meet up near our cars, then head to Christine's house to hang out.

"That was so cool how they intercepted that ball right at the end," Marcus says, skipping a little to keep up with me. He looks nice in a light blue polo shirt and Windbreaker. "And the half-time show went really well, don't you think? Mr. Parker did a really good job choreographing this year." I nod and try to follow along with what he's saying, but I'm distracted, thinking about Dave and Jamie and what that means to Dave and Ana.

I hear Christine's car before I see it. The light from a streetlamp illuminates two dark shapes sitting on the hood. Christine and Tyler. I can see Riley coming across the parking lot from the other direction, talking to some cheerleaders, but Ana doesn't seem to be by her car. I squint. We're almost there before I see where Ana is. She's standing by Dave's car, just on the other side of hers, with her arms crossed over her chest.

I quicken my step. Something's wrong. Marcus must sense it too because he stops chatting.

"There wasn't anything weird going on," Dave is saying, leaning against the hood of his car. They're just far enough away that they probably think they're out of earshot . . . but they're not. "She's a friend, someone I've known for years."

"I saw it, Dave! She was all over you. I saw it with my own eyes."

Tyler and Christine glare at the ground, trying to pretend they can't hear what's going on. I toss my bag and my instrument case onto Christine's backseat and walk around to the front. Marcus plunks down on the curb in front of the car.

"She's always had a crush on you. You're just too blind to see it."

Dave laughs, low and quiet, and in the light from the streetlamp behind him, I can see him shaking his head. "Why are you being like this? I already told you nothing is happening with Jamie or anyone else. I care about *you*."

Dave's voice breaks on the last word. And in some way, I do feel for him. He is obviously crazy for Ana. We all know that. But he did have his arm around Jamie. Even if it was just a friendly thing . . .

"You have a funny way of showing it."

If Marcus ever started flirting with another girl, it would rip me apart. It's kind of hard to tell who's right here. Maybe they both are.

"Look, I'm tired of this," Dave says, his voice low. "We fight all the time. I love you, but we can't go on like this."

Tyler leans back onto his arms, slowly, and I can see that he's as uncomfortable about hearing this as the rest of us are.

"Let's go," Riley mouths to me. I nod and start to walk toward the stadium, and Marcus follows.

"Then stop." Ana's voice is shrill. "Stop being so frustrating. Stop canceling on me and flirting with other girls and being so selfish. You're making me crazy."

Christine sees us and slides off the hood and moves toward us.

Dave is quiet, but I can see his shoulders hunch up. He turns and begins to walk around his car and opens the driver's side door.

I freeze.

"Don't walk away from me." Ana starts to follow him, and he stops but shakes his head.

"I'm sorry, Ana. I love you, but I can't do this anymore." Dave steps into his car and shuts the door. No one says anything when he starts the engine, or when he turns on the lights, or when he carefully backs up and drives away.

The air feels heavy. Ana stands still, frozen under the street-lamp, staring at the empty parking space. I look at Riley, who seems as terrified and confused as I feel. What are we supposed to do? We just watched our best friend get dumped.

Slowly, I turn around, walk toward Ana, and put my arms around her. She doesn't react, but I pull her toward me, and eventually she begins to cry. I hold her for a while and whisper prayers for strength and comfort into her ear.

They call it the Passing of the Peace, and it takes forever. At Ana and Riley's church, they pause the service for two minutes so you can shake hands with the people in the pew in front of you. But at Church of the Redwoods, it sometimes takes half an hour. Everyone gets up from their seats and hugs everybody else, and people get wrapped up in conversations, and, well, they just wait for everyone to be done before they move on. I used to think this was normal, but I've been going to church with the Miracle Girls more and more, and I slowly came to realize that everything about the church where I grew up is different. And while there's something nice about having other kids my age, and a real building, and some kind of normal teaching, Church of the Redwoods will always be home to me, a sacred space.

The Miracle Girls wanted me to go to church with them today, but Dreamy was sniffling this morning, wiping her nose on her sleeves as she got ready for church, so I told them I wasn't going to make it after all.

I want to support Dreamy. It's just that being here is strange. Right now Dreamy's talking with Mrs. Scholl, a jolly overweight woman with long, gray hair who gave me a sticker book when I had the flu when I was five. She keeps shooting me pitying looks, and I want to disappear.

Dreamy and Ed helped start Church of the Redwoods, back before Nick was born. My parents met in the streets of Berkeley, protesting the Vietnam War, and they both came to faith through some weird hippie thing called the Jesus Movement. Basically, it was a bunch of flower children who found Jesus, and if you listen to Dreamy and Ed talk, it changed everything about the church. It certainly changed everything for them, anyway. More than thirty years later, here we are.

I mean, here Dreamy and I are. This is the first Sunday I can remember at Church of the Redwoods without Ed, and there's a deep ache gnawing at me. He should be here. I take a deep breath of the sweet, cool air and pull my sweater tighter around me. It doesn't feel right. Nothing about this feels right anymore.

I sit alone, watching as people I've known my whole life throw their arms around Dreamy, pulling her in tightly, laying their hands on her and praying. I am glad that she has this community, these people to stand by her when she needs it most. I just wish things were different.

I bow my head and whisper a prayer to God. Why hasn't he answered me? Why is he taking so long to fix everything? Is this some kind of test?

12

We are not calling our country Bob," I tap my pen on the plastic table. Between worrying about Dreamy and Ed and worrying about Ana and Dave, it's almost a relief to be back at school today.

"But it's such a likable name. Have you ever met someone named Bob who wasn't nice?" I stare at Dean, but he goes on. "Bobs smile a lot and send their grandmothers birthday cards. Bob is the golden retriever of names." He leans back in the plastic library chair and threads his fingers together behind his head. His signature pose.

"Bob is a name for a person, not a country." I shake my head. We've been in the library since school got out, but we're not any closer to finishing our project. Riley's brother, Michael, is typing away at a keyboard in the bank of computers by the wall, and he keeps looking up and glaring at us when we get too loud.

"Well, I haven't seen you come up with something better."

"I don't think we should be spending so much time on the whole name thing. We're supposed to get through currency and legal system today." I shove my copy of the schedule in his face.

"I guess we could call it Zoeville."

I glare at him, though part of me wants to laugh a little. "Can we stop being ridiculous please? I have to go soon."

"Zoeville or Bob. Your choice."

"I am not choosing between those names."

"We'll arm wrestle for it, then." Dean sticks his elbow on the table, hand straight up.

"I was thinking we could base the currency on a renewable resource, like wheat, instead of gold." I spent a lot of time researching how money works last night. It turns out a dollar bill is only valuable because it represents a tiny chunk of gold the government owns. The bill doesn't have any value on its own. It's only a representation of the stuff that's really valuable, but if currency was based on something we could all grow, I suspect we might be able to get rid of poverty altogether.

"Bob it is, then." Dean puts his arm down and picks up his pen, then leans over the form Mrs. Narveson gave us to fill out by next week.

"Wait!" I scream too loudly. The librarian, Mr. Wallace, gives me a dirty look from behind the counter, then turns back to his crossword puzzle. "That's our official record. We have to turn that thing in for a grade." Dean drops his pen and puts his hand out in an offer to arm wrestle again. I glare at him, but he doesn't flinch.

He begins to wiggle his arm to tempt me.

"Whatever." I rest my elbow on the table and lean in a bit, and he grabs my hand and levels his eyes at me.

"Are you ready?" Dean's hand practically engulfs mine. Marcus's hands are thin and bony, but Dean's is big and warm. "If I win, our country is Bob," he says. He tilts his head a little, composing his face to look very serious. "If you win, we're Zoeville. Ready?"

I nod, but he's already pulling on my hand.

"Hey!" I pull my hand back toward me, but he's got a solid grip. I twist my arm a little bit, trying to get a better angle. Mr. Wallace clears his throat, but Dean looks at me, one eyebrow raised.

"Zoe?" I turn my head, yanking my hand away. Marcus stands behind us, his eyes wide. Dean smiles up at him without a care in the world.

"We were just naming our country," I say quickly. "This is Dean. My history partner?" Marcus steps forward, his face pale in the fluorescent lights, and Dean stands up and holds out his hand. "Dean, this is my boyfriend, Marcus."

"Good to meet you, man," Dean says with a devilish look in his eyes. Marcus shakes his hand a little uncertainly, then steps back and studies us. "Zoe's always talking about you. It's cool to finally meet you." He gestures to the empty plastic chair across the table. Marcus's jaw relaxes, but he shakes his head.

"Zoe, my mom is waiting. We were supposed to be out by the band room ten minutes ago."

"Oh my goodness. I'm sorry!" I begin to grab at the papers scattered across the table. "I was supposed to meet Marcus after he finished his lab. He's working on this cool thing with steam." I'm talking too much, and my hands are moving too quickly, but I get the papers shoved into my bag and sling it over my shoulder. Marcus waits, his hands in his pockets.

"I'm sorry. I have to run," I say to Dean, who smiles and nods.

"No problem. Sorry to keep you." He smiles at me, then shifts his eyes to Marcus. "And I'll see you around, Marcus."

Marcus puts his arm on my waist. I want to explain that we were just playing around, that it wasn't at all what it looked like, that Dean is just my stupid slacker history partner, but I don't. We both stay silent as we walk out the door.

13

Mrs. Farcus drops me off at home, and I see I'm still dealing with Situation Normal: All Messed Up. Nick is on the computer, doing some kind of pointless graphics thing, I have a voice mail from Ed telling me all about his new handyman gigs with a sad voice, and Dreamy is hunched over the picnic table, hands shoved into a five-gallon bucket. Her long brown ponytail hangs limp down her back. I watch as she moves her hands around for a bit and then lifts a wooden screen out of the bucket, squinting in the bright sunlight.

"Zoe!" She drags the back of her arm across her forehead and steps inside the open glass door. "Check this out." She holds the papers, still wet, in front of me. "I'm testing out different scents. What do you think?"

I reach for a sheet and hold it up to my nose. It smells like vanilla.

"I like this one," I say uncertainly. Dreamy has been recycling paper by hand for years, well before it was a cool hobby, turning old tissue paper and newsprint into note cards and fancy stationery.

"I talked to Linda Cunningham down at Seaside Gifts yesterday." She takes the vanilla from my hands and gives me another. The smell of evergreen reaches my nose. "She said she might be willing to take some of my cards on consignment, so I wanted to try out a few different types."

I reach for another and take a whiff of lavender. It's really strong, like she emptied a whole bottle of lavender oil into the pulpy mix. I run my hand over the textured surface, noting the thick grain of the paper.

"She thinks I could sell them for two or three dollars each. Can you believe that?" My mom's sleeves are pushed up around her elbows, and her forehead is dotted with sweat. Her eyes are wide, her face hopeful.

"I like this one." I hand it back to her. Truthfully, it's not much different from her others, or from cards I've seen in stores, but it seems to make her happy to hear it.

"Oh good." She brushes a lock of hair behind her ear with her free hand. "I really want this to work." She takes the lavender sheet between her fingers and smiles nervously.

"I'm sure it will," I say with as much certainty as I can muster. Dreamy sighs and turns back toward the door.

"I'll keep experimenting," she says, nodding her head toward the patio.

When the heavy glass door slides shut behind her, I start making plans. Things have been tight for a long time, but if our income is dependent on paper, I have to do something more than just try to get them back together again. I can get a job. I don't have a car, but it's only a twenty-minute bike ride to downtown. Maybe Bayside Books is hiring.

The phone on the wall across the kitchen rings.

Oh! Maybe Half Moon Bay Coffee Company is hiring. That would be so cool. I love coffee, and I'd get to see the Miracle Girls all the time and still make some money to help out.

The phone rings again, and I walk into the kitchen and pick up the receiver from the wall.

"Hello?" I try not to sound too impatient, but no one ever calls for me on this line, so what's the use in picking it up?

"Hi. May I please speak with Nick?" The woman's voice on the other end sounds stilted and professional.

"Sure. Can I tell him who's calling?"

She hesitates for a second. "It's Heather."

I rack my brain, but the name doesn't mean anything to me.

"Heather Boyd."

"Okay, hold on just a second." I set the receiver on the counter. "Nick! Phone!" I scream.

You know, even working at the ice cream shop wouldn't be bad. It closes really early, and it would be cool to have access to dairy products whenever I want—especially since Dreamy only allows those nasty Tofutti things in her freezer.

A minute later, Nick finally shuffles into the kitchen. He yawns and takes the receiver out of my hand. "Hello?"

I walk back into the living room to give him a little privacy. We haven't exactly grown closer since he moved home, so I don't really feel like it's fair to pry into his life. I press my body to the windows and watch Dreamy as she frantically works on her paper project.

"Oh," he says. I turn away from the window at the tone of his voice. "I told you when I left." He waits as she says something more. "Well, I don't know how to fix it. I told you that," he says into the phone, his voice rising. I lean back a little and steal a glance at him in the kitchen. He makes his hand into a fist, his veins popping out on his lean arm.

In a flash I remember something from when he lived at

home, back when I was still a small child. He used to come home late at night smelling like alcohol and acting like this, irritable and angry. Ed would make him touch his nose with his pointer fingers.

"It's not my problem anymore. That's all there is to it." He switches the phone to his other ear and shakes his head.

I thought he had pulled his life together out there at the ranch. His stories of riding under the big sky and caring for the cattle made it seem like he'd found his place in the world.

"I'm hanging up now. I don't work for you anymore. Remember? I don't have to sit here and listen to this." Nick slams the phone back on the hook, and I whip back around to the window. For a moment, the air is still.

Nick mutters a curse word under his breath and storms over to the front door.

"Wait." I chase behind him. He stops, but doesn't turn back. "Where are you going?"

"Somewhere else." Nick turns around, his eyes red. "Tell Dreamy." He grabs Dreamy's key ring from the hook, yanks open the door, and fades into the night.

14

I slide into our old broken picnic table Wednesday afternoon and dump the contents of my paper sack out on the table: some nasty fruit leather, a Tupperware container with almonds, and something with a weird mushy texture that I can't quite identify.

"Zo." Christine plops down and points at my lunch. "When are you going to tell Dreamy that stuff makes you gag?"

"What?" I hold up the Tupperware and give it a shake, making the almonds rattle. "I like these." Dreamy has been packing me disgusting vegan lunches since kindergarten. I stopped eating my lunch in middle school, but it would be weird not to know it's there for me, waiting in the little brown bag. Besides, there's usually one thing in the sack that I like, and that helps me not feel so guilty.

"And they say I'm the crazy one." She pulls out a sandwich and sighs. Christine used to eat Yoplait yogurt every day, but she kept it in Ms. Moore's mini fridge. Now that Ms. Moore's gone, she's had to switch to solids. Christine moves over a little as Ana and Riley appear, holding lunch trays. Ana looks thin and pale and has dark circles under her eyes.

"How're you holding up?" Stupid question, but I hope it shows concern.

"Fine, I guess." She bites her lip, and I can see she's fighting back tears. "You?"

I shrug, put the almonds aside, and start digging in my purse for spare change. At some point, Nutter Butters became an integral part of my lunch.

For a moment we're all silent. The sounds in the background seem to swell—people laughing, two girls in an argument, the noise of plastic trays hitting hard wooden tables.

Christine takes a deep breath. "I have a Ms. Moore update." She shoots for a nearby trash can and sinks her brown paper lunch sack. "I heard it when I was in the office for my session with Mrs. Canning."

"What is it?" Nutter Butters only cost four quarters. I know I have them in here somewhere. I stopped asking Dreamy and Ed for money last month, but I've gotten pretty good at scouring the couch and underneath the floor mats in the van.

"Our meeting with Lovchuck worked." Christine smiles. "She talked to the superintendent, and the school board is going to hold a public meeting."

"Oh," I say, unable to keep the disappointment out of my voice. A meeting? Like that will do any good.

Riley takes a small bite of her burger and shakes her head. She's never been very interested in food. "I was hoping it'd be something more."

"Wait," Christine says, putting both hands on the table. "Don't you see? This is a good thing. Before, they were treating it like a closed case." Christine takes a sip of her bottled green tea. "But now they're at least giving the public"—she points at herself and then to us—"a chance to be heard. This means Ms. Moore has a shot."

"That's great," I say. "We'll go and make sure they hear our support."

"No!" Riley waves her hand. "We'll do more than that. We'll e-mail and call people." She points around the courtyard. "Let's talk it up to everyone and get a lot of people to come."

Ana gives her a high five. "This is perfect. I'll handle the AP students. Zoe, you take the band. Riley, you talk to the cheerleaders and the jocks. And Christine, you're on the artists. Try to rein them in." I feel the tiny ridged edge of a quarter and grasp it in my palm.

"Exactly," Christine says. "Show our support in numbers. The meeting is in a month, so we need to get organized."

"Plenty of time." Ana laughs a little. I sort of doubt this is actually enough time to pull it all together, but this is the most animated I've seen Ana in weeks, so I just nod. Maybe Ms. Moore's cause will be good for her, help her refocus on the present.

Aha. I locate another coin at the bottom of my bag. I pull it out and feel the weight of two quarters in my palm. This whole public meeting thing is crazy, but who knows, maybe it's just crazy enough to work.

15

coast down the hill into the parking lot of the Sea Witch. This isn't the classiest motel at any time of the year, but the low wooden building looks run-down and depressing on this bleak October day. The paint is peeling, and the roof looks a little wonky. There are a few cars scattered in the parking lot, but for the most part it's fairly deserted. If Ed thinks staying at this place is preferable to staying with us, things are really bad.

My bike makes a clanking sound as I climb off and walk it across the parking lot. Ed was going to stay here while he looks for an affordable apartment, but he moved out a long time ago and I haven't heard him talk about checking out rentals yet. We talk on the phone a lot, but it was Christine's idea to invite myself over for dinner tonight. I need to talk to him, really talk, and face-to-face is the only way this is going to work.

I lean my bike against the wall outside Room 12. There's an orange rust stain on the door. I knock, and a second later Ed is standing at the door, wearing his old denim shirt—wrinkled, but clean. He throws his arms around me and ushers me inside.

"It's not a palace, but it works," he says, gesturing around at the dark room. It's small, with a bed in the middle and a tiny bathroom at the back.

"Not bad." I sit down on the bed and run my hand over the polyester bedspread. It has that damp feeling places around here get without proper ventilation.

"Your brother didn't want to come?" Ed tries to smile, flashing his crooked front tooth.

"He had a lot of stuff going on." I stare at a bleach stain on the mottled carpet.

"Well," he says quickly. "Then it's just me and my girl. Nothing wrong with that." He points to the tiny table in the corner of the room. There are half a dozen white Chinese take-out boxes spread across the top. "I got us dinner." He flushes a little.

I survey the offerings. He's got rice and half a dozen kinds of vegetables, as well as fortune cookies and little Styrofoam plates and plastic silverware.

"It looks great." I step toward the table. "And it smells delicious." I lower myself into a padded beige chair. Ed sits across from me and starts to dish out broccoli and beans and spicy tofu while I pour us cups of Sprite from the two-liter bottle he has chilling in the room's small refrigerator.

"So," he says, breaking apart his cheap wooden chopsticks, "how's your mom?"

"Fine." I'm not sure how much I'm supposed to say. "She's good." I play with my chopsticks. "We're all good."

"That's good," he says, though his face falls a little. "I'm doing well too. Handyman work is going well."

I mash my rice into the puddle of sauce on my plate. I like the rice to be good and soaked.

"And the horses?"

"They're good." I study the grains on my plate. The air

smells a little funky in here, like mold and feet and soy sauce. "They miss you."

"You know we've had Old Gray Mare since Nick was a toddler?" Ed rubs his chopsticks together. "I've never been away from them for so long."

"Wow. I didn't know she was that old." I pick up a piece of broccoli. That horse has been frail as long as I can remember.

"That was a long time ago." He gets a far-off look in his eyes. "She was why we first built the stable, you know. We were going to have a whole business." I nod. I knew my parents started out hoping to have a business with the horses, giving riding lessons and leading tours through the woods and along the beach. "At one time we were going to build a new house too."

I raise my eyebrows, but my mouth is full.

Ed shrugs. "Back when we first bought the land, when we were first married, we put up the dome to get started. We built it ourselves so we would have something to live in until we got on our feet." He stabs at a piece of tofu. "Then we were going to build a big place, out in the woods." He shakes his head. "I think we still have the plans for the real house somewhere."

"I never knew that." It's weird to think of my parents being young, in love, full of dreams. Everything is so different now. "What happened?"

"We were waiting for the stable to take off. Then your brother came along, and everything changed. I started doing landscaping to help out."

We both chew in silence for a minute. The low hum of the fluorescent lights is the only sound.

"Ed." I pile more snow peas on my rice to give my hands something to do. He smiles, waiting for me to go on. This is what I came here for, so I might as well say it. "Why don't you come back home?"

Ed doesn't answer for a moment. He taps his chopsticks on the edge of the Styrofoam plate, then lays them down carefully and crosses his legs.

"I'd love nothing more." He sighs. "But it's not that simple." He reaches for his plastic cup but doesn't take a drink, just holds it in his hand. "Marriages are complicated. Your mother and I . . . we've got some problems to work out."

"I know." I smile at him. In the dim lighting he looks pale and tired. "But we miss you. All of us."

"Your mother said that?" His eyes light up a bit, and for a second he looks so hopeful that I can't bear to tell him the truth. Dreamy hasn't exactly said as much, but it's so obvious.

I take a deep breath. Ms. Moore said to fight. She didn't say anything about not fighting dirty.

I nod. "We all want you to come home."

16

Dean's bedroom doesn't look anything like Marcus's, not that I thought it would. Not that I thought about that, I mean . . . it doesn't look like anyone's bedroom that I've ever known.

The Farcuses don't allow us to be in Marcus's bedroom. They've never said this rule out loud, but one time when he was trying to show me his new fish, his mom mysteriously popped into his room and hung around until we left.

Our project is due in two weeks, and we have a lot of work left, but the school library closes at four, so here we are.

"Whoa," I say under my breath as I step inside. In the corner of Dean's room are a black electric guitar, a video camera on a tripod, and a saxophone. The guitar has a skull and crossbones sticker on it, and the sax is dented and scratched. "I didn't know you played."

"I dabble." Dean flops onto his bed. "I used to play sax."

I've been trying to put my finger on exactly what it is about him that makes me so unnerved, and I've finally figured it out. He's too casual. He never worries about the right thing to say or do or what I think of him . . . he just does. I walk over and pick up the guitar while I figure out what to do with myself. There's a bed in the middle of the room and some books, assorted shoes, and CDs scattered around. But there's nowhere else to sit.

I slip the strap over my head, and the guitar hangs low on me. I hold down a string with my finger, and it pinches my skin. "I always sort of wanted to learn the guitar."

"Turn around." Somehow he doesn't make it sound like a command, so I do it. "It looks pretty good on you."

"Really?" I press three strings down and strum. A horrible noise comes out.

"You're no Debbie Harry, but you look good."

I lean in toward the old, scarred corkboard over Dean's bed. There are lots of pictures tacked up in a messy way, jumbled one over the other: Dean and his parents dressed up inside a church, Dean with some friends, Dean and some cousin or something, Dean dressed up in a tux, posing with a girl at a school dance.

"Did you go to a prom?" I squint at the girl in the photo. She's pretty, if you like the Barbie look.

"Yeah right." Dean snorts. "That'll be the day. Prom is for losers." Dean squints at the photo. "That was this thing I had to go to for school. They pick like fifty kids and make them dress up like dorks and parade them around in front of congressmen and stuff." He rolls his eyes. "It was lame and I tried to ditch but my mom insisted."

"Sure." I glance back at him.

He holds his hands up in the air. "Seriously, I'm not into all that ra-ra school stuff." He walks over and jabs his finger at the picture. "Pure torture."

I study his face. Something tells me Dean doesn't want to admit it was a very big deal to be selected, even if his date does look like Skipper's evil twin sister.

"Knock, knock." I turn my head as a woman walks into

the room. She's tall, like Dean, with the same olive skin and jet-black hair, and she's wearing hip, thick-framed glasses.

"You must be Zoe," she says. "I'm Mrs. Marchese." Mar-kay-sey. Even though I've never said it aloud, I recognize his last name from class. He must be Italian or something. I let the guitar hang from my neck and shake Dean's mom's hand.

"I heard you're quite the musician. Do you play guitar too?" A large gold cross dangles from around her neck, catching my eye. Something about it looks different, not like the crosses you see at churches in California. It's very ornate and dramatic, almost artsy in a way. "Dean just took it up, when he dropped the sax."

"I've being playing it for two years!" Dean unlaces one of his shoes and tosses it on the floor. "You have to admit I'm getting better."

"But you were good at the sax." Mrs. Marchese shakes her head. I can't quite place the look on her face. "Well, you'll be good at the guitar too . . . eventually." She winks at me while Dean unlaces his other shoe and throws it gently in her direction. She laughs, grabs it off the floor, and chucks it at him.

"Fine, fine. I know when I'm not wanted." She walks over to the bedroom door and opens it wide. "Nice meeting you, Zoe."

I fight the urge to make an excuse and follow her out of the room.

♡

By ten o'clock my mind is fried, my breath stinks like Chee-tos, and all of my uneasiness with Dean and his room has long since faded away. I've been sitting on the floor at the foot of the bed, but now my back is aching. I lie back, my spine instantly soothed by the change in position, and shut my eyes. Just for a moment. I'll only shut them for a moment.

"My brain hurts."

I hear Dean scoot to the edge of the bed. A shadow falls on my face as he leans over me. "I can't believe I got stuck with you as a partner."

"Ha," I mumble. "I know you're trying to mess with me. I'm not falling for it." Dean stayed on the bed all night, and this system has worked out perfectly. No awkwardness, no close proximity. "I saved this team with my brilliant constitution writing skills."

We went into this evening a little behind schedule, but now we're all caught up and maybe even a little ahead. We worked out the kinks in our economic plan, which pegs our currency to the price of wheat. Then Dean hashed out a solid outline for our twenty-page paper and assigned different sections to each of us, and I drafted our constitution. As nervous as I was about this partnership, we've turned out to be a pretty good team.

My eyes feel glued shut, and I stay perfectly still, letting the exhaustion wash over me. Between band practice, doing this project, worrying about my parents, and plotting to get Ms. Moore back, I've been running myself ragged. I let my head roll to the side and open my right eye a little. The sax in the corner glints at me, so I shut it again.

"Why'd you give up the sax?" Maybe if we talk about something other than Zoeville for a minute, my brain will rest up. "Didn't fit with your new image?"

Dean laughs. Every fall a few underclassmen drop the marching band as they face the inevitable fact that no A-lister ever wore a plumed hat.

"No. My brother played the sax." He falls quiet, and I open my eyes to see why. He stares at a spot on the floor a few feet from us. "It was Fletch's thing, with Dad."

"He stopped too?"

"Died." Dean swallows

"I didn't know." I fight the urge to say I'm sorry. Christine hates it when people say that when they realize her mom is dead. I guess when you lose a loved one, you hear "sorry" so often it starts to sound hollow. "You must miss him." I slide across the floor into Dean's shadow so I can make eye contact with him without squinting at the overhead light.

Dean collapses down on his hands and watches me. "Yeah." He nods slowly. "It's been almost three years, but I still miss him." He dangles an arm over the side of his bed and pulls at a thread in the carpet, making it longer than the rest.

"I'm so sorry." I shut my eyes and berate myself. Why did I say that? I told myself not to say that. "I mean—" A feeling, something tracing down my arm, stops the words in my mouth. I want to open my eyes and make sure it is what I think it is, but what if it stops? The feeling continues, so faintly that I'm not positive it's happening, and then on the third stroke down my arm I make out the smooth, hard edge of a fingernail. When the heat from Dean's hand meets the cool of my forearm, a chill shoots through me, like an electric current.

I should leave. I should stand up, grab my books, and go. They're by the door in a stack. I can see them in my mind.

But . . . his brother is dead. Dean is opening up to me and talking about something so painful and raw. I can't bolt on him now.

He opens his palm and cups my forearm as he gently runs his fingers down the soft fleshy part of my arm, all the way to my wrist. Each hair on my arm is alive. Neither one of us says anything as his fingers trace the small twin bones of my wrist and then flit over my outstretched palm, pausing there for a moment. I hold my breath. Is this happening? Will he? He links his fingers in mine.

I bolt to my feet. "I have to go." In an instant, I'm across the room and stuffing my books in my backpack. "I'm really tired." I stand up but keep my back to him. "No need to walk me out."

"What about"—I hear Dean get up from the bed and edge closer to the door—"the fair citizens of Zoeville?"

"Bye." I scramble out of his bedroom, rush quickly down the stairs, and let myself out the front door silently, hoping not to disturb his mom. I run to a dark portion of the yard, under a big valley oak tree, and press my back to its rough, uneven trunk. I pull out my phone and call home, affect an airy tone, and ask to be picked up. Dreamy tells me Nick is on the way.

I cover my face with my hands and try to take deep breaths, listening intently for the sound of a door opening, but nothing happens. After a few minutes, my heart slows a little.

As I wait for Nick in the shadows on this chilly October night, I ask God again and again for just one thing. I need to take it all back.

17

E d."

"Butterbean. Happy Thanksgiving."

"Happy Thanksgiving to you too." I try to make my voice sound casual, like I just had an idea. "Hey, I was thinking, why don't you come on over for dinner tonight?"

"Oh." Ed sucks in his breath. "You know I would love to see you, honey. But I . . . I'm not so sure my coming over there is a good idea."

"Sure it is." I'm instigating a sneak attack. It's Thanksgiving. They have to play nice today. "Dreamy's got the Tofurky in the oven, and she's making those sweet potatoes you love, and—"

"That's sweet, Zo." Ed clears his throat. "But I can't come to the house. That wouldn't be good."

"But the horses—"

"Zoe. I'm afraid not."

"Oh." The air whooshes out of my lungs.

"But I would love to see you. Why don't you stop by after the big feast?" His voice is a little too chipper, but I pretend I don't notice.

"Okay. Sure. See you then."

♡

I carefully balance the overstuffed box in my left hand and turn the doorknob with my right. I get the door open, step inside, and lean back until it shuts.

"Zoe, is that you?" Dreamy calls from the kitchen.

I freeze where I am. She can't see me from there. "Yeah?"

"We're eating in ten minutes, okay?"

"Okay." I sneak into the dining room and set the heavy box down. After Ed said no, I had to revise my plan a little, but even without him, I can still pull this family together. Dreamy has been cooking for a week while Nick has been program-ming or whatever it is he does in there all by himself. I don't know what happened on the ranch, but it must have been pretty bad for him to prefer being alone all the time. This means it's up to me to remind them what Thanksgiving really means. It's about people with obvious differences brokering a day of peace and sharing a meal together.

But getting everything together took longer than I thought. There's so much stuff in the garage it took me a long time to find what I needed. Now if I can keep Dreamy out of my hair a little longer, I'll be able to make it all come together.

"Nick! Thanksgiving!" Dreamy yells. The smell of cinna-mon and sugar is wafting through the air. I don't have a lot of time.

I pat my back pocket and find the matches. I strike one and light a couple of Dreamy's homemade beeswax candles, then lower the lights.

I blow out the match and walk back over to the box, dig-ging deep inside the dusty jumble, looking for the best album. It's covered in a metallic green, gold, and white fabric, and the pictures inside are yellowed. I open the front cover to a picture of Dreamy, as big as a house, pregnant with Nick. Below her is a shot of Ed with a dog I don't recognize. Ed has giant lamb-chop sideburns, and he's wearing tight, cowboy-looking jeans. I run my fingers over the pictures, tracing their familiar faces gently. Nick thumps down the stairs behind me. I grab two more albums out of the box and scurry over to the table, putting them under my chair.

"It's so fancy in here," Nick says as he walks into the room. He takes his usual seat and grabs a dinner roll from the basket.

"Here's the Tofurky." Dreamy comes in, holding the loaf-like brown tofu that smells surprisingly good. She slides into her seat and takes a deep breath.

"Wow." Dreamy looks around and takes in the elaborate place settings. "Thank you, Zoe." She pulls a knife off the table and begins to carve the "turkey." "Everything looks lovely."

"Did you notice that it's Great-grandma's china?" I hold up my plate with the delicate silver rim. "You got that for your wedding, huh?"

Dreamy motions for me to hand her my plate. "Yup." She puts a few pieces of "meat" on it.

"And where is this tablecloth from again?" I blink my eyes and try to pull a confused expression onto my face.

"Your father gave it to me," Dreamy mumbles and picks up the sweet potatoes. She dishes a huge glob onto her plate. "I'm not quite sure how these turned out. I'm using a new rec- ipe this year."

"For which anniversary?" I finger the handmade lace. I know the whole story backward and forward. Ed gave it to

Dreamy for their first wedding anniversary. She admired it at a craft fair, and he sneaked away and bought it for her.

"Nick, sweet potatoes?" She hands the Pyrex dish to Nick and picks up the green beans.

I glance over at Nick and see his face stuffed with a vegan roll, oblivious to what I'm trying to do. His skull is impossibly thick.

"This is so"—Nick swallows the huge chunk of food in his mouth—"good. Thanks, Dreamy." He shovels another huge bite in his mouth, making me lose my appetite.

"I saw this article in *Vegetarian Times* last week, and I knew we had to try it." Dreamy slips a small bite of her stupid potatoes in her mouth.

How can these two be so focused on the food? Can't they see there is an entire chair just sitting empty at our table?!

"Why don't we say grace?" I say through my teeth. Dreamy knits her brow at me. This was usually Ed's job. He always said grace. I extend my hand to her, and she blots her mouth with her napkin.

"Of course." She takes my hand. "That's a wonderful idea."

Nick raises an eyebrow and slowly holds out his hand toward me.

I bow my head and wait for a moment. I peek up to make sure they have lowered their heads and closed their eyes too. "Thank you, Lord, for this meal, and for the time we get to spend together as a *family*," I say, adding a bit of emphasis to the last word. "And please bless Ed. Bring him home soon. Amen."

Dreamy clears her throat and opens her mouth, but she doesn't say anything. She quietly reaches for the cranberry relish—Ed's favorite—and passes it to Nick.

He sets it down, scoops a little onto his plate, and continues to wolf down his food as if he's just returned from wandering in the wilderness.

For a few minutes we eat in silence, and the sounds of knives and forks clinking against real china are the only noise.

"Well," I say, looking for some kind of transition. I reach under my chair. "I was thinking it might be fun to go through the old albums today."

"Oh, don't worry." Dreamy waves her hand in the air. "I'm going to organize them soon."

I pull up the one from the first year of their marriage. "I don't want to organize them." I turn to a random page and see a picture of Dreamy and Ed dressed up as John Lennon and Yoko Ono. Ed is probably the world's biggest Beatles fan. They're both so young in these photos. In fact, they were younger than Nick is now. "Look at these pictures. They're amazing."

"Where's Marcus today?" Dreamy asks, her voice thin. She's leaning her head in her hand, her elbow on the table.

"At his grandmother's." Marcus's family goes to see his grandmother in Sacramento all the time.

"That's nice." Dreamy lifts a forkful of food to her mouth but only takes a tiny bite. "You should call your grandmother."

"Yeah." I will not let Dreamy throw me off task. "Nick,

there are some hilarious shots of you in here too. There's this one where you're wearing Ed's boots, and they're practically up to your thighs."

"Really?" Nick finally stops chewing and raises his head from the plate. "Let me see." My heart soars as he reaches for the album.

"There are some other good ones." I grab another from under my chair. "There's this one from the eighties where—"

"Enough!" Dreamy bangs her hand on the table. Nick and I stare at her, wide-eyed. She has dark circles under her eyes, and the laugh lines that used to show the fun she took from life now just make her look old and weary. "Please stop." She lowers her voice to a whisper. "You'll ruin them . . . with the food."

She reaches out her hand, and Nick gives her his album. I stash mine under my chair, feeling my cheeks burn.

We eat in silence for a few more minutes, Dreamy moving food around, Nick shoveling it in as fast as he can. Every breath seems to echo through the house. Dreamy takes a long drink of water, then clears her throat.

"This was"—she stands up and gives me a wobbly smile—"really fun. But I've got to get started on that kitchen."

"Yeah." Nick yawns and pats his belly. He stands up. "And I've got to finish this site by Monday." He reaches for another biscuit.

My heart sinks as I watch the two of them retreat back to their private worlds, filling them up with nonsense and numbness.

I sit there for a while, staring at the empty chairs across

from me, trying to hold back tears. The whole meal lasted less than half an hour.

Part of me knows they did the best they could. They have their own demons to fight, and they're doing it the only way they know how. But when I look at Ed's empty chair, I can't help but think they didn't even try.

18

'm staring at the ceiling in my bedroom, going over all the ways I could have done things differently, when my phone trills to announce a new text message. Probably Marcus. I pull it out of my bag and push the button to bring it up. It's . . . I stop. It's from Dean.

My heart starts to beat faster, and my legs feel a little weak as I open it.

Happy Tofurky Day.

I stare at it for a while. Why would he send this to me? I scroll up and down, but there's nothing more to the message.

I feel myself smiling. It's kind of cool to know he was thinking about me. I guess it would be rude not to answer. I start typing.

Thanks. How's your T-day?

I hit send before I can change my mind, then lie back down, holding the phone in my hand. I sneak a peek at it a few minutes later, and again, but there's no reply.

I could have pushed the photos less. I could have talked

about Ed more. Does Dreamy even know what's going on with him? About the new handyman jobs he's been doing to make ends meet? I could have . . .

I flip my phone open almost before it rings.

"Please save me," Christine moans into the phone. I try to hide my disappointment. "They're making me play games."

I laugh. Christine can be so dramatic sometimes, and if I know her as well as I think I do, she's really calling to make sure I'm okay.

"Candace is campaigning for charades, and Emma wants to play Cranium." She pretends to retch. "I hate Cranium." Emma is Christine's stepsister.

"Wow. Sounds like a party. So this is the first official New Lee Family Thanksgiving?"

"Something like that." She snorts. "Oh no, now they're trying to make Tyler play Taboo. What is it with these people and their electric timers?"

"Tyler's there?" I run my hand along the nylon thread stitched across my bedspread. I've had this thing forever.

"Yeah, he came over after dinner. Please come too. The more people I have, the less likely it is I'll have to demonstrate the hula or something." Christine went through a rough time when Candace and Emma moved in last year, but things seem to have calmed down since the wedding in May. I think Christine actually kind of likes Candace and Emma, though she would never admit it.

"You should suggest Pictionary. You'd clean up."

"So you'll come?"

I sit up. Christine's family is fun, if a little crazy. And it's not like there's anything going on here.

"Sure. Why not."

"Oh, thank God. Please hurry. They just broke out the markers."

♡

"ZOE!" Christine's stepsister, Emma, shrieks when she answers the door. "Come in!" She ushers me in and closes the door behind me. She hangs my coat and purse on the rack by the door, but I grab my phone out, just in case. "Christine, guess who's here?"

"I don't know," Christine calls from the living room. "Could it be Zoe?"

"You're just in time!" Emma leads me down the hall to the living room. She's taller than last time I saw her, and her brown hair is longer now, more wavy and less curly. "We're about to start playing Cranium. You can be on my team." She's still a spaz though. It's good to know eighth grade hasn't changed her that much.

"Zoe. So good to see you!" Candace gets up from the couch to give me a hug and ushers me into the living room. They all look quite comfortable tonight, sprawled out on the couches, laughing. Christine's dad is hunched over, snapping batteries into the electric timer, and Tyler is leaning back on the love seat next to Christine, his feet up on the table. He looks totally comfortable here. I pull my phone out of my pocket and press a button to light up the screen. No response.

"Hey, Zoe." He waves, and I sit down uncertainly on the couch.

"Hey." He's almost too comfortable, like he's spent a lot of time here.

"Zoe's on my team." Emma flops down on the couch next to me.

"You're ditching me?" Tyler pretends to stab himself in the heart. "I thought we were a team, Emma." He twists the fake knife around.

"You snooze, you lose, bucko," Emma says, shrugging. She turns to me. "What color do you want to be? Let's be red. Red is the best anyways, and I'm always red."

"Welcome to the funny farm," Christine says, rolling her eyes at me, but she's smiling. I try not to think about how quiet my own house is today. A year ago Christine would have done anything to avoid spending a holiday with Emma and Candace.

"Are Ana and Riley coming?"

I ignore Emma, chatting away in my ear. My phone buzzes, and I grab it quickly. Marcus. I'll call him back later. I send him straight to voice mail.

Christine shakes her head. "Ana's serving dinner at the nursing home, and Tom's in town, so Riley's out with him."

Christine's dad snaps the cover of the timer back on and holds it up triumphantly. "I did it." Mr. Lee is not one of those Mr. Fix It dads like Ed.

"We're going first." Emma starts to clap, then reaches for the big ten-sided die.

"Emma, you need to calm down and be patient." Candace wags her finger at her. "This is not how a big sist—" Candace claps a hand over her mouth, making a hollow thud.

We all turn to her and study her beet-red face. Emma is the *little* sister at the Lee household, not the big sister. But why would it matter if Candace got them confused? Who cares?

Mr. Lee starts shaking in silent laughter.

"What?" Emma asks, jumping up and down. "What? What, what, what, what? Tell me!"

"You might as well tell them now." Mr. Lee nudges his wife and snickers again.

"I really can't believe I did that." Candace shakes her head, grinning from ear to ear. "I guess it's on my mind today with all of us hanging out like this."

"That's okay." Christine stands up and heads toward the kitchen. "You don't have to tell us. Don't force yourself."

Candace studies Christine as she pulls a plastic cup down from the cupboard and then glances at Mr. Lee. He nods. "I was going to wait to tell you guys, but, well, I guess the secret is out now."

Christine's eyes widen, and her face drains of color.

Emma leans forward. "OMG! What already?"

Candace reaches for Mr. Lee's hand, and he smiles at her. "We're expecting a baby!"

Emma's shrieks nearly blow out my eardrums. She starts clapping her hands and bouncing around on the couch. She begins to spin in circles singing, "I'm going to be a big sister! I'm going to be a big sister!"

Christine slowly wanders back into the living room with an empty plastic cup in her hand. "When?" She sets it on the coffee table.

"We're due in May."

I let my breath out and try to process the fact that while

my family is falling apart, Christine's family is expanding yet again. She leans back against the couch, and slowly, almost imperceptibly, Tyler reaches for her hand.

♡

I'm crawling into bed when I finally get a text back from Dean. I flip my phone open and stare at it while it takes about a hundred years to load.

> Cool. Wanted to wish everyone a good day. See you around.

I read it over several times. Did he send his earlier text to everyone in his phone book? I scroll through my phone and pull up the message. It's impossible to tell. But why would he mention Tofurky unless he was talking specifically to me? And yet, his new message doesn't make sense unless he sent it to a bunch of people.

I pull up a text Ana sent to the Miracle Girls about Ms. Moore last week. Riley and Christine wrote back, but I can only see that she sent the original message to me.

My phone falls to the bed. What if I'm the only loser who wrote him back?

I snap off my light and crawl under the covers, burrowing down into them and pulling my old quilt up over my head. He probably thinks I'm obsessed with him now. I press my eyes together as tight as they'll go. I want to block out this whole, horrible day.

Eventually, slowly, I begin to pray, mumbling my requests out loud, asking for God's blessing on my family, on Ed, and on Dreamy. I pray for reconciliation and forgiveness. I pray for Christine and the changes her new family is about to face. And I pray for Dean, wherever he is, that he will forget I ever existed.

I'm finally drifting off to sleep when I realize I never called Marcus back.

19

Whatever happened to those bonds your great aunt Emmeline left you?" Dreamy peers at Ed over her reading glasses. "I want to make sure those go to you. Or you can sign them over to the kids."

"Didn't we cash them in for Nick's graduation party?" Ed's face is ashen, and he seems even thinner than normal. The skin on his face almost hangs. Is he eating enough?

I trudge past them into the kitchen for some Thanksgiving leftovers. I open the fridge and sigh. I had real pumpkin pie at Christine's house last night, and now the soggy vegan substitute at my house is just plain depressing.

"You're right. Okay, let's move on." I hear Dreamy rustle some papers. When I came home last night, she was still up preparing for this. They're trying to make sense of a lifetime of combined finances. Listening to them has turned this grim holiday weekend into a torture session, but I can't tear myself away.

I opt for the candied sweet potatoes and pull a spoon from the drawer. I'm not supposed to eat out of the dish, but who even cares anymore?

"Okay, on to the house. How are we going to divide that up? I read some articles at the library and it seems that—"

"Well, I'm not going to live at the Sea Witch forever." At first Ed seemed to be kind of blindsided by the divorce, but lately he's been voicing grievances of his own, hinting at old hurts and scores unsettled, and I've realized that they both have issues to work out. "I can tell you that much. I built this house with my own two hands."

As I shovel my third bite of sweet potatoes into my mouth, the doorbell rings, but my parents don't notice.

"What is *that* supposed to mean?" Dreamy gives a loud sigh. "I was right there next to you, helping you build this house, every nail."

"I'll get it," I yell, but no one responds. Nick must be hanging out in his room, avoiding everything yet again.

I shove the casserole dish back into the fridge as the bell rings another time. I dash to get it, blocking out the rise in Dreamy and Ed's voices. I've been around them fighting enough to know that we're only a few minutes from an all-out screaming match. Whoever it is, I need to get rid of them.

I peer through the peephole and almost gasp when I see Marcus. How long has it been since we've hung out? I crack the door just enough, then wiggle through the opening, and shut it behind me.

"Hi." I give him a quick wave and glance nervously behind me. Can he hear their voices through the door? I can, but I'm listening for them.

"Hey." Marcus leans in and gives me a hug that I can barely return. I'm really not in the headspace for this. He needs to learn to call before he comes over.

We wait for a long moment, and it dawns on me that he

thinks I'm going to invite him in. "So . . . how was your grand-ma's?" Ed's booming voice is clearly audible in the silence that follows. They're at it now for sure.

"It was good . . ." Marcus moves his head, trying to make eye contact with me. "What about"—he coughs—"your Thanks-giving? Did you guys have a big meal?"

"Yep." I take a few steps away from the door, hoping he'll follow me. It's a bright November day. The air is brisk and sharp and there's not a cloud in the sky. "A crazy vegan feast."

"It must have been good to finally have all four of you at the table." Marcus walks behind me. I don't know where I'm leading him, but I'm glad he can't see my face. "I mean, now that Nick is home."

"Um, something like that." I plop under a tree in our front yard and rub my hands together a little. It's too cold to sit out-side for long, but at least we're out of earshot of the fight.

Marcus sits down next to me, taking pains to find a spot without any twigs or pebbles. "You know, I see Nick around a lot, but I haven't seen Ed in a long time."

"Umm . . ." I try to think of something truthful I can say in response. I guess I haven't quite managed to tell Marcus everything. I've tried a couple times, but it never seems to come out. "He's here now." I gesture at his beat-up Datsun.

"Zoe." He takes my hand. I can feel him trying to look at me, but I keep my head bowed. "What's going on?" He rubs my hands, keeping them warm.

It hits me that they're in there talking about who gets the house. It's our house, the weird white bubble that represents us, the funky, free-spirited Fairchilds. You can't divide it up.

And why hasn't Ed moved home yet? When he first decamped to the Sea Witch, I thought it was going to be a temporary thing, that I could make them see how silly they're acting. Ed would understand how much he needs us, and Dreamy would realize how empty our house feels without him.

"Please tell me." Marcus shakes his head. "You've been so distant and closed off. I'm really worried."

I raise my head and see his warm brown eyes staring back at me. Why haven't I told him? Marcus is so good to me. Maybe I don't want to disappoint him with my messy life and imperfections.

"My parents are . . ." My lips quiver so much that I have to pinch them together to steady them. Marcus squeezes my hands and keeps his gaze locked on me. "They're saying they're going to get a divorce." As soon as the d-word leaves my mouth, the tears well up in my eyes. Marcus pulls me into a hug and rubs my back as I sob harder than I have in ages. This is why I love Marcus.

"But they're not going to . . ." I glance back at my house. From this distance, it's the picture of quiet domesticity, the same loving household I've always known. "They're not going to go through with it. I've got a plan."

Marcus gives me a lopsided grin. "I'm sure they'll work it out. Dreamy and Ed love each other very much." He puts a hand on my knee. "But if they don't, you can come to me."

"They will! They're going to figure this out!" I don't mean to yell, but Marcus isn't listening to me.

"Okay, okay." He holds his hands up. "They'll work it out." He scratches his head and looks at me warily.

I lace my fingers through the parched brown grass and grip the dying roots. All we need is a couple of good rains, then Ed will start landscaping again and we'll have more money. Dreamy won't be stressed if she can pay the bills. "You really think they'll work it out, right?"

"I do." Marcus nudges me so that I'll look at him. "I really do."

20

I peer into the smudged windows of El Bueno Burrito and hesitate. Thanks to its fake Mexican theme, it looks dreary and depressing, the way only an off-brand fast-food restaurant can. I shut my eyes and say a prayer for strength. I might as well go in. It's not like they'll be hiring anyway, and then I'll know I've exhausted every option. I walk past a few occupied orange plastic tables and approach the counter.

After several weeks of halfheartedly searching online postings, I decided to get serious about finding a job. It's the Christmas season, and stores always need extra help this time of year, and well, we need the help too. I started job hunting at the Half Moon Bay Coffee Company. That was three hours ago, and I was stuttering and shaking so hard that I had to repeat myself three times. Now I've almost gotten used to the humiliation.

"Hi," I say to the tall, skinny guy working the register. I see a patch of hair on his neck that he missed when shaving. "Are you guys hiring?"

I wait for him to say no. Half Moon Bay Coffee Company, Bayside Books, the record store, and four different gift shops all told me the same thing.

"I'll go get the manager." His voice is squeaky. Ah yes, this trick. I've already encountered it several times. He's going to let the manager tell me no.

As he disappears behind the swinging door to the kitchen, I steel myself so I won't cry. Stupid small town. Stupid, stupid Half Moon Bay, where all the good jobs are taken—and the bad jobs too. I don't even like burritos.

The manager walks over to the front counter, followed by the tall guy.

Maybe I can make money by selling stuff on the Internet instead? Or by starting some kind of green company? Oh. I could collect cans and scrap metal and recycle them. That has to be worth something.

"Gus is the name." The manager sticks out his hand eagerly, and I shake it.

"I'm Zoe."

"You need a job?" He's a very average man: average height, brown eyes, not fat, not thin. In fact, he's almost completely forgettable except for his nervous energy and his brown brush-like mustache.

"Yeah." I start to back away from the counter. "But I know you're probably not hiring. I'll check back in the spring."

"No, wait." Gus waves his hands in the air. "We need someone."

I stop in my tracks. "Really?"

"Hold on. I'll go get my interview forms." He dashes into the back. While he's gone, I try to smile at the skinny guy, but he won't meet my eyes so I stare at his Adam's apple, mesmerized by how it moves up and down his neck.

Gus runs back in, wagging a piece of paper in the air. "Please, please," he ushers me over to an empty table. "Do you have time for the interview right now?"

I walk over to the table, taking in the ugly orange tile, the hideous piñatas hanging from the ceiling, and the smell of greasy meat that lingers in the air. "I guess so." I pull out the chair across from him and sit with my back to the door. The tabletop feels sticky.

Gus takes a pen from his pocket and clicks the ballpoint out. "Zoe, may I please have your last name?"

For the first fifteen minutes, Gus meticulously ticks boxes, fills in blanks, and gets his little form just so. I answer his questions, smile a lot, and try to look hirable. No matter what he offers me, I need to take it. I focus my thoughts on buying groceries for the family, shopping for a nice blouse for Dreamy, splurging on some new work boots for Ed. We need this. I can do this. But my hands are slick with sweat.

"Now I know you probably have your heart set on cooking." Gus shakes his head solemnly. I shiver. The idea of touching raw meat creeps me out. "But you have to work up to that. For now we need someone to run the register. Are you good with numbers?"

The door to the shop opens, distracting him for a moment.

I cough. "Well . . . I'm a fast learner." There. That wasn't a lie.

The people walk up to the counter, and I almost gasp out loud when I spy a familiar flash of über-blonde hair. Riley? Riley and Michael?! Jeez louise. What are the odds? I slump down a little in my chair.

"Are you good with machines? The reg can be a little tricky." Gus's excited voice snaps me back.

"Well . . ." I don't think there's really any way to spin this. One time I exploded a mug in the microwave, I can barely operate our TV remote, and don't even get me started on computers. Nick got all of those genes.

I glance nervously at Riley. She hasn't seen me yet, but her brother, Michael, seems to be counting the tiles on the floor. What if he looks up?

"Wonderful, wonderful." Gus makes some notations, and I decide to keep my stupid mouth shut. "You start Saturday, Zoe. Welcome aboard."

My mouth hangs open.

"What do you say to that?" Gus bounds out of his chair and grins at me like a maniac. It dawns on me that he wants me to show some enthusiasm.

"Awesome," I say quietly. Maybe if I hurry things along here, I can sneak out before Riley sees me. I thought no one ate here. I don't mind working somewhere cool and seeing people, or even somewhere lame if no one ever visits, but I don't want to work somewhere lame that people *do* go to. I'll die of embarrassment. What if . . . but he wouldn't. Not his style.

Gus gives me an awkward high five and sort of accidentally slaps my shoulder, but he doesn't seem to notice.

"Can you get here at seven?"

"What?!" I sputter before I can stop my mouth. "A.m.?"

Michael turns at the sound and squints across the room. His face lights up, and he points at me. Marvelous.

"We're doing these new breakfast burritos that people are crazy for." Gus stares around the cramped, grim burrito place and smiles with pride. "Let me run to get your W-4 and some other HR forms to fill out." He disappears into the back room, and I lean against the table, trying to look nonchalant, like maybe I just polished off a nice veggie burrito and I'm on my way home.

Michael tugs on Riley's arm until she turns to him. He points at me, and I give a shy wave back. Busted.

"Zoe!" Riley walks over and hugs me. "Your mom does this too?"

"What?"

She holds up two white paper sacks. "You know, makeshift Mexican. Mom sends me and Michael for burritos about once a week, whenever she gets too busy." Like most of the rich families in town, they live within walking distance of downtown, not out in the boonies like us.

"Who was that man?" Michael says, skipping the part where we exchange niceties. Last summer he attended a special program for autistic kids in San Francisco, and he's gotten a lot better, but he can still be a little blunt.

"Um, the manager." Maybe they won't ask more questions. I don't know if I'm prepared to answer them.

Gus strides out of the back room at just that moment. I have no luck today, I swear.

"Hi there." He waves frantically at Riley and Michael. "Gus, the manager, here. Just wanted to say thank you for stopping by!"

"We come every week." Michael's tone is a little harsh, but Gus doesn't seem to notice.

"Great! I love it!" Gus turns to me. "And here are your forms, Comrade Zoe. See you bright and early Saturday morning!" He gives me one more high five for good measure.

"Thank you," I say, ignoring Riley's stunned face. "See you then." I put my arm on Riley's back and move her to the door. There's something kind of off with Gus. It's good to love your job, but he loves his job a little too much, if you ask me.

It's just meat inside a flat pancake. It's not rocket science or anything.

Gus waves until I finally get all three of us outside and shut the door.

"You got a job, Zo?!" Riley shrieks.

"When will you work? You have to go to school." Michael makes momentary eye contact with me. "It's a state law."

"Why didn't you tell us?" Riley laughs a little, shaking her head. "Are you sure you can handle it?"

I bite my lip and take a few steps away from the building. "The marching band is winding down now." I grab my arms and hug myself to stay warm. It's going to be a cold bike ride home. "And you guys are busy a lot. I just thought it'd be fun." Chill bumps raise on my arm.

"You can drop out at sixteen, but only if your parents consent." Michael leans in close and studies my face. "Are your parents going to consent?"

"I'm still going to school." I shrug a little at him. "I'll only be working a few nights and Saturdays."

"What about your parents?" The exterior lights from El Bueno Burrito fall across Riley's burning stare. "Do they know about this?"

I rub my hands together and blow into them. "Yeah, they're . . . it'll be fine." I'll tell them now that it's settled.

"I'm cold. I want to go home." Michael pulls his Windbreaker from his waist and threads his arms through the sleeves.

I need to change the subject, distract Riley. "Speaking of, where on earth has Tom been?" This really isn't the time to talk about this, but that's what comes to mind. Lately Riley's mentioned Tom less and less. If I didn't know better, I could swear that . . . "College must be as fun as they say."

"Ha ha ha," she laughs loudly. "Oh yeah. He's great." She opens up her bag of food and sniffs. Michael begins to pull her arm, but she doesn't seem to notice. "He's really awesome."

I can tell there's more to this story, and I want to ask her all about it, but something about her forced laugh and ear-to-ear smile stops me. If she wanted to talk about it, she would. "That's good." I nod and smile at her reassuringly. But maybe I should nudge her to talk about it. Is that what a friend would do? "He should come down. I'd love to see him."

"Oh, he will." Riley allows herself to be led away a few feet. "I'll make sure of it."

Michael walks around behind her back and pushes with both of his hands. "Let's go." He's not angry, just determined.

"Tell Dreamy I said hi," she says over her shoulder.

"Sure!" I wave at them and smile as they walk away. "Of course I will."

I wait for Riley and Michael to disappear around the corner of the shopping center, then unchain my bike. I swing my leg over the middle bar and take a deep breath for the long, cold ride home.

21

"Ms. Moore always took time to make sure we understood the symbolism in the stories we read." Riley is cool, calm, composed. She smiles out at the audience as if she does this sort of thing all the time.

Of the four of us, we decided Riley was the best choice to speak at Ms. Moore's hearing. I'd rather go to school in my underwear than get up in front of a group of people like this. We still don't even know who filed the lawsuit, but we hope to pick up some clues tonight.

"She taught us that when you just look at the surface, you're only getting half the story. It's when you dig in, read carefully, and try to understand the meanings and images behind the words that you can begin to understand what a book is really about." Riley glances down at her page of notes and then back at the crowd. She makes it look so easy.

"More important, she taught us that people are like that too. When you look beyond their actions and try to understand their motivations, what makes them do the things they do, things often look a whole lot different." Riley pauses and takes a deep breath. "It's time to look deeply not only at what Ms. Moore taught us, but why. She truly cares about her students. Now it's time for us to do the same for her. It's time to bring Ms. Moore back to Marina Vista."

Riley steps away from the microphone and ducks her head as the crowd in the theater begins to clap. She walks down the steps back to our seats, and a few guys whistle as she makes her way up the aisle.

"Thank you, Riley," Ms. Lovchuck says, taking her place behind the podium at the center of the stage. "Anyone else?"

The theater is packed tonight, and every seat is filled. Christine's dad, a local politician, is sitting in the back row with the head of the school board, taking furious notes. There are even people standing at the back and squeezed into the aisles. I'm not sure if our outreach effort helped or hurt our cause. Our e-mails and posters brought out Ms. Moore's supporters, but they also inspired her detractors and a fair number of people who simply love a good scandal. The whole meeting has the air of a bad episode of *Jerry Springer.*

Someone pops up in the front of the room as Riley plops into the seat next to Christine.

"Kayleen. The microphone is yours." Ms. Lovchuck gives her a canned smile and steps back offstage.

Kayleen, the bubbly blonde cheerleader, adjusts the microphone, clears her throat, and starts to read from a sheet of paper. "When I found out that I got the new English teacher, Ms. Moore, my freshman year, I was excited." Marcus grabs my hand and holds on to it tightly. I squeeze it back.

"But I quickly realized there was something odd about her. Something unusual. Her assignments got weirder and weirder—"

I try to stand up and protest, but Marcus grabs my arm and pulls me back down.

"Let it go," he whispers.

Kayleen looks up from her paper. "Can anyone tell me what having all the guys in our class—and none of the girls—put on wigs and read Shakespeare aloud has to do with learning?" A few people snicker and one person claps. I swing around in my folding chair and try to see who it is, but it's impossible to know.

"Great writers like Shakespeare deserve our respect, not fake sword fights and cross-dressing." I make my fists into balls and dig my fingernails into my palms. Is Kayleen some kind of idiot? Ms. Moore told us why she did that. In Shakespeare's day, women were not allowed to be actors. For the female parts, men would wear wigs and dresses and talk in high voices. She wanted us to see what it would have been like to see the plays in context. Plus, if I know Ms. Moore, she was probably also saying something about the rights of women.

"And then there is her syllabus. My friends at other schools are reading classics like Mark Twain, Herman Melville, and Ernest Hemingway." Kayleen holds her paper a little closer to her face. I shake my hands, trying to calm down and stay relaxed. I want people to see that I have complete confidence in my position. "Why are we reading books by writers neither I, nor my parents"—Kayleen looks up and smiles at a slim, attractive couple—"have ever heard of, people like Chinua Achebe, Sandra Cisneros, and Amy Tan?"

I lean forward and try to catch Ms. Moore's eye. I want her to know that I recognize Kayleen is distorting the truth, but she doesn't see me. She's sitting by a portly, older gentleman in a very expensive-looking suit. Marcus said he's her lawyer, and she's probably been advised not to speak at all tonight.

Kayleen clears her throat and takes a deep breath. "Thank

you for listening to my speech. I tried to report the facts and avoid emotions."

I snort, unable to control myself. If Kayleen had been paying attention at all in Ms. Moore's class, she would have learned that calling something a fact doesn't make it true. I grip my hands together.

"You may hear a lot tonight about the kindness of Ms. Moore, and she probably is a good person. But what Half Moon Bay and the teachers, parents, and student body of Marina Vista need to decide is if she's a good teacher." My leg starts to bounce up and down.

Kayleen lowers her paper and locks eyes with me.

"And I'm afraid the answer to this question is no."

I want to spring from my seat, fly across the room, and scratch Kayleen's eyes out. I restrain myself—barely.

"We can, and should, do better by our students. Thank you." Kayleen lowers her head in some kind of bow, and a few people begin to clap forcefully. My heart sinks. I can't believe people are clapping for her. That speech was . . . that was unbelievable. It was wrong. It was . . .

And before I know what I'm doing, I'm standing up and pushing my way toward the aisle.

"Go, Zoe!" Ana calls. She's still pretty upset about the big breakup, but there was no question that she'd come tonight. So much is on the line. I feel every eye in the theater on me as I make my way to the front of the room.

Kayleen sits down next to her parents, but Ms. Lovchuck hasn't even made it to the podium when I storm onto the stage. My footsteps echo in the huge room, and she retreats, standing by the big curtain at the edge of the stage, waiting.

"Hi," I say, leaning down a little. I adjust the microphone. Being tall isn't always so awesome.

"Louder!" A man in the back says, and my cheeks flush red.

I fumble with the mic stand, twisting the middle joint, trying to extend the pole. There's a garbled sound as my hair drapes over the mic. Finally I get the stupid thing to work.

"Is this better?"

Some people nod and mumble yes. I clear my throat and glance at my hands, which is dumb because I know I didn't bring anything with me. It's not like I really thought this out, and I don't exactly know what I'm going to say here. I only knew I had to speak out.

"Ms. Moore has been like a second mother to me, a friend—even a sister," I say quietly. I scan the crowd, but of course he's not here. He doesn't even know Ms. Moore, but my stomach still drops a little. "Whenever I had trouble with schoolwork, with friends, or with other stuff, I always knew I could go to Ms. Moore. She'd be there for me with a kind word, some wise advice, or just an ear to listen."

I hear two people in the third row talking and some programs rustling. Everywhere I look, eyes are wandering. I say a quick prayer for eloquence. I need God to make my tongue mighty like Aaron's in the Bible. Ms. Moore's always been there for us, and I can't let her down.

I grab the mic out of the stand and take a few steps. "And you know, honestly, a few of the stories I've heard tonight are sickening, really." I shake my head, thinking about Kayleen's little performance. "Some people check into their job in the morning and check out in the afternoon. But Ms. Moore lived, breathed, ate, and slept her role as a teacher at Marina Vista." My voice gets louder with each sentence. "She was tireless, starting the Earth First Club, pitching in with counseling when Mrs. Canning—"

Mrs. Canning smiles warily from the audience.

"When Mrs. Canning's schedule got overloaded. But probably the best part about Ms. Moore was that she taught us to dream big."

Kayleen nudges Ashley, and they smirk back at me, but it only fuels me to keep going. I know I'm right, and that gives me the courage to keep talking.

"I was born in Half Moon Bay, and I've lived my whole life in this little town. But thanks to Ms. Moore, I have learned about the horrors of oppression in Africa, I have read what it's like to grow up in this country as a young woman from Mexico, and I have sat with aging Chinese women and heard them tell amazing stories."

I feel adrenaline pulsing through me as I speak. The audience stares back at me, but at least they seem to be paying attention. I shut my eyes and pray that my words can make a difference.

"I may only be Zoe Fairchild, the little redhead girl you grew up with, but by reading the stories of other people from worlds far beyond the borders of Half Moon Bay, I have become a citizen of the world." My voice warbles on the last few words. Whenever I get upset, I start to cry, but I can't let myself do that here.

"Ms. Moore, if there's one thing I've learned from you— aside from the fact that Shakespeare plays were originally acted only by men, some of whom wore wigs to portray the women's roles"—I can't resist finding Kayleen's smug, perfect face and giving her a cold, hard stare—"it's that you have to know right from wrong and stand up for what's right." The words feel as though they are being pumped from my heart, through my bloodstream, and onto my tongue. It's as effortless as breathing.

Marcus smiles and shakes his head at me. I avoid his eye. It's not that I . . . I just don't want to get distracted. I clear my throat.

"And you were what was right in my life, in all of our lives. I will not stand by and watch you get pushed aside."

Slowly someone starts clapping, and I follow the sound. Marcus rises from his chair.

"It's . . ." Marcus keeps clapping for all to see. "It's about loyalty." I look away and sweep my hands over the crowd. "About standing up for those who've stood by you."

Marcus puts his fingers in his mouth and lets out a high-pitched whistle. Christine and Riley stand up next to him and start to clap, and Ana joins them a second later. I take a deep breath and keep my eyes away from Marcus.

"Ms. Moore, I learned all of that from you. It's a lesson I'll never forget."

She smiles at me, and I beam back at her. I mean every word of it.

"'Is Ms. Moore a good person?'" I shrug and laugh. "Of course. Not even her detractors can deny that. But is she a good teacher?" I shake my head at the crowd. "No, she's not."

I hear a small gasp in the audience and then some murmuring.

"She's the best teacher Marina Vista has ever had." I hold my breath and listen to the sound of Marcus and the girls clapping.

Other people join in, and slowly everyone sitting in the chairs, except for a few with arms crossed over their chests, rise to their feet and clap and cheer. Out of the corner of my eye, I see Marcus staring at me like I'm a hero, as if I'm the most righteous and noble woman who has ever walked the earth.

I steal a glance at Ms. Moore, but she has her face buried in a tissue. I have to bite my lip so I don't start sobbing on the stage—for her, for all the ways life is cruel and unfair, for all the ways I've failed everyone.

♡

We're on our way to the car at the end of what feels like a very long night when I hear a hoarse whisper.

"Hey."

I know that voice. "Ashley?" I match my hushed tone to hers. "I'm not in the mood, okay?" I rub my itching eyes and shake my head. It feels like hours have passed, though the hearing ended a few minutes ago, after only a couple more people spoke.

"Look—" Ashley peers over her shoulder and then leans in closer to me. Marcus is only a few feet behind us. "I know who did it."

I rock back on my heels. What kind of cruel joke is she playing this time? "Did what?"

Ashley shakes her head and pulls me closer to her. "I know who got Ms. Moore fired."

My eyes go wide. Obviously we figured out it was Kayleen tonight, but I didn't expect her friend to rat her out.

"We need to talk." She fingers her program, folded into the shape of a fan. "Just you and me. Can you do lunch on Monday?"

I would swear this is a setup, but something about Ashley's face says she's not putting me on. I'm usually pretty good at reading people. It's my thing. "Okay," I say, taking pains to sound noncommittal just in case she really is messing with me.

"Don't tell anyone about any of this." Ashley takes a few steps and looks around again. "I mean it."

22

My door squeaks open.

"Hey," I say, not looking up. "I'll be right down to help with dinner. I need to finish this problem."

Dreamy doesn't answer me. I raise my head.

"Oh . . . Nick?" I shake my head. He hasn't actually set foot in my room since he's been home. "I thought you were Dreamy."

"Listen, kiddo, can I get some help?" Nick crosses his arms over his chest and then uncrosses them. They dangle awkwardly at his sides, and I have to fight the urge to hand him an object to give him something to do with his hands. "I need some help with the horses. Dox in particular—"

"No." I put my pencil down on my desk. "Not going to happen." Dreamy and Ed called Nick the day Alfalfa nearly dragged me to the grave, but I don't think he's really ever understood what I went through. Nick's just like Ed. They think horses are innately good creatures that couldn't hurt a fly.

"Zoe, Dox has an infection. I need your help so I can give him his medicine." He frowns at me. "And honestly, I don't think Dreamy has done much of . . ." He kicks at something imaginary on my floor. "I've been feeding them, but I don't know what else has been done."

While I inherited Ed's wild red hair, Nick has Dreamy's thick, dark mane, and though he's deeply tanned, there are dark circles under his eyes.

"We have to do it for Ed." Nick turns and waits to see if I'll follow him.

I sigh and start looking for my shoes. I don't want to be anywhere near the horses, but what can I do? "I'm only going to help you with Dox. That's it." I shove my sockless foot in a sneaker. "I'm willing to do anything around this house except mess with those horses."

"Thank you." Nick's tone is a little weird. He seems really worried for some reason. I shove my other foot in my shoe and follow him down the stairs.

Wordlessly, we walk through the dark living room and slip out the sliding glass door. I hesitate for a moment. The ugly purple hot tub Ed got last year seems so ridiculous now. Nick starts down the stairs, and I give in and follow him. It's a good ten-minute walk, and we don't say a word the whole way. I watch my breath come out in little puffs in the early December air.

He opens the stable door, and a horrible stench hits me. Ed usually gets out here every day and cleans the horse stalls. Nick has been coming out here as much as possible, but it's a lot of work. Suddenly I feel like a failure. Ed was probably depending on us to take care of his horses. "I'll start in the stalls." I grab the old shovel near the door.

"Thanks, kiddo." Nick begins to gather hay and carrots for the horses. I hear old Alfalfa neigh. He was a good friend once. I wish things hadn't ended like they did, but, well, maybe everything happens for a reason. Without horseback riding to occupy my time, I had to make real friends.

Nick leads Alfalfa out of his stall to brush him down, and I slip into his stall to start shoveling. Poop smells really bad in general, but horse poop smells seriously awful. I try to take shallow breaths, but it's heavy lifting. As I shovel, I wonder how Ed does this every day. "Nick." I walk to the edge of Alfalfa's stall. He is brushing small circles in Alfalfa's coat with the currycomb. "This is crazy. We've got to do something about Dreamy and Ed."

He laughs a low, quiet chuckle and shakes his head. "I don't think it's up to us, kiddo." Alfalfa shakes his head too. Traitor. Now my horse is agreeing with my stupid brother.

"But they'll listen to you." I frown at my sneakers, already caked in horse manure. "They think I'm a baby." I try banging my shoe against the stall, but the gunk is stuck in the tread. "They won't listen to me."

He stops brushing Alfalfa. "They're not going to listen to me either." Nick hangs the currycomb on the rack on the wall and grabs the dandy brush. Grooming a horse is a lengthy process, but I could probably still do it in my sleep. "People have to work through their own relationship problems. We can't help them."

I lay the shovel handle against the stall and grab the other dandy brush from the wall. "Yes we can." There's no way my brother is tricking me into shoveling poop while he grooms the horses. He can shovel out the stalls by himself, or we can do it together, but I'm not doing the worst task just because I'm his younger sister. "Let's make them a special dinner."

He laughs. "Zoe, this isn't a movie." Nick runs the brush down Alfalfa's body and flicks the dirt into the air.

I take a step back and dangle the brush from my hands. "Like you even know." The only girl Nick ever dated in high school was a geeky German exchange student named Caroline, and I'm pretty sure she asked him out.

"I know more than you. Let's leave it at that." He flicks the brush down Alfalfa's side, and a cloud of dust kicks up. I roll my eyes.

"I've been dating Marcus for almost a year." Okay, I'm rounding up, but it's not like he can top that record.

Nick laughs long and hard. "You have no idea." He keeps chuckling as he walks over to the rack and grabs the body brush. "Why do you think I'm here, anyway?"

"You missed us?"

He opens his hand, and I throw my dandy brush at him. He catches it and hangs it on its hook. "I miss you guys and everything, but . . ." He strolls back and sets straight to work on making Alfalfa's coat gleam. "Forget it."

I slip my hand in the black strap and step closer to Alfalfa. I hear Dox neighing a little, anticipating his turn. "What happened?"

"Nothing." Nick looks at me for a moment. I nod my head and try to appear very grown-up, like the kind of person he can confide in. He dips down to work on Alfalfa's back leg and lets out a breath. "Look, the truth is, I met someone. We got pretty serious, but it didn't work out."

I can only see Nick's muddy, worn work boots through the horse's legs. They're caked in Colorado red clay and look like fossils, artifacts from another time. "So why did you come home?"

Nick rights himself and stares at me, searching my face for something. "Sometimes people need space." He strolls over to the rack. "And that's what Ed needs right now." He pulls the hoof pick off the wall and hangs up the body brush. "You'll understand that someday."

"Whatever." I walk back to the stall and pick up the shovel. On second thought, maybe I would be happier working on my own. He always does this, treating me like I'm still five years old.

I sink the shovel's blade into a huge pile of manure and lift it up. Stupid horses.

"Just give them their space," Nick says.

I toss the manure into the wheelbarrow and frown.

I know a lot about space, actually. More than Nick would ever guess. And I think having some space from the person you love is stupid. It doesn't accomplish anything. It just . . . makes people crazy.

23

'm zoning out in third period when Mrs. Narveson totally loses it.

"And it was this battle that led a young lawyer to pen a poem entitled 'The Defense of Fort McHenry.' Later to be put to music and called—" Mrs. Narveson clears her throat. "Me, me, me . . . ," she sings and touches her throat like an auditioning opera star.

People around me wake up a little and begin to murmur. We're getting harder to shock, and third period has really been dragging today. Let's just say that the War of 1812 is not the most interesting topic, even in Mrs. Narveson's wacky hands. But this, this is something different. She almost looks like she's going to . . .

"Oh—h say can you see, by the dawn's early light."

People turn to look at each other. Is this crazy teacher singing "The Star-Spangled Banner"? She's finally lost her mind. Well, at least I don't have to take notes for a second. I give myself a shake and try to wake up. Now that I close at El Bueno Burrito twice a week, I'm pretty exhausted. Never mind that once I get home I still have to finish my homework.

"Whose broad stripes and bright stars, through the perilous fight."

She's really going to do it. She's going to sing the whole

song. Mrs. Narveson's eyes are nearly popping out. I steel myself for the infamous high note that has brought many a professional singer down a notch or two.

"O'er the land of the freeeeeeeeee." She doesn't even shy away from it. She grips the podium and belts it out, and oddly enough, she nails it. "And the home of the brave."

The class is utterly silent for a second or two. I hear someone cough. Then slowly there's a sound beside me. Clapping. I turn and see Dean clapping, not in a snide way, in a real way, and other people join in.

Soon everyone is cheering and beating on their desks, and Mrs. Narveson turns a little pink. After a minute she raises her hands, and the class settles down.

"And that concludes the War of 1812. If you missed anything"—she pauses and glances at her notes—"just remember: no trade with France, England tries to scold America, war breaks out, Brits torch the White House, Francis Scott Key gets creative, and the United States finally gets a little recognition. Are we clear?"

We stare back at her, mouths gaping. Was that even English?

"Good." She puts a check mark next to THE WAR OF 1812 on the chalkboard. "Next item of business."

She walks to her desk, grabs a stack of papers, and then turns back to us. "I'm finally ready to hand back your Build-a-Nation projects. I was very pleased with the results. There were some very, ah, creative"—she winks at me—"approaches to government. I was pleased with your work, for the most part, and I hope you'll be pleased with your grades."

Wow. It's taken her six weeks to grade these things. Granted we've been working on other projects that are much smaller in scale, but I haven't been doing so well on them. It turns out that pretending to work with your partner is a little easier said than done.

She takes a binder-clipped packet off the top of the stack and hands it to Emily Mack, who squeals and turns to her partner. There is some mumbled conversation as a few people flip through their projects, and she continues to hand out papers one group at a time. Kayleen doesn't even bother to share their paper with Christine, but Christine doesn't seem to be too concerned about it. She's putting the finishing touches on what looks like a band taking the stage at a rock concert in the margins of her notebook.

"Very well done," Mrs. Narveson says, holding out a stack of papers to me. I take it uncertainly. There's a big red A at the top. "A strong and interesting execution." I flip through the pages for a second, reading the notes she's put in the margins.

"Ahem." Dean doesn't even really pretend to clear his throat.

I hold the papers out to him. I can feel my face flushing, and I keep my eyes on my desk.

"Not bad." Dean's fingers brush mine as he takes the pages out of my hands. "Nice work, Zoe."

I know he's goading me, but I glance up at him. I can't keep myself from looking. He's leaning back in his chair, smiling at me. Or is he smirking? Okay, it's definitely a smirk. His eyes say that he's laughing at me, but my stomach flips a little bit. I turn away quickly and start to put my notebook into my bag. A second later the bell rings, and I'm running toward the door.

Ashley keeps peeking over her shoulder and casting furtive glances toward the door. She wanted to meet somewhere out of the way, somewhere we wouldn't run into other people. She was very specific about that. Why she picked the library, then, is beyond me. I was too curious about her motive to argue much about anything, let alone her odd choice of location. Ashley and I aren't exactly the best of friends. She's pretty much been nothing but awful to me—to all of us, really—since the first day of freshman year, when she laughed at my broomstick skirt. But for her to meet me here, now—she has to want something.

"Look," she says, apparently convinced no one cool is anywhere nearby. "I didn't mean for this to happen."

I run my finger along a line someone has carved into my plastic chair and wait for her to go on, uncertain how to react. What is she talking about?

"I know you guys are close to her and stuff. I just . . . I didn't mean to get her in trouble." She takes a deep breath and watches me. "My dad was . . . he was going through some stuff last year. Legal stuff. And he was kind of dumping it on me, and in a weak moment I told Ms. Moore."

The smooth gash in the plastic suddenly feels jagged beneath my hand.

"She called him in for a conference, said some things she shouldn't have, and the next thing I knew she was gone. It wasn't what I meant at all."

"But . . . what? It was you?"

"I like her too, you know." Ashley smoothes down the hem of her skirt. "The people in your little Miracle Club or whatever aren't the only ones who thought she was cool. You didn't think Christine was the only student who had counseling sessions with Ms. Moore, did you?"

I continue to stare at her, too stunned to answer.

"Never mind." She picks up her bag and shakes her head. "I saw that you guys were trying to get her reinstated, so I thought you might want to see this stuff." She gestures toward a stack of papers in her bag. "But I guess I was wrong. Forget I said anything." She turns to go.

"Wait!" I nearly shriek before I remember that we're in a library. "Ashley, wait."

She pauses, turning her head back. Her clothes hang loose on her thin frame. I never noticed how translucent her skin is. Maybe it's the fluorescent lighting in here, but she's frailer than I ever realized.

"What is that stuff?"

Ashley waits, biting her lip. She looks at the door, then back to me, and finally she nods and lowers herself back into the chair. Slowly, she pulls a folder out of her bag. I take it and flip through the stack of papers. There are some printed e-mails, a few stapled packets of what looks like transcripts of phone calls, and a couple of pages of notes.

"These are his records. All the evidence he's submitted to his lawyer about the things Ms. Moore said to him."

"Oh wow." I'm too overwhelmed to muster a more intelligent response. I'm trying to process what she's just told me. "Okay. Well—" I cough. "Maybe I'll call the Miracle Girls and see if we can all go over this stuff."

Ashley shakes her head. "No. You can't tell them! You can't tell anyone. You promised!"

What? I think back. I guess I did promise her I wouldn't tell anyone about our meeting, but did she really mean I couldn't tell anyone *forever*?

"Don't worry—my friends are really trustworthy," I say, even though I know it sounds lame. "They're . . . they'll want to help. They're loyal, and they love Ms. Moore too. Ana is super organized and really takes charge. Christine is a great artist, really good at making posters. Riley—well, you know Riley's great." Ashley looks at the ground. "And . . . maybe we can work together or something."

Could the Miracle Girls work with Ashley Anderson for this? How would that ever work? What about the horrible things she's said about us over the years?

"Why don't you just tell your dad the truth? Tell him you want Ms. Moore back?"

"Look." She runs her fingertips across the smooth surface of the table. "I know your family is all happy Jesus people who love each other to bits, but that's not how it is for everyone, okay?" She laughs. "My dad and I don't exactly have that kind of relationship."

I study her face. Is she making fun of me? Her lips are pursed together, and she appears to be totally serious. I can't decide whether to be thrilled because that's how it looks from the outside or to cry.

"But you could—"

"I've tried, okay? Don't you think I tried that?" She shakes her head. "After everything he's already invested in this, he's not backing down."

24

think we need a toast." Ana holds her glass in the air and shushes us with her hand. "To the Miracle Girls, the ultimate best friends." She laughs, clinks her glass against the rest of ours, and takes a sip of her Diet Coke.

Ana planned this whole big girls' night out and even made a reservation at a nice Italian restaurant downtown and convinced us to dress up. My feet are throbbing under the table after working all day at El Bueno Burrito, and I'm going to have to make it up to Marcus tomorrow for canceling our date night at the bookstore, but it was worth it to get us together.

"And to swearing off musicians," Ana says. I haven't seen her this animated since . . . well, before the breakup. Mostly she just mopes around or glares at Dave and Jamie hanging all over each other across the room at youth group. "Good riddance!" She chuckles, but her laughter somehow seems a little too forced.

"So do you guys want to get appetizers?" She scans the menu. "The fried calamari here is—oh wait."

I scan the prices and bite my lip. I've been working at El Bueno Burrito long enough to get paid, but I gave almost all of it to Dreamy. It's going to take a while before I build up a cushion.

She cringes. "Sorry, Zo. I forgot you can't eat seafood. We

could get a cheese plate or something instead. They have this amazing stinky blue cheese that melts in your mouth."

Christine leans forward and props her elbows on the table. "Why would I want to eat food that smells like feet?"

"So no on the cheese." Ana takes a sip of her water and continues to look over the menu. "I'm going to get the pasta primavera." She closes her menu with a snap and nods. "How about you guys?"

"You know, I'm not that hungry anyway." I watch as a heaping plate of pasta passes by on a tray. "I think I may just have a drink or something."

Riley raises an eyebrow. "You sure? We could split something if you want." She looks perfectly relaxed in a loose, peasant-style black dress and boots. She has a long strand of pearls looped around her neck, a look I swear I saw in the magazine at the grocery store last week.

"I'm okay." I quickly read the list of appetizers, looking for something I can order to throw them off my trail. "Maybe I'll get a . . . cup of minestrone or something too." At eight dollars a cup, minestrone is the cheapest thing on the menu. "I'm just not very hungry." I can see in their faces they're not buying it, but they're going to be kind and act like they don't see what's really going on.

Christine is already doodling on the paper tablecloth with a blue crayon, doing a pretty good representation of the four of us huddled around a table. She's drawn a basket in the middle of the table next to a sign that says Breadsticks Go Here.

I feel my cheeks burning, but a moment later the waiter comes to take our order, and the conversation shifts to Riley's trip to see Tom in Santa Barbara next weekend and how hard the whole long-distance dating thing is.

"Speaking of Tom," Ana says as the waiter sets down a bowl of breadsticks. I try to not make it too obvious as I reach for one. "I've been thinking." She flushes. "Now that I'm . . . I'm kind of the only Miracle Girl without a boyfriend."

Christine raises her hand. "Yo."

"Oh, but you and Tyler aren't fooling anyone," Ana says, waving her hand. Christine picks up the green crayon in front of Riley and begins to print in big block letters *B-O-Y*.

"Still just friends," she says, concentrating on her printing. *F-R-I-E-N-D*.

"Okay. Well." Ana scrunches her chin down into her neck. "I found out Dave and Jamie are officially dating now, and since I'm the only one without a boy *friend* or boyfriend or whatever, and you know, prom isn't that far away, and . . ."

"It's like five months from now!" I laugh, but Ana grimaces.

L-E-S-S. Christine draws a big arrow pointing at herself.

"I, well . . ."

"But we're definitely going. Don't even think of not going, ladies," Riley says. "Prom is a big deal."

"I was wondering if you know any guys you could set me up with."

Christine chokes on her water. I pound on her back.

"Ana." Riley tilts her head a little. "Do you think you're ready? It's only been a month or two and you and Dave were together forever."

"Of course I am, and I'm so ready to move on and meet a guy." Ana nods, but her words sound a little too rehearsed.

"One who's mature and cares about important things, like literature and art."

"That's a pretty tall order for a high school guy." Riley takes a crayon from the middle of the table and toys with it.

"He doesn't have to be in high school." We eye her. "Riley's dating a college guy. Why couldn't I date a college guy?" She dips a breadstick into a puddle of olive oil on her plate.

"You totally could," Riley says softly. I see Christine visibly relax. There's always been this weird competitiveness between Ana and Riley. "You could have any guy you want. You're smart, and pretty, and someday you'll find the right person."

I reach for my third breadstick. These things are so addictive, and so free. We're going to need some more.

"I mean, look at Zoe and Marcus," Riley says, pointing at me. "That took a long time to develop. It wasn't like they rushed into anything, and now look how happy they are together."

Ana's face goes pale, and tears begin to well up in her eyes.

"Really happy." I shove the breadstick into my mouth.

"Any guy would be lucky to have you," Christine says quickly, adding a halo above the drawing of Ana. "It's just that . . ." She trails off as tears begin to spill out of Ana's eyes.

"It's just that—" Riley picks up Christine's thought. "Are you sure you're ready for this? Are you really over Dave?"

"I'm over him," she says quietly, but I know better than to believe her. I reach out and lay my hand on Ana's back. She's breathing deeply, trying to get her emotions under control.

"It took you by surprise, didn't it?" Riley asks, almost under her breath.

Ana doesn't respond, but then, slowly, she nods. "I never really thought we'd break up, you know?" Her voice comes out a little squeaky.

"I know," Riley murmurs.

"I knew we'd been fighting, but I thought we'd get past it." She takes a sip of water. "It really never occurred to me that it might end."

I tear a breadstick in half. It sounds kind of stupid. I mean, we're only sixteen. We're way too young to be settling down for the rest of our lives. But at the same time, I kind of understand what she means. When you're with someone for a long time, it's hard to imagine *not* being with them. It seems like you'll go on forever, the same as always, because that's the way it's always been.

"We're with you. It hurts, but we'll be here until it gets better." I hand her my napkin, and she swipes it under her nose. "We'll help you through this."

"Plus, we'll go to Dave's house and beat him up if you want," Christine says.

Ana laughs so hard that she seems in danger of snorting. "Thank you," she says, wiping the napkin across her face. She takes a few breaths, keeping her eyes on her plate. "I'm sorry. Here I am freaking out when Zoe's parents are breaking up." She shakes her head. "Plus, Tom is halfway across the state and . . . and Tyler is being all . . . whatever. At least you have Marcus," she says to me, biting her lip.

"Yeah." I try to smile. "Thank God for that."

25

The bell rings, and Mrs. Narveson is already standing behind her little podium at the front of the room.

"THEME!" she yells. The thing about her class is, if you're not ready the moment class begins, you'll fall behind. "Westward expansion led to the growth of the new nation and allowed for the spread of slavery." Despite her craziness, Mrs. Narveson is actually surprisingly logical and methodical, and she always lays out the argument she's going to make at the beginning of a lecture, just like she wants us to do in our papers.

By the time I have the theme copied down, she's already explaining how the balance of free states and slave states was carefully maintained as new territories entered the union. I hear furious scratching beside me, but somehow I doubt Dean is working so hard to capture every word Mrs. Narveson is saying. I've never seen him actually take notes in this class. I wonder what he's working on.

It's the last week of school before Christmas break, and I'm like a zombie. I work Tuesday and Thursday nights, plus Saturday mornings, and I'm almost getting the hang of things. Somehow, so far I'm managing everything: school, band, work, the Miracle Girls, the fight to save Ms. Moore, the fight to save my family. And Marcus. He's been so understanding.

I've filled half a page with notes and two full pages with doodles by the time Mrs. Narveson declares her lecture finished and assigns us tonight's reading.

"Oh, and before I forget!" She walks over to her desk on the side of the room and picks up a stack of manila folders. "I hold your futures in my hands."

The hair on my arms rises. Ooh, this must be our next big project. I smile at Dean, but he's writing something on his sneaker.

"The winds of change are blowing through our classroom." Mrs. Narveson pretends she's trudging through high winds to get back to her podium. "All that you know will soon be taken from you, and you must start life all over again." She shuffles the folders at the front of the classroom. "SURVIVAL!" she booms, then turns and writes it on the chalkboard in her signature all-caps. "This is what it means to be American!"

Okay, survival, winds of change . . . What could it be? Maybe we have to pretend we're pioneers on the frontier and survive in the wilderness next semester? No, there are too many liabilities with that. Winds of change? What if it's a Dust Bowl project? Something to do with alternate energy sources? Like windmills? Well, no matter what it is, I'm sure we'll get an A.

"The first big change is you must leave your family behind and form new bonds in the New World." She wiggles her eyebrows at us. Leave our families? "That's right: new partners. You can never get too comfortable in America."

My heart starts slamming in my chest. New partners? Granted, my partner and I haven't actually worked together since October, but I was just getting up the courage to patch things up with him. It was all just a misunderstanding, and we can work through it. With all the change going on in my life, the last thing I need is a new partner.

"We're going to do alphabetical order . . ." My heart sinks farther. No matter what she chooses, first or last name, we won't be together. "By the fourth letter of your last names, just to keep things interesting." I list the letters quickly in my head. R and C. Shoot! I have zero luck.

Mrs. Narveson reads down the list slowly. Christine gets paired with Jake, a soccer player who is the shortest guy in the whole junior class. After Kayleen, I'm sure she's ecstatic to get a new partner. At least someone is, I guess. I get partnered with this Goth girl named Courtney who we've been going to school with since the dawn of time, but I don't really know.

"Dean, you'll be with Kayleen," Mrs. Narveson says.

From my vantage point, I can see Kayleen's face light up, and I bite my lip. It's not that I care, really, if he's not my partner. It's no big deal. But he was really smart and we did get an A. I just want . . . I glance at Courtney in the back corner. She has her head down on her desk, and her pants are fifteen sizes too big for her. I only want to do well in this class, and someone like Kayleen doesn't deserve Dean—a partner like Dean.

Mrs. Narveson takes the chalk and scratches out CAPTAINS OF INDUSTRY on the board.

"Brother against brother, old teammate against old teammate." She smiles like it gives her great pleasure to see us so uncomfortable. "For your first project next semester, we're going to look at the Industrial Revolution." She grabs a stack of folders from her podium and then begins to weave her way through the classroom, passing them out. "You and your

partner are forming a labor union to protect your fellow workers in a factory. I've assigned each team to a different industry,
and you're going to have to make some tough choices about
which causes to support and which to neglect for the greater
good."

She drops a folder on my desk with my name at the top.
I peek inside and find a huge stack of information on the
assignment. It seems that Courtney and I work at a shirtwaist
factory, whatever that is, in New York.

"Smart teams would get started on this over winter break."
Mrs. Narveson wiggles her eyebrows as we groan in unison.
"You're going to have to make your case to the fat-cat factory
owners, and I am the sole member of—"

The third period bell rings over Mrs. Narveson's voice, and
she stops midsentence. She's like a faucet that goes on and off
at the sound of the bell. I yawn. How on earth am I going to
make it through three more periods?

"Got to run, Red. Forgot something in my car." Christine
grabs her bag and waves over her shoulder as she dashes out
of class.

I wave lazily, then stand up from my desk slowly and stretch
a little. Dean is kneeling down next to my feet, looking for
something in the front pocket of his messenger bag.

"Looks like you're going to miss me a lot next semester."
I motion at Kayleen's back with my head so he gets what I
mean.

"I doubt it." Dean shoves his textbook into his bag and slings
it over his shoulder. He shrugs at me and waltzes out of the
classroom as I stand there with my mouth gaping open. Obviously I was kidding. He didn't have to be so mean about it.

I shove my things into my bag, grab my stupid pencil, and trudge to the door. What an annoying jerk. He acts like we don't even know each other.

"Zoe!" Marcus flies around the corner the moment I step out of the room.

"Ah!" I jump.

"I have something to tell you." On the *t* in *tell*, Marcus launches a tiny spit bubble my way and it lands on my cheek. I wipe it off as something catches my eye.

"It's about Ms. Moore." He tries to catch his breath. He must have run all the way over here.

Dean slams his locker and wraps some girl in a hug. Air whooshes out of my lungs. She's some rocker chick. I put my hand against the rough stucco wall to steady myself.

Marcus steps toward me. "You okay?"

"Huh?" I focus back on Marcus, who is crestfallen. "I'm sorry. What were you saying? About Ms. Moore?"

This is good, what I wanted, after all. I wanted him to leave me alone.

Marcus follows my gaze across the hall, and we both stare at Dean making out with the girl for a moment. She's really very short.

I roll my eyes. "I can't believe they're making out in the hallway. How gross can you be, right?" I touch Marcus's hand and he turns back to me, but he has a funny look on his face.

"You didn't call me back last night."

"I know. I'm sorry." I sigh and will my eyes to stay glued on Marcus. But in my periphery, I can see that Dean and that girl have not come up for air. "I didn't even walk in the door until eleven."

Marcus glances behind him again. "Is that your history partner?" He looks from Dean to me, then back at Dean. Something in his eyes looks sad.

"*Was.*" I shrug. "He was my history partner, but we just got assigned new partners for next semester. I got *Courtney.*"

Marcus turns back to me. "Really?" I nod. Finally Dean and the girl pull apart. That was one for the books. Her lipstick is smeared, and he wipes it off with his thumb. They walk away holding hands. "It's good that he's finally made some friends."

"Yeah, good for him." Some friend. Maybe he was inspecting her tonsils with his tongue. Friends do that I guess. "Now what were you saying about Ms. Moore?"

Marcus smiles at me and holds out his hand. "Let me walk you to class."

I take his palm and try to ignore that it's slick with sweat. We head in the general direction of our fourth period classes.

"The district council voted last night." We weave through the crowds, dodging small clusters of people. "It was four to three in favor of reinstating Ms. Moore, pending the lawsuit. Isn't that great? That's why I ran all the way over here."

"What does that mean?"

"It means if she wins, she gets to come back!"

26

The jingle bells over El Bueno Burrito's door ring out as our second customer in six hours leaves. The tip jar contains thirty-four cents. I was so bored I counted.

"Zoe, let's talk about how you can up your game." Gus takes a step toward the register and mans my normal post.

"Um, okay." I stop scraping crusty cheese off the counter. "Feliz Navidad" has been playing on endless repeat for weeks, and the tacky holiday decorations taped all over the window are starting to curl around the edges. It's totally dead in here, and Gus is hovering. He's a nice enough guy, but it's better when he's busy—when he's bored, he drives me bonkers.

"We want the customers to feel like this is their hangout, their . . . home away from home, if you will."

I try not to laugh. It's the week before Christmas, and no one wants to eat burritos. They're all at their real homes, gathered around the fireplace with their perfect families, not here, ordering fake Mexican food.

"I want you to try making small talk with them when they come in." Gus presses a few buttons, making the register drawer slide open. "Say, 'Happy Holidays. Did you get all your shopping done?' "

Ryan, the lanky guy who was working the register the day

I applied, has been promoted to fry cook, but he hasn't had to grill anything for the past hour. Once Gus came out of the back, though, Ryan began to frantically clean his station. He's been rubbing a dirty rag over the cooktop for thirty minutes.

"And don't forget to smile, Zoe." Gus stares at me. I take a deep breath and then try to give a very convincing smile.

"That's better. And it's really important with regulars to learn their order." Gus rifles through the bins on the shelves under the register and finds a little notepad. "Write it down, and then say it to yourself a few times. Starbucks invented this trick, and I think we know how that worked out for them." Gus nudges me with his elbow.

The jingle bells chime, and I move to try to reclaim the register.

"Okay," Gus whispers as he steps aside. "Let's practice what we've learned."

Here goes happy. I look up and try to make eye contact with our customer—then freeze. My stomach drops. No, no, not now. Any time but right now, with my manager watching, when I'm wearing this stupid red and gold visor.

Dean strolls inside, clutching a yellow plastic bag in his hand. He's got a knit wool cap pulled down over his dark hair, and his cheeks are flushed from the cold.

"Zoe?" His face widens into a smile, and my cheeks burst into flames. I'm probably literally on fire.

I look down at my stained El Bueno Burrito apron. Even the smiling sun embroidered on it looks tacky and embarrassing. I feel Gus nudge me with his elbow. Right, the friendliness routine.

"Hi, welcome to El Bueno Burrito," I say, faking a chipper

tone. What would Riley do in a situation like this? I try to picture her face. I think she'd lift her chin up and pretend it didn't bother her. But I'm wearing nasty old jeans and a T-shirt that smells like refried beans, and my face is greasy from the heat of the kitchen. "How's your holiday shopping going?"

"I didn't know you worked here." Dean's face is a little bewildered, but then he seems to notice the tall man hovering behind me. "Oh, um, the shopping is going well. Thanks for asking." He steps up to the register, and I try to keep my chin up and smile as if I'm happy to see him. He gives me that smug look that always unnerves me. It's like he knows how attractive he is, like he can see the butterflies flying around in my stomach.

"Oh," says Gus, stepping forward. "You're one of Zoe's *amigos,* eh?"

Dean's eyes dance in delight, and I pray that the floor opens up and swallows me whole. "Yes, sir."

Gus pats my shoulder. "She's the best. I'm so glad you stopped by to see her."

"I was hungry." He tilts his head back and stares up at the plastic menu board above the register. "But seeing Zoe is a bonus."

"Well, I'll leave the shop in your capable hands." Gus sighs, his ultimate friendliness fantasies having played out in front of his very eyes. He walks toward the back and stops as he passes Ryan. "I think that stove top is clean now. Why don't you come with me, and we'll check out the walk-in freezer together."

Ryan's shoulders sink, and he follows Gus to the back.

"What's good here?" Dean lays the yellow bag down on the

counter and studies the sign. It's been so long since we had a normal, friendly conversation that my mouth feels like it won't work. I swallow hard and give it a try.

"It's pretty hard to mess up nachos." I recognize the bag from the Music Hut, the little music store down on Main Street. "That's about the only thing I would trust."

"Can I get a Baja Burrito?"

"Living on the edge, I see." I punch a few buttons on the register, but end up hitting the one for the Antojito Burrito and have to start over. I'm getting pretty good at this thing, but I can't seem to get the buttons to work right all of a sudden. "That'll be $4.50."

Dean digs into his back pocket and pulls out a black leather wallet. He flips it open, and I catch a glimpse of a faded photo tucked into the billfold. It looks like Dean, but the guy in the photo has sharper angles in his face and lighter hair. He pulls out a five-dollar bill and lays it on the counter.

"Ryan!" I call as I push the right buttons to open the register. I slide the bill into the correct slot, face up, and pick out two quarters in change. I hold them out, and Dean takes them carefully from my hand. His fingers are warm and rough.

I walk around the edge of the counter and peer into the back to see if I catch sight of Ryan or Gus. All is silent. Poor Ryan. Gus is probably making him restock and reorganize the walk-in, everyone's least favorite job. There should be a law about forcing teenagers to freeze for several hours, but of course there isn't.

I look from the walk-in, back to Dean. Well, I have no choice, do I?

"Be right back." I roll my eyes and walk to the kitchen,

which is separated from the front by a small counter. Okay, I know how to do this. There's some chicken Ryan cooked earlier. It only looks a little dried out. A scoop of thick refried beans. A spoonful of guacamole, and some sour cream. Lettuce and tomato. I roll it all up. It doesn't look as neat as when Ryan does it, but it should work. It isn't until I've wrapped the whole thing in a sheet of foil that I realize I forgot the cheese. Well, hopefully Dean's not picky. I can hear him drumming on the counter as I round the corner back into the main room. I reach under the counter and pull out a paper bag and begin to shove the burrito inside.

"Hey, I never said that was to go."

"Oh. You're staying here?" I narrow my eyes at him. No one ever stays here to eat. It's totally depressing.

"Are *you* staying here?" He tilts his head a little and smiles. What is this nice-guy routine about? I thought we mutually hated each other's guts?

"I'm on the clock until ten." I play with the string of my apron, twirling the end around a little.

"Then I'm staying." Dean crosses his arms over his chest. "Tray me." I shake my head and pull an orange plastic tray from underneath the counter. He places his burrito squarely in the middle of it. "You coming?" He nods his head toward the row of empty tables along the wall.

"I can't." I smooth my apron down over my jeans. "I'm working. I have to—"

"You have to what?" Dean motions around the room. "There's no one here. Why are you so afraid of me, Zoe?" He stops and waits, watching me. I suck in my breath. I'm not afraid of him. It's inappropriate. I'm at work, and he's . . . he has a girlfriend. I mean, yes, I've missed him as a friend, but now is not a good time. Dean is grinning at me, like he knows he's got me now. "Come sit with me for a minute."

I shake my head just as Gus reappears from the back.

"What's going on here?" He puts his hands on his hips and furrows his brow.

"I'm sorry, I didn't mean—" I swallow and try to keep myself from babbling. "Our *customer* wanted me to take a break and sit with him, but I declined." I shoot poison darts out of my eyes at Dean. I can't get fired. I need this job.

Gus's face breaks into a smile. "I'm joshing ya." He takes his hands off his hips and starts rubbing them together. "Just a little humor to raise worker morale." His tie is pulled a little to the right. "I'm going to send you home early, Zoe." Gus gives Dean a thumbs-up, and I realize he thinks this must be my boyfriend. If only he knew the truth. "Ryan and I will finish up."

"Really?"

"Consider it an early Christmas present from the management." He *loves* referring to himself as the management. It makes him feel important.

"Cool. I'll go clock out." I turn to Dean. "I guess I'm going to leave early or whatever, so if you want to get going . . ."

"I'll be here," Dean says. I try to pretend I don't feel the way my stomach flips.

♡

I step outside into the cool night air and say a quick amen that I don't have to hear those depressing jingle bells any more tonight.

"Where are you headed?" Dean asks, zipping the front of his leather bomber jacket. It's the kind of thing that would look ridiculous if anyone from around here tried it, but somehow looks right on Dean.

I kick at the curb. "Home, I guess."

"Fair enough." Dean turns, and my heart sinks a little. Of course he's going to leave. He probably has big plans with rocker chick tonight. He starts walking down the pavement. "You coming?"

I stare at him, and he shrugs. "I'm walking you home. Unless . . . you don't have a car, do you?"

I watch him for a minute, but he keeps walking down the sidewalk. "You live this way, right?" he calls over his shoulder. What does he mean he's walking me home? Why is he being so weird tonight? We haven't even had a real conversation since that night in October at his house. He shoves his hands into his pockets, his record bag swinging from his wrist, and doesn't look back.

He can't walk me home. It would take forever. He must not know I live out in the boonies. Plus, I have . . . and he has . . .

But for some reason I can't bring myself to yell for him to stop. This is just a friendly gesture. Friends can walk each other home. There's no law against that.

He's almost at the end of the sidewalk, in front of the shoe store, when I decide what I have to do. I go to the bike rack, unchain my bike, and run after him. He doesn't seem surprised when I wheel my bike up next to him. He steps out into the parking lot and starts across it. I blink as a pair of headlights comes around the end of a row of cars and blinds me for a second.

"What'd you buy?" I finally ask.

"Coltrane." He hands me the bag and takes my bike. "Take a look." I pull a big, thin cardboard sleeve out of the bag. It's an old record. I didn't even know people had record players anymore. A serious-looking African-American man stares out from the cover. "It's a Christmas present for my dad." I run my fingertips over the smooth surface of the record sleeve. "Coltrane and Thelonious Monk played this legendary series of shows at New York's Five Spot."

"Five Spot?" Is this something I'm supposed to know?

"It was a famous jazz club in the East Village." I don't know anything about Coltrane, but judging from the picture, it looks like he played the saxophone, which makes an eerie kind of sense.

A silence passes between us, and I hand back his bag, and he passes me my bike.

Dean adjusts the wool cap on his head. "Is something going on lately?"

I adjust my grip on my handlebars. "What?" I step carefully along the sidewalk.

"I don't know," Dean says. "You seem . . . different some-how, sad or something. I thought maybe it had something to do with Christmas." He's quiet for a moment, and the moon glints off his shiny black hair. "It's always hard at my house. I guess that's why I notice it when other people are depressed too. Christmas is supposed to be this holy time, but the last thing I feel like doing is talking to God."

Part of me wants to tell Dean that nothing's changed. If I seem different it's because things have been weird for us ever since he tried to . . . and then got this little girlfriend, which didn't help matters. But then, part of me also knows there's some truth in what he says. After our disastrous Thanksgiving, maybe I am kind of dreading Christmas without Ed. I really thought he'd be home by now. But how could Dean know that?

"It doesn't really feel like Christmas without him, you know?" Dean says.

I take a deep breath and look up at the night sky, black velvet and dotted with tiny silver stars. I don't answer him for a minute, but he doesn't seem to mind. And then somehow, for some reason, walking along the wide main road away from town, I start to tell Dean about Dreamy and Ed. I tell him about the fighting, the horses, the strain of money, and about Nick coming home and being a shadow. The sidewalk ends and turns into dirt along the side of the road, and I tell him about the Sea Witch and how Ed didn't come home for Thanksgiving. Dean just listens.

When we turn onto the road that winds through the woods and up to my house, I'm still telling him about how Dreamy handmade all of our Christmas cards this year and how the notes she tucked inside didn't say anything about our family falling apart.

It feels like we just left El Bueno Burrito, but we must have been walking for at least an hour, probably more. A blister is starting to form on my heel, and the moonlight is shining down on us when we walk up the long dirt driveway toward my dark house.

We both get quiet as we get closer. I lean my bike against the porch railing.

"Wait." I try to keep my voice down as something dawns on me. "How are you going to get home?"

He grins, his face bright in the pale moonlight. "I have my car."

I scan the driveway before I can stop myself. Of course it's not here. "Where?"

"Back at El Bueno Burrito." Dean's smile is almost guilty. "I guess I'd better start heading back."

My eyes widen. "You can't do that."

"Sure I can." Dean reaches up and touches my hair, brushing a lock back from my face. He yanks on it, lightly, and drops his hand. I let out my breath slowly. He smiles at me, then turns a little, back toward the driveway.

"No, wait." I dig in my bag for my keys. Why can I never find these things when I need them? I thrust my hand all the way to the bottom of my bag and feel around. There's my phone and my iPod. Aha. I feel smooth, cold metal and curl my fingers around the sharp teeth of my house key. "I'll run in and grab Dreamy's car keys, and I'll drive you back in the van." I'm technically not allowed to drive anyone else around until I've had my license a full year, but what are the chances anyone would find out?

"It's okay." Dean shoves his hands deep into the pockets of his jacket. "It's a nice walk. I'm enjoying the night."

"But—"

"Good night, Zoe." Dean turns and starts to walk away, whistling quietly. I watch him until he gets to the end of the driveway, then step inside the quiet house and close the door.

27

"Hi, Zoe." Michael says the right thing as he answers the door, but he forgets to make eye contact.

Riley whispers something in his ear, and he smiles, then runs into the house. She opens the door wider, and I follow her inside. We agreed to meet on the eve of Christmas Eve, which I always thought deserved a name of its own. This year I could call it Last-Minute Panic Shopping for Marcus Day. The guy is impossible to buy for. I spent three hours downtown and still showed up at Riley's house empty-handed.

"Hey, guys." I wave at Ana and Christine, and they mumble something over a bad Christmas TV special. We're all pretty much in Christmas break comas.

"Zoe, how are you tonight?" Mr. McGee stands up and nudges Michael. This is called modeling. It's important to show good social behavior so that Michael can learn it.

"I'm good. Thanks for asking," I say, making sure I'm doing the modeling thing too. There's a game board spread out on the table. "Are you playing chess?" Mr. McGee is tall and thin and has brown hair with two small patches of gray at his temples. It's funny. He's always struck me as a little geeky, while Mrs. McGee is so . . . like Riley. Popular, loud, outgoing. I wonder how they met.

"Okay, we're all here. Let's get to it." Ana stands up and yawns.

Riley and I exchange a look.

"Didn't you tell them?" I ask.

"It's complex," Riley says through her teeth. It just made sense for Riley to tell them. It's her house, not mine.

"Tell us what?" Christine narrows her eyes. "If this is some kind of prank, I'm out. I'm on good behavior until Christmas. I think Candace and Dad are seriously considering getting me an iPhone as an I'm-sorry-there's-a-puking-baby-on-the-way gift."

"Well . . ." I take a breath, but the doorbell rings.

"I'll get it!" Michael pops up from the kitchen table and dashes to the door. Within seconds, a familiar voice pierces our silence.

"Um, hi, Michael." Ashley's normally sure voice sounds a little unsteady, even from here.

Ana falls back on the couch. Christine's eyes become as big as saucers. I think fast while Michael practices small talk.

I scramble over to them and whisper, "She knows something about Ms. Moore's case. She's going to help us."

Ana shakes her head quickly back and forth. "She'll double-cross us."

Riley steps toward them. "Trust us. Okay?"

Ashley walks into the room, and I can almost hear her gulp. Ana and Christine stare at the floor.

"Glad you could make it," I say and wave her into the living room, trying to affect a normal tone. I've been dreading this moment ever since Ashley called and said I could tell the girls—and only the girls.

"Ashley?" Mr. McGee pushes himself up from the kitchen table. "Um, hi." He shakes his head in disbelief. "I haven't seen you in *ages*. How . . . are you?" Riley glares at her dad.

"Well, ha ha." I have no idea why I'm laughing. Riley's ex-best friend is standing in her living room, and her father just pointed out that they hardly even talk anymore. "I guess we should get started, Riley."

Riley seems frozen in place for a moment as the past catches up to the freaky present. I motion to her bedroom with my head.

"Want to go hang out in your bedroom?" I try to smile at Mr. McGee and Michael to show that everything is fine, but they've already turned back to their game. Men.

"Yeah," Riley finally says. "Room."

She starts to walk down the hall and slowly, one by one, we rise and follow her. No one utters a peep, and I find myself whispering a quick prayer that this works out. Ashley is the missing piece to saving Ms. Moore. The Miracle Girls need her.

We all file in, and Christine shuts the door. I plop onto the bed with Ashley and Riley. Christine takes the white wooden chair, and Ana perches on the floor, as if she might dart off at any second.

For a long moment, no one says anything. I study Riley's room. There's something different about it, but what? There's still the same surf-themed décor with warm, greenish-grayish walls, white wood furniture, and lots of knickknacks and mementos. I glance at her huge poster of Kelly Slater, the pro surfer she's borderline obsessed with. Wait. That's it. The poster used to have a small roll of photo-booth pictures of

Tom and Riley pinned to the bottom of it. Where'd they go? Actually there used to be a lot of Tom stuff in here, and now everything is so tidy.

"I'm glad you made it," I say to break the awkwardness. "There was . . . a miscommunication so Ana and Christine . . . didn't know you were coming."

"I asked Riley not to say anything." Ashley traces the subtle pattern in the sand-colored duvet. "I wasn't sure I could really do this."

Ana bites her lip and bores her eyes into the floor. Ashley picked on Ana more than any of us, and Ana has a long way to go to forgive her for calling her God Girl for years. Actually we all have a long way to go. She's double-crossed us enough times to make us permanently wary.

Ashley takes a deep breath and lowers her arms, holding out the papers she gave me the other day. "I loved Ms. Moore too. She was my counselor until—" Christine looks up sharply. "Until my dad got her fired. I want to help get her back." She grips the papers tightly. "Zoe said I could trust you guys. But the stuff in these papers . . . I don't know. I need to make sure you guys won't spread this around."

"You can trust us," I say, trying to sound confident. Ashley may not be my favorite person, but I know she's being sincere. I can feel it in my bones.

"We won't tell anyone what's in there." Riley nods a little. "I can promise you that."

The tension in the room builds. Christine clears her throat, and we all turn to her. She opens her mouth, then stops, and we wait for a second. "I, uh"—she clears her throat again—"admire you for coming here. Whatever we see or hear today will remain in this room."

A huge weight slides off my shoulder. There. If Christine is on board, Ana will play along too.

"You shouldn't call people God Girl." Ana purses her lips, and I can see the tears welling up in her eyes. My heart starts to pound. "It's mean."

Ashley blushes a little . . . and it looks almost real. Maybe this ice queen has a heart buried inside of her after all.

"Sorry," she mumbles.

No one says anything. Ana stares at Ashley, her face a mix of emotions, and it feels like a showdown at high noon. Can we move beyond the past to fix our shared futures? I swallow, and it seems like everyone can hear.

"Promise me you won't do it again?" Ana juts out her lip.

Ashley raises her head and locks eyes with Ana. "No matter what happens. I promise."

"Okay." Ana nods, but she still seems on guard. "I'm in."

♡

Two hours later, we've combed through every single document in the folder three times, and the mood in the room has grown grim. It's become pretty clear that the whole lawsuit depends on one little incident and the delicate matter of who is telling the truth.

"Okay, let's go through it again, one more time." Christine is sprawled on the floor next to Ana. "Don't leave anything out."

Ashley, Riley, and I are collapsed on the bed, looking at

Riley's smooth white ceiling. No cottage cheese bits or water stains to stare at here.

"It was just a normal counseling session with Ms. Moore." Ashley's voice has grown quieter and quieter during the course of our meeting. She seems to be shrinking before our eyes. She's already confessed it was Ms. Moore who first reached out to her when her essays in English class turned dark. "School was winding down, and I was talking to her about my parents' divorce."

From the beginning, people have said that Ms. Moore got fired for telling off someone's dad. For a while Christine was afraid it was her dad that had complained, but after digging through the papers and looking up the laws and school district rules, we learned that though Ms. Moore did yell at Ashley's dad, you can't actually get fired for that. Ms. Moore gave him an earful about all the stress he was putting his daughter through with the divorce, and we found the letter of reprimand from Ms. Lovchuck in Ashley's file, but that's not enough to get her fired. It was something else.

"I was telling Ms. Moore that my father had told me to swear to his divorce lawyer that my mother was an unfit parent and I was better off living with him, and I just sort of lost it." Ashley's voice fails her, and I wonder if I should put a hand on her arm to comfort her. She's opening up, but she's still Ashley Anderson and I'm still Zoe, right?

No one says anything, and I listen to the sound of Ashley's uneven breathing. These files contain very detailed notes about Ashley's home life, and the story behind them is tragic. All those times she said something horrible or did something vindictive, it never really occurred to me there might be something that was making her deeply unhappy, something that had nothing to do with any of us.

"I started sobbing uncontrollably, and I think I had a bit of a panic attack." I turn my head a little and see a tear slide out of her eye. "Ms. Moore came around the table and kneeled next to me. She tried to talk to me. She kept telling me to put my head between my legs and breathe slowly, but I was freaking out. I coul—" Ashley's voice catches in her throat. "I couldn't get any air, and it felt like I was going to pass out. Then she put a hand on my shoulder and gave me a little shake."

Riley hands her a tissue from her bedside table. It's printed with little surfboards. This whole house looks like a staged model home.

Ana comes over to the bed. "You okay?"

Ashley sits up, blots her eyes, and smiles warily. "Yeah, thanks."

Ana nods slowly and waits for a moment. "So how hard did she shake you? And how on earth did your dad find out?"

"I didn't know he was suing her. I should have known he would take care of it his own way." She drags the tissue across her eyes, smearing her mascara. Ashley takes a deep breath and sighs. "So he was all upset about what she said, and he asked if she'd ever touched me and I said, 'No, not really.'"

"Uh-oh." Christine sits up.

"Exactly." Ashley points at her. "He kept asking me questions and sort of putting ideas into my head, and then he made it known what he wanted me to say."

Riley shakes her head. "I'm so sorry, Ash."

I glance at Riley. It's a little jarring to hear her use this nickname so comfortably. She's been Ashley Anderson, Satan in cashmere, since high school started. Ash. That one little syllable betrays so much history.

Ana squeezes onto the end of the bed. "Okay, shake my shoulder as hard as she shook your shoulder." She leans forward so Ashley can grab it.

Ashley gently cups her shoulder and gives it a quick shake.

"That's it?" Christine pops to her feet. "This should be a snap to disprove. All you have to do is take the stand during your dad's trial and show everyone what really happened."

"Oh no. I'm not doing that." Ashley grabs her head with her hand. "My dad will kill me."

Ana and Christine exchange a worried look.

I bite my lip. "You have to. We'd be right there with you. We could help you through it."

"He's my dad. I can't. He'll . . . hate me forever. I came to you guys because I need to figure out another way to fix this. Without him knowing it was me." Her eyes well up with tears, and her lip quivers.

"And we won't let you down." Riley shrugs at the rest of us. "We'll find another way. We'll move mountains or make miracles happen . . . or something."

28

'm getting ready to go last-ditch Christmas Eve shopping with Ana when the doorbell rings. My heart skips around in my chest. I had a feeling he'd pick today to come back. I knew Ed couldn't stay away on Christmas. He's sick of living in that rat-hole apartment he rented, and he's coming to make a grand romantic gesture to win Dreamy back. They're strolling off into the sunset in my imagination when I pad down the stairs and run to the door, yanking it open. Only it's not Ed.

"Hello?" The gray blanket of fog refracts the sunlight, and I blink. The girl on the doorstep is thin and short, and her dark brown hair is pulled back in a neat ponytail. She's wearing tight jeans and cowboy boots, and a sheepskin coat much too heavy for winter in Half Moon Bay.

"Hi." She smiles sheepishly and slips her hands into the pockets of her coat. "Does Nick Fairchild live here?"

"Yeah." She's pretty, in a kind of tomboyish way. I open the door a little wider and spot a blue pickup truck in the driveway. "But he's not here right now." Nick has been going out at weird times recently. Two days ago he was even wearing business clothes and a tie. Right now he's out buying cinnamon for Dreamy.

"Oh." Her face flushes. "Well . . ." She kicks at the wooden porch a little bit. "Do you know when he'll be back?"

"Soon." I step back and examine her. She doesn't look like a serial killer or anything. "Do you want to come in and wait?"

"I'm Heather." She holds out her hand.

"I'm—"

"Zoe, right?" She smiles at the confusion that must be apparent on my face. "Nick talked a lot about you." I stare at her some more. "I used to work with Nick," she adds quickly. "In Colorado. We worked together at the ranch . . . ?"

"Oh right." I usher her inside and close the door to block out the cool, moist air. Nick's mysterious phone call comes back to me. Heather was his boss. Though somehow that doesn't really make it any clearer what she's doing on our doorstep on Christmas Eve. "He's talked a lot about you too," I say, even though he hasn't ever told me anything about her. It just seems like the thing to say.

She sits on the edge of the couch and stares at the domed ceiling above in wonder.

"Was Nick . . ." How do I ask this nicely? "Did he know you were coming?"

"No." She clutches her hands in front of her. "He didn't. It was . . . it was probably stupid anyway, but I just . . . I don't know. I wanted to say Merry Christmas I guess."

It's the flush in her cheeks that makes the pieces fall into place. The messy breakup. His abrupt departure from the ranch. The weird phone call from his old boss. The fact that she apparently just drove out from Colorado to wish him a Merry Christmas.

"I'm sure he'll be glad to see you," I lie. He's just starting to pick up the pieces of his life again. Maybe this wasn't the best idea. "Can I get you something to drink or anything? We have water, and some seltzer I think, and some weird sugar-free lemonade thing."

"Would you mind? Seltzer would be awesome."

I nod, then walk into the kitchen. Dreamy's hunched over a patch of ground she planted in the fall, but her back is to me. I pull a glass off the shelf and fill it with ice, then crack open a bottle of seltzer and pour some into the glass.

The front door slams. Heavy footsteps sound across the floor. I snap out of it and walk out of the kitchen. I should warn Nick that he has a visitor before he does something totally embarrassing. "Nick, I—"

It's too late. He's clutching a small plastic grocery bag, staring at Heather. She gives a slight wave from the couch, but lowers her hand when he doesn't respond. His jaw clenches.

"Heather." He tosses the bag onto the side table and lets out a long breath.

"Hi." She no longer looks sheepish.

Nick glances at me, and I look away as if maybe I don't even know they're there. He clears his throat.

"Let's go for a walk," Nick says, so low I almost don't hear him. Heather nods and stands, smoothes down her pants, and follows him out the front door.

I stare at the closed door long after they're gone.

What Heather did is crazy. There's no doubt about that. I don't know if it's going to work out with her and Nick, or if he even wants it to. But she did it, and that means something.

29

"ight maids a milking, seven swans a swimming," Dreamy sings from the kitchen.

I press my eyes shut and pray for strength. We're all dealing with the fact that Ed isn't here in our own way, and I suppose I need to respect her method, annoying though it may be. I glance at the clock. It's three o'clock, and he hasn't even called to wish me a Merry Christmas. Ed's spending the day in San Mateo with Uncle Hugh and Aunt Sarah.

"FIVE GOLDEN RIIIIIIINGS!" I turn up the volume on the TV. I'm watching *It's a Wonderful Life*. I'm not sure how I never noticed it before, but this is one dark movie. Sure, in *A Christmas Story* they chop the head off that goose at the Chinese restaurant, but that's a cakewalk compared to the suicide attempts and near financial ruin in this little doozie.

Dreamy is suddenly hovering over me.

"You know what I think would be nice?" She smiles too much. I can nearly see her silver fillings.

"Why don't you and Nick play that board game you used to love?" As if on cue, we hear footsteps padding down the spiral staircase. "Remember that, Nick?" she says, raising her voice. "What was it called?"

"Well," I roll over onto my back and try to muster a smile. "I think I'm going to finish my movie."

"What was that game called?" She picks a piece of lint off Nick's old sweater when he stops in front of her.

"I don't know . . ." He scratches his stubble and smiles. Though she left as quickly as she appeared, there's been something different about him since Heather's visit.

"Chutes and Ladders!" Dreamy pats him twice on the arm. "You should play that."

Nick raises an eyebrow at me, and I flare my nostrils ever so slightly. Chutes and Ladders? Is she serious? I haven't played that game in ten years.

"Maybe later." He walks over to the couch, and before I know it, he's reaching for me. "For now I need Zoe's help." I point the remote at the TV and start raising the volume, but he takes it out of my hand and clicks it off.

"You in?" Nick walks to the back door, and I nod.

I follow Nick wordlessly outside and to the stables. I knew this was what he meant when he said he needed help, but anything is better than hanging out in that stupid bubble, watching my mom pretend that everything is fine.

Nick's steps slow down as the stable comes in sight though.

"Hey," I say, catching up to him. "I thought I was the one afraid of horses."

"Zoe, I—" He stares straight ahead and sighs. He starts to say something and then stops himself. "I have something to show you."

His tone makes me uneasy, and we walk quickly the rest of the way in silence. Once we arrive, he pushes the door open and hesitates. "I don't know if you'll even care. But I wanted you to know."

I peer into the stable and take a few steps into the weak

light. Same poop smell, same caving roof, same lack of Ed . . . everything seems to be the same.

"Dreamy sold Dox."

I freeze, a trapezoid of light glinting on the hay around me. My heart beats a little faster.

"She did what?"

It's not like I loved that horse. Well, maybe I did, a little, because of what he meant to Ed. But mostly this means things are still bad, worse than I thought. I've started chipping in for groceries, and I buy all my own clothes and school lunches, but I guess it's not enough if she's still selling off horses. Maybe I need to cut back more. I've been saving a little, hoping to eventually get enough for a car, but I can stop that. Maybe I should get rid of my cell phone, though the thought of giving up my lifeline to the world outside these woods is horrible.

"She did it a few days ago. I wasn't sure if you'd been out here since then." Nick shuffles behind me, making a rustling sound in the hay. I hear a jingly noise, but I ignore it. "Or if she tells you stuff like that because you don't like the horses . . . or whatever."

I listen but don't turn as Nick gets one of the horses out of its stall. They walk up behind me slowly, as if not to scare me. Horses have very distinct breathing, lots of contented sighs and rolling the bit around in their mouths. Nick puts something in my hand, and even in my numb state I know what it is. A lead rope. I hold it and don't move. I can feel Alfalfa's familiar presence behind me, but I'm paralyzed with fear.

Even though the accident was two and a half years ago, it feels like it happened yesterday. I remember holding on as Alfalfa reared up, and the breathless feeling of falling. I can still see the world rushing by, my foot stuck in the stirrup, the twigs tearing my skin, my head bumping on roots and rocks. I remember very clearly the feeling of facing down death.

Nick gets Old Gray Mare bridled and set up with her own lead rope. He walks up next to me, and she obediently follows him.

"C'mon, kiddo," Nick whispers into the silence of the barn. "Let's go for a little walk. No riding. Just leading."

I notice that I've been standing in this small square of light so long that my left shoe is now in the shadow.

"A walk in the woods. No big deal." Old Gray Mare breathes out in a tired, happy way. She really is a sweet old girl, a nice calm horse. Ed always said the others looked up to her.

I raise my face and study Nick in the shadows. In my mind my brother was always larger than life. These past few months I've seen a different side of him, that of a flawed, hurting human. I nod, slowly.

Nick starts walking to the door. Halfway there, he stops and looks back to see if I'm following. I stare at my feet, unsure of what they will do, but they move a few steps, slowly, and then the steps come easier. Alfalfa falters for a moment behind me and then falls into rhythm with my gait. We walk in step, in time, together.

For a while we stroll through the woods in silence, and maybe it's because of how far from the modern world we seem, or because of the chill in the air, or what a cruel holiday it's been, but my thoughts go to a different place, another time. I try to put myself in the shoes of two everyday people, walking to a town far from home to be counted for a census. I think of a woman—no, a girl. Maybe my very age, being forced to grow up and face the challenges God has put in her path. They said she rode a donkey because she was very pregnant, but she must have led it sometimes too, to stretch her legs. Did she ever wish things could go back to how they used to be? Did she ever wonder if God really knew what he was up to when he chose her? What if she failed and everything fell apart?

Eventually we reach the clearing, where the horses used to love to stop. They would drink from the little brook that fed the pond about a half a mile from here. But today there's no brook, and the grass is brown. Nick drops Old Gray Mare's lead, and she begins to pick over the brambles and dried-up weeds. I drop Alfalfa's lead and steel my nerves as he passes very close to me and joins Old Gray Mare.

"You did it." Nick's eyes dance in the fading afternoon light.

I nod. I guess I did do it. Nick sort of tricked me. He distracted me and didn't give me any time to overanalyze it. But I don't feel like talking about the horses right now. I can't put it into words yet.

"Why did Heather come here?" I say suddenly.

Nick sighs deeply and lowers himself down on the grass. He folds his hands behind his head, shuts his eyes, and smiles. "I'm not quite sure."

"What did you guys talk about?" I plop down next to him but keep the horses in my sight. They seemed content over there, picking through the field for something to eat, but you never know.

He shakes his head a little. "Everything . . . nothing. All that stuff." Nick pulls a long brown weed from the soil and holds it up to his face. He tosses it and sits up. "Can you keep a secret?"

My heart races a little. Nick and I have never really had secrets. "Of course." He watches me, and I smile to encourage him.

"I left Colorado because I asked Heather to marry me and she said no."

My eyes go wide, and Nick laughs at me.

"It's okay." He flops back down and shuts his eyes again. "When she said no, I was devastated. I hopped the first ride I could find back home and called Dreamy and Ed from the road." He drops his head to the side and squints at me. "I just needed to get away. But seeing her again made me realize that she was right to say no. Granted, now she's changed her mind. She wanted to start things up again, but we have no business being together. And well, once I saw how bad things had gotten here . . ."

The horses seem to neigh in agreement across the clearing. The sun glints off Alfalfa's shiny brown coat and highlights his goofy white spots.

"So, you did love her but now you don't?" How could you propose to someone and then realize it was all a big mistake?

"I did love her." Nick plucks another long weed and puts it in his mouth. "But it wouldn't have worked. She wasn't ready then, and I'm not now. I couldn't leave home, not with the way things are here. You have to be in the same place at the same time to really hold on to each other." He chews on the end of the weed. "Sometimes love isn't enough." He shuts his eyes and leans back and smiles up at the big gray sky.

30

I see a figure forming in the darkness, and even though I know who it is, my heart beats faster.

"Well," I say, trying to wrap things up with Ed. I took the call on the back deck because I didn't want to censor what I said for Dreamy. I don't have to pretend it was a happy Christmas if I don't want to. "I hate to talk and run but . . ."

Marcus slowly comes into focus in the shadows beyond the deck.

"Merry Christmas, little girl." I can hear in Ed's voice that he doesn't want me to go either, which is a small consolation.

My eyes water for a moment, but I choke back the tears. "Merry Christmas, Ed. Come home soon." By the time I snap my phone shut, Marcus is sitting in front of me, but I can't bring myself to look him in the face.

"Here," he says quietly. He hands me a small square package, wrapped in bright green paper with smiling reindeer on it.

I grip it to my chest and try to figure out how to tell him. I just need a little more time. I guess all this stuff with Dreamy and Ed has me really messed up. I really did try to find a gift for Marcus, but Christmas shopping has been close to impossible, and nothing jumped out at me. Plus with money being so tight . . .

"Should I open it?" I blush for being such a coward. Why can't I admit that I simply don't have a present for him? He'll understand. He always understands.

Marcus's eyes are hard and cold. "I saw him."

"What?" My voice is louder than I mean it to be. I try to cover it up by laughing a little. "Saw who? Ed?"

"No, *him*." He shakes his head slowly. "Dean."

My palms begin to sweat. I probably wouldn't feel that bad if Dean had only walked me home that one time, but it's happened a few times now, so I'm not sure which time Marcus is even referring to.

Really, it's not my fault. I can't make him *not* come to El Bueno Burrito. It's a public place. Dean shows up at closing and escorts me home. It's just a friendly thing. Besides, all we do is talk. We talk about Grace, his rocker girlfriend, and about Marcus, and New York, music, everything.

"Yeah. Dean is my friend. I'm allowed to have friends, right?"

Even though Dean has a car, we always walk for some reason. I don't know why, but neither one of us has ever mentioned him driving me home. There's something about the walking part that feels right.

"Since when?" A puff of cold air blows out of his lips. "You always say he's an idiot and a jerk. Now you're friends with this idiotic jerk?" He thrusts his hands into his coat pockets. "I mean, really, Zoe. I'm trying to be patient here, but what am I supposed to think?"

I stand up too. I have never, ever cheated on Marcus, and for him to suggest . . . well, but that was Dean's fault.

That was before we were friends. He was new in town and confused.

"You're supposed to trust me." I have been good to Marcus. I was the first person to see what an awesome guy he is, back when people thought he was just some band geek. I've been loyal to him, even when I had the chance to not be. I would never hurt him. "And give me a little space when I'm going through . . ." I wave my hand wildly at my house behind me. "Whatever."

Marcus glowers at me and takes a few steps back into the shadows. "Space is not what we need."

I roll my eyes. Smothering is just in Marcus's nature.

"Merry Christmas, Zoe." He turns his back on me and disappears into the frigid night.

♡

At one in the morning, I admit to myself that I can't sleep and pad downstairs to the living room. The Christmas tree that Dreamy chopped down herself and strung with white lights and red berries looks oddly cheery in the gloomy light.

I try to read the book about solar power Dreamy got me, but it's dry and dull. I look for something on TV, but there are infomercials on every station. In desperation I even crack open one of the books Mrs. Dietrich assigned us to read over Christmas break, something called *Tess of the d'Urbervilles*, but it's horrible. Finally I cave in and find the little reindeer-paper-wrapped package and pull it from under the couch where I hid it.

I plop down on the floor, take a deep breath, and open the card.

Zoe,

Dreamy helped me with this. Seemed like what you needed the most this year.

Merry Christmas,

xoxox

Marcus

P.S. I did a whole collection of them, but this is the best one. I'll give you the rest tomorrow.

I scratch my nose. Well, that was as clear as mud. I slide my finger under the paper and slip the paper off and find a DVD. That's odd. Marcus is good with computers and stuff. I wonder if he dubbed an old out-of-print movie for me? That would be kind of sweet, I guess.

I find the remote, mute the volume, and pop in the disk. I did mention to him that *Love Story* somehow disappeared from my collection. Light flickers onto the screen. I slide away from the TV and lean my back against the couch.

The first shot is of a young couple, waving and smiling. My parents, only they're not my parents, they're young, and thin, and lovely. Ed leans over a crib and pulls out a roly-poly baby with a head full of red hair.

I grab my mouth to stop my lip from quivering.

Dreamy grabs the baby's hand and makes me wave to the camera. In the video I'm giggling, laughing, and my parents are cooing over me.

Dreamy stops to hear something the cameraman says and then laughs. She pulls Ed in, and they kiss for the camera. Then they lean in and kiss both sides of my cheeks.

After a few more minutes, I shut it off, worried that my

sobs will wake Dreamy and Nick. I lie back on the floor and let the shag carpet dig into my back while the tears roll into the hollows of my ears. I can't believe how much I had and never knew. I wish I could go back to the happier times and really savor them. I didn't think they would someday come to an end. It seemed like we'd be together forever.

31

M s. Lovchuck seriously loves assemblies. She likes the power trip of standing in front of us with a microphone, telling us what to do. I'm in the special band section near the front, and I usually love attending these things, playing our fight song and helping get the crowd excited, but today I'm kind of distracted. There's something wrong, and he's sitting three rows behind me in the trombone section.

After our horrible Christmas, I went over to Marcus's house and patched things up as best I could, and I even bought him the game Star Trekopoly. I think we both recognized it was a lame gift, especially compared to what he did for me, but it seemed to cheer him up a bit, and now we've settled back into a sort of uneasy rhythm. There was a moment there when I thought I was going to . . . but then he was so forgiving about the whole present thing, and I was reminded all over again how much I don't deserve him, how hurt he would be if things ended, how I'll never find anyone who loves me as much as he does. Still, things have been kind of weird for the past few weeks, so it's best if I keep my eyes focused on the gym floor and ignore what's going on behind me in the trombone section, or, worse, across the gym where Dean sits, arms crossed over his chest, watching me. I don't see Grace.

In fact, I haven't seen her at all lately. Has she been missing school?

As soon as the cheerleaders finish their final cheer and Ms. Lovchuck dismisses us, I stuff my piccolo case into my bag and start down the stairs without even looking back. If I hurry, I can get out of this gym without any awkward questions.

The wooden bleachers shake as hundreds of students rush for the doors, and the smooth, glossy floor of the gym feels blessedly stable under my feet. Some kid named Ben, who just transferred in, is right in front of me, looking confused. I catch a glimpse of Ana from across the floor, and she waves, but then is swept up in a group headed toward the doors on the other side of the gym.

"There you are." I feel a hand on my shoulder and whip around to see Dean grinning at me. "I went to El Bueno Burrito Saturday, but you weren't there." He steps into a small space beside me.

"Yeah, someone called in sick on Wednesday." I bite my lip. He came to the store, and I wasn't there. "So I had to switch days." We're pressed forward in the crowd, and he leans in to me a little bit. "Sorry." I don't know why I'm apologizing to him, but it makes me feel better to say it.

"I'm sorry too." He reaches into his back pocket. The closer we get to the doors, the more the crowd presses in on us. "I came to talk to you about next Saturday night." Dean flips his wallet open and pulls out two small pieces of paper. I squint but can't read the tiny writing.

"Next Saturday?" I blink as we step out into the cool February sunshine.

"Yeah. You're coming with me, right?" Out of the corner of my eye, I see that he's grinning at me. "It's in the city, but I figured we could drive up and get dinner—"

"What are you talking—"

"Zoe!" I know it's Marcus before I turn around. Shoot. He must have booked it across the gym floor. "There you are." I force a smile onto my face as he slips his hand into mine. He stares straight at me, and somehow squishes his way in between us. "I wanted to talk to you. Do you still need a ride home after school, because I have to go to—"

"Hey, Marcus." Dean nods at Marcus and gives him an easy smile. Marcus looks at me for a split second before returning a pinched smile.

"Hey." Marcus turns back to me. "So I'm supposed to ask you whether you need a ride." His palm is sweaty, and I have the strongest urge to pull my hand away, but I don't, because of Dean, or because of Marcus, or something. "Home."

"Um." I wince as Marcus presses my hand to the left, trying to steer me away from Dean, and I let him because I don't know what else to do. "Sure. Or I could see if I could get a ride from Christine."

"I can give you a ride," Dean says smoothly. The muscles in Marcus's arm tense.

"No, that's okay," Marcus says. The crowd is thinning now as students stream away from the gym in different directions, so there's no need for Marcus to be pressed so tightly against me, but he holds on. "We already planned it this way. I only wanted to be sure we were still . . . on the same page."

"Either way. So, Zoe, next Saturday . . ." Dean takes a step closer to me. He holds up the tickets, and I shoot him a panicked look. I can see in his eyes that he knows exactly what he's doing. "I'll pick you up at seven." Dean smiles at me from ear to ear.

Marcus clears his throat.

"I don't even know what you're talking about," I say quickly. Marcus lets a breath out through his nose. "I never said I would go."

"Why aren't you taking your girlfriend?" Marcus asks, his voice higher than normal.

Grace. My stomach falls. Why *isn't* he taking Grace?

"I want Zoe to come with me," Dean says to Marcus, shrugging. "It's my dad's new band's first real show, and I know how much Zoe likes music, so I thought she'd enjoy it."

It doesn't even bug me that they're talking about me in the third person, as if I weren't here, because my mind is swirling. There's no good reason for him not to bring Grace, unless . . .

"I only got two tickets, but I could see if there's any more . . ." Dean lets his voice trail off, and an uncomfortable silence hangs in the air. That would be so awkward, and we all know it, and that's exactly why he offered it. It was safe. Marcus would never take him up on it.

He hasn't mentioned Grace in a while, and I haven't seen her around. He mentioned something about things being weird with her the other night when we were walking home. Truthfully, I've never really thought they had that much in common.

"I didn't say I would go," I say, with a little more volume than necessary. I glare at Dean. "I never said anything about coming along." Marcus's arm relaxes a bit.

The courtyard is almost empty now, except for a few students rushing toward the J-wing with big cardboard boxes in their arms. At some point the three of us stopped moving.

"It's at this new jazz club in San Francisco. There's a cover, but I'll take care of that." He tucks his hands into the pockets of his jeans. "They're playing some old school songs, the stuff my dad listens to."

I look from Dean's face—olive, handsome, smug—to Marcus's red, pinched face. I have to make him understand that I didn't do this. I didn't want this.

But then I let my eyes travel back to Dean, his tall frame, the defiant slope of his shoulders, and I realize that maybe I didn't agree to go with him, but I kind of want to. I picture the two of us, out in the big city, at a grown-up club, listening to his father's music together. Marcus doesn't understand how much this means to Dean. Just last week on one of our walks home, Dean opened up about his music, about how his father was always out playing in the evenings when he was a kid, about how he and Fletch took up the sax because of how much it meant to their father. He didn't say it, but I know hearing his father play reminds him of his brother. It's a part of his past, a part of what made him who he is now. I want to be a part of it too.

"Maybe we could go for just a little bit." Even as I say it, I know how stupid it sounds. Dean's not going to skip out on his dad, but it makes me feel less guilty somehow. "And then I could come over to see you when I get back," I add quickly. "Or we could hang out earlier or something." The bell rings, and the last few shadows scurry across the quad, but none of us move.

"What about bookstore night?" Marcus's voice squeaks a

little bit on the last syllable, and it takes me a second to realize he's tearing up.

"Well . . ." My heart sinks. I totally forgot about bookstore night. How could I forget that? "Maybe we could go another night instead, just this once?" A fresh wave of guilt washes over me as I watch Marcus's face crumble.

"I could find somebody else to go," Dean says. "I didn't mean to make things difficult." He adjusts the strap on his bag, and a part of me wonders whether that's exactly what he meant to do.

"Zoe?" Marcus takes a step forward and turns to face me, still holding my hand. He looks into my eyes, and I can't help it, I have to look away. This is killing him, and I don't know how to make it better.

"We're just friends, Marcus." I don't mean to whisper, but my voice barely makes a sound. No one says anything, but Marcus releases his death grip on my hand and slowly pulls away. I bite back tears as Marcus steps away, and suddenly I realize that somehow I've made a decision without meaning to, without fully comprehending what I was doing.

"I . . ." Marcus stops and takes a deep breath. "I guess you should go then."

I turn to Dean, his arms crossed over his chest, watching. He takes a small step forward, edging his shoulder behind mine. I can feel the heat of his skin through my shirt.

"I'm sorry." My voice comes out in a low wail. Marcus just nods.

"I'll always love you, Zoe." He ducks his head, but not before I see tears pooling in his eyes. "I hope he is who you think he is." He turns on his heel and walks away before I can even process what he's said. A tear leaks out of my eye.

"But we're not—" I start, but I don't finish my sentence. He's not going to stop to listen, and I don't even know what I was going to say. Marcus's footsteps echo in the empty quad as he hurries away.

Without a word Dean puts his hand on my arm. It feels warm, and strong, and because I don't know what else to do, I lean back, just a little, and let my back touch his chest. I don't even know how long we stand there.

32

Oh," Ed says. Dreamy and Nick startle too. They're all sitting stiffly in the living room, and there are papers scattered on the coffee table. "I thought you were going to youth group with the girls, Butterbean."

Even though I can see that something horrible is going on, I allow myself a few moments to enjoy the sight of my father back in our house. If this were a snapshot, you'd never know how dysfunctional the real life behind it is.

"It's over." I swallow and start walking. Ed looks at his watch and mumbles. Dreamy collects the papers into a pile and bangs them on the edge of the table. "The others went out afterward, but I wasn't feeling up to it."

Ed laughs awkwardly. "Well . . . it's good to see you. Are we still on for lunch next weekend?"

It's so obvious what's going on here. He's come to pick up the divorce papers. Dreamy must think that no one can hear her talking on the phone. Come on.

I cross my arms over my chest. "I'd rather do dinner tonight. Why don't I order some Thai?"

Nick flinches and hops to his feet. "I can't. I've got . . . to run an errand. Thanks though."

"Yeah, tonight doesn't work for me either." Dreamy grabs a few pillows from the floor and tosses them back on the couch.

She picks up an empty plate and walks into the kitchen. "I was going to organize my checkbook."

I shoot a pleading look at Ed that he takes pains to ignore.

"I'll see you soon." His voice cracks a little. He stands up slowly, grabs a manila envelope from the table, and then shuffles to the front door. His jacket is slung on the back of one of the dining room chairs.

His face shows that this is killing him too, so I decide not to push it. I can't bear to see my father cry.

"Hold up." Nick darts across the room and shoves his feet into his old work boots. He pats the front of his coat, looking for his wallet. "Can you give me a ride downtown? I'm meeting some people."

Ed's face brightens a little. "Sure." He opens the door a little, then pauses and turns to me. "Um, bye," he says quietly over his shoulder. Nick joins him at the door, but just before he closes it behind them, he winks at me.

33

The club is dark and noisy, but I try to act like I know what I'm doing as I duck around a low table and slide into a velvet booth. There's an ottoman across the table, but Dean doesn't even hesitate before he plops down next to me on the booth. I guess it's so he can see the band. If he sat on the ottoman, his back would be toward the stage.

"That's him," he says, nodding at a dark form hunched over a speaker on the stage. His shape becomes clearer as my eyes adjust to the dim lighting. He appears to be plugging in some cords, though it's hard to tell from here, especially because several other people are rushing around the stage, setting instruments in stands and running wires along the floor.

A loud, brash song trills out from Dean's back pocket, and he grabs his phone quickly. I see a picture of Grace flash across the screen for a split second before he silences the call.

"Maybe you should get that?" I gesture at the phone. "Take it outside or something. I can wait here." I watch him carefully.

"No," he laughs in a sad, somber way. "Now is definitely not the time." He powers his phone down and puts it back in his pocket.

So they must have broken up too. Poor Grace. I hope she took it well. At least they haven't been together very long.

"You want a Coke or something?" He gestures toward the long, dark wooden counter that takes up one side of the room.

"Sure." Before I can say more, he stands up and walks toward his dad. I watch as he leans in to say something to him. Mr. Marchese looks in my direction, then the two of them head toward the bar.

I've never been anywhere like this. It's the kind of place adults go, but Dean seems perfectly at ease. I wonder how many evenings he's spent at hole-in-the-wall jazz clubs, listening to his dad play.

For a moment I try to imagine my parents in a place like this, and it almost makes me laugh. I wonder how they'd feel if they knew I was here. Ever since their problems started, they've been too distracted to ask many questions about where I'm going and what I'm up to. Still, it feels very grown-up and exciting.

"Zoe"—Dean sets two drinks down on the low table in front of me—"I'd like you to meet my dad. Dad, my friend Zoe."

I stand up and thrust my arm out, and he grasps my hand and shakes it.

"Nice to meet you, Zoe." His voice is deep, a little scratchy, but warm. "Dean tells me you're a musician."

"Not a real one." I run my hand through my hair to smooth it down. "I just play the piccolo."

Dean's dad laughs. "Nothing wrong with the piccolo." He jerks his thumb at the stage behind him. "I should get going," he says as several guys in dark suit jackets take the stage. "Nice to meet you, Zoe." He turns and starts walking, but calls over his shoulder, "Enjoy the show." Dean smiles and sits back down on the bench.

"He's nice," I say and lower myself down beside him.

"Yeah, real jim-dandy." Dean's eyes dance as he gives me a wry grin.

"Whatever." I roll my eyes, kicking myself. It was kind of a silly thing to say, but what are you supposed to say about someone else's dad? I certainly can't say that he's handsome, or how much Dean looks like him, or how much I hope to talk to him—the missing piece in the puzzle that is Dean's family history.

"You know what's nice?" Dean asks as he leans forward to grab our drinks. "Being here with you." He takes a frosty glass in each hand and holds one out to me, and our fingers brush as I take it from him. Dean smiles, and my heart does that little flip it makes whenever he looks at me. "Are you doing okay?"

He raises his soda to his lips and watches me over the rim of his glass. Dean knows about my parents, and he knows about Nick, and about Ms. Moore, but I know what he's really asking about. He wants to know if I'm okay about the Marcus thing.

"Yeah." I let out a long breath and take a sip of my Coke. It's cold and sweet and strangely refreshing. "I'm fine. It's just . . ." I trace my finger along the edge of my glass, leaving a trail in the condensation. The truth is, I feel horrible about Marcus. I'll never forget the look in his eyes as he walked away, brokenhearted. I hate that I did that to him. But somehow, despite all that, being here with Dean still feels right. I guess maybe I've liked him for a while, if I'm honest. There's something electric in his touch, something in his eyes that draws me in like no one else ever has before. "It's been weird."

"You know I'm here for you," Dean says, ducking his head a little. He pulls his arm from the back of the booth and gives me a fist-bump, then lets his hand gently rest on my knee for a second. "If you want to talk."

"Thanks." I want to do more than just talk, and I inch my body closer to him, but Dean doesn't lean in to kiss me or lace his fingers through mine. I move my hand a little closer, waiting for him to reach for it, and my body tenses in anticipation. But he just smiles, crosses his arms over his chest, and slouches down against the back of the seat. He lets his shoulder rest gently against mine as the band begins to play.

34

glance at my watch and say a silent prayer of thanks when I see that I'm five sweet minutes from getting out of El Bueno Burrito. Getting up early on Saturday definitely stinks, but it's the one day of the week I don't have to help close this place down. The sour mop, the gross bits of food everywhere, counting the money—closing is the absolute worst.

This has been the longest week of my life. Nick was out all the time, doing who knows what, Dreamy and Ed are dividing up their assets, and Marcus is avoiding me. Never mind that Dean is still playing tricks with my mind—are we friends? Are we more? And still God doesn't seem to be giving me any miraculous signs from above about how to fix my problems.

I tap my fingers on the stainless steel counter and try to remind myself that every minute I'm here means I'm that much closer to a car, let alone food for the week, but I still watch the second hand strike out the final minute and sigh in relief. I give Ryan a high five, clock out, ditch my soiled apron in the laundry bucket, grab my things out of my locker, and then stroll out the front door into sweet freedom.

The sun is high in the afternoon sky, and I blink a few times when I step out. I recognize Ms. Moore's boxy Honda in the parking lot. Huh. She doesn't usually work Saturday mornings. I make a split-second decision to treat myself to a mocha and say hi to her. I pull open the door, and the sweet smell of old paperbacks and coffee drinks hits me. She definitely has the better job.

I walk up to the front counter, but there's only one bored-looking guy standing there. Where is everybody? A quick bolt of laughter peals through the store, and I follow it, weaving my way through the stacks to the children's area. There, on the brightly colored rug, standing around the neon green beanbags, four bookstore employees huddle around Ms. Moore. I duck behind a long bookshelf and press my face to the heavy gardening books to eavesdrop.

"Tim." Ms. Moore leans in and gives a balding guy a hug. "Thanks for giving me a chance to come in here and shake everything up."

He laughs, his big belly shaking a little. "I've never had someone fight me so hard on the classification of memoir."

She hugs a quiet woman who is wearing a baggy sweater that ties at the waist and then a blushing college kid.

"Have fun in Boston," the guy squeaks out, and my ears prick. Boston? Is Ms. Moore going on vacation? This is an awfully heartfelt good-bye if she's coming back in a week or two.

"Cross your fingers for me, everyone?" A few of the employees hold up crossed fingers, and Ms. Moore begins to make her way to the front door, clutching a small cardboard box. "I'd love to get back to teaching."

She waves a few more times, distracted by their well-wishes and good-byes, and nearly walks right past me.

"Zoe!" She flinches as I step out into the aisle. "What . . . um, hi there."

I cross my arms over my chest. If I didn't know any better, this would look exactly like a good-bye party. "What's going on?"

Ms. Moore glances back at the store employees and tries to smile. "Come on." She motions to the door with her head. "Follow me."

I stay still for a second, watching her walk to the front of the store. Ms. Moore is originally from the Boston area. If she were to give up on this whole strange adventure, Boston is exactly where she'd go.

Ms. Moore props open the door of Bayside Books and smiles sheepishly at me. I give in and trudge to the front, moving as slowly as possible. I can't believe it. I can't believe we've been fighting so hard for her, and now she's going to give up.

I follow her in silence to her car. She hands me the box, which contains two ceramic mugs, a few paperback books, and a framed picture of an old couple, then pops her trunk.

"Here." I put the box in her trunk, then turn and start to walk away. How could she do this to us? She lets me get a few feet away without saying anything, and for a second I worry this is how we will leave things forever. She clears her throat.

"Zoe, I was going to tell you."

I freeze. Likely story. I storm off, more determined this time.

Ms. Moore slams her trunk. "There's a lot I have to tell you, actually."

I stop again but don't turn around. "Would you like to come over for a while? I don't work for Marina Vista anymore, so it's okay. Besides . . ." She lets out a long breath, and I finally face her. "I have something for you."

She gives me a half smile, but there are dark circles under her eyes. This isn't how I want things to end.

Without a word, I follow her to her car.

♡

Ms. Moore hands me a mug of hot tea, and I perch on the edge of her brown couch. It's overstuffed like a marshmallow, and I sink into it. The furniture in her apartment is a little outdated, but it feels comfortable somehow.

"I was going to tell you, Zoe. I only just found out, and nothing is definite yet."

I snort a little. It looked pretty darn definite to me. Why else would she quit her job at the bookstore?

Ms. Moore grips her hand-painted ceramic mug. She takes a sip of her tea, and I notice the subtle lines around her eyes. Sometimes I forget that she's not one of us. She's an adult, with adult-size problems. "I got a job interview at a private school in Boston. And I want to visit my family while I'm up there, so I needed the time off. But the bookstore couldn't accommodate that, so I quit."

I take a sip of tea to try to steady my quivering chin. I will not cry in front of Ms. Moore. I will not.

"Please try to understand. It's the kind of thing I've always dreamed of doing, being able to teach what I want, having a real budget to work with . . ." She frowns at my pained look and puts a hand on my shoulder. "I don't have the job yet, so it's not definite. But I do feel like I have to explore this opportunity. I've been out of work for almost a full year, and teaching is the only thing I've ever wanted to do."

I set my mug down and rub my hand over my face. I guess

I hadn't thought about the toll this must be taking on her. I'm sure she misses teaching, but she's probably also struggling to make ends meet.

"I would have never left without saying good-bye."

"You taught us to fight for what we wanted. You said you were fighting for this. What changed?" I ask in a small voice. Her apartment smells like old books. "Why leave now? We're making progress."

Ms. Moore sighs. "I don't know how much I'm allowed to tell you, but the school board is planning to settle out of court." She puts her mug on the coffee table and kicks off her worn white athletic shoes. "They're not going to renew my contract unless the case is dropped."

"But he didn't have a case! This—" I grab her shoulder and give it a small shake. "Is not the kind of thing you get fired for."

Ms. Moore smirks a little. "How did you find out about that?"

Oops. Ashley didn't want us talking about the details with anyone. I shouldn't have said that. "It's not important." I push up my sleeves, but the worn-out elastic won't hold them, and they slide down again. "What's important is that this whole thing goes to trial and Mr. Anderson loses and we have a chance to clear your name."

"Mr. Anderson is suing the school, not me. I can't make it go to trial." She tucks a section of hair behind her ear. "Plus, if I understand what's going on over there, Ashley won't testify against her father." She walks across the room to the book-shelf and scans for something. "And I wouldn't want her to. I'm only a teacher. Her family is forever."

I lean my head back and exhale. How am I going to save someone who doesn't even want to save herself?

She pulls a binder off the bottom shelf and flips it open, rummaging through the pages and finally pulling out a folder. "Here it is. I was going to frame each of these and give them to you guys." She walks back to the couch, clutching the folder to her chest. "But I don't know if I'll have time now." She lowers herself onto the couch next to me and slides the folder over.

My heart slams around in my chest as I take the folder. I pray that this is not what I think it is, but of course it is. I lift the top paper off the stack and suck in my breath when I recognize my own handwriting.

These are the essays we wrote that first day in detention. Ms. Moore assigned us to describe the day our lives changed. We were just a bunch of shy, isolated freshmen, all aching and hurting in our own ways, and this is how we learned . . . about each other. We learned that the four of us had more in common than we ever imagined.

I run my fingertips over the page, feeling the indentations where my pen pressed into the paper, and skim the first paragraph. It feels like I wrote this in another lifetime. My essay is about the day Alfalfa dragged me through the woods. I thought I was dead for sure. You don't get dragged half a mile behind a horse and survive, but somehow, miraculously, I did.

That day changed everything. Every moment of my life has been different since I slipped off that saddle; even though I walked away with just a few scratches, I am scarred permanently by it. As I flew through the woods, my head scraping along the ground, I realized what it would be like to die, and it scared me. I stopped riding after that and withdrew into myself. I have lived every day since then knowing that God saved me for a reason, feeling the unbearable weight of divine responsibility pressing down on me. I slide my eyes over the paper and tears begin to sting my eyes.

"Yours is not the only one in that folder," Ms. Moore says quietly. I don't move, afraid that motion will send tears splashing down onto the paper. "The others are there too."

Slowly, I scoot my essay aside, and even through my tears I recognize the drawings in the margins of Christine's paper. The familiar doodles bring another wave of grief, and I feel it again, that eerie sense I had that day, that something much bigger than us is behind this. The letters on the page begin to blur, and I start to wonder if the day I was dragged wasn't really the event that changed everything after all. Maybe it was only the means. I let my eyes rest on Christine's dark, angry handwriting. Perhaps being saved that day was only the beginning of my miracle.

I was so lost and confused, and then . . . it was like we were called to be there, in Ms. Moore's classroom in detention, like it couldn't have happened any other way. God saved all four of us for something.

Maybe he knew it would take all four of us to save her.

"How did you know?"

I lift the corner of Christine's paper and see Ana's precise letters on the sheet below it. I've wondered about this for years. How did she know that we needed each other so much? We were so different back then: the pink-haired freak, the type-A new girl, the jaded cheerleader, and of course, the red-haired, pudgy band geek. We had absolutely nothing in common on the surface, and yet she saw something.

"Teacher gene." Ms. Moore laughs. "You either have a sixth sense about these things or you don't."

Goose bumps raise on my arm. All of the Miracle Girls have experienced something like a sixth sense here and there, a certain sureness that comes over us. I always thought it was because we got a second chance at life. I wonder if Ms. Moore . . .

"Reread yours." She nods at the paper in my hand. "I don't think you'll recognize that scared little girl anymore."

I glance down at my paper and scan my words. I hardly described the accident at all. I describe the weird way my mind flashed back to the day we first got Alfalfa, but then I spent most of the page writing about how dangerous horses are and how quickly a huge mistake can happen. I sound like a nervous wreck.

"You see what I mean?" Ms. Moore smiles at me. "You've all grown up so much. Christine's family has made a fresh start of things. Ana and her parents actually communicate with each other now. Even Riley learned that she's not invincible."

I bite my lip. "But I'm still . . ." Since that day when Nick and I took the horses for a walk, I haven't been near the stable.

Ms. Moore puts a hand on my knee. "You've changed. You've faced so many obstacles, and you've . . . you're filled with a self-confidence that I've never seen before. It's like you're not afraid of anything anymore." I nod because I can't bring myself to correct her.

"You even stood up to me today." Ms. Moore pushes herself

up and walks into the kitchen, then comes back with the tea-kettle. She pours a little more water in my mug. "I was so proud of you. This new Zoe—she's not afraid to go out and get what she wants." She gives me a weak smile, and her eyes water for a second. I pick up my paper again and lay it carefully on top of the stack.

I swallow slowly and bore my eyes into the carpet. She's right. Again. I have to go out and get what I want because it's not going to just turn up on my doorstep.

No more sitting on the sidelines. No more Mr. Nice Guy. Zoe Fairchild is not going down without a fight.

35

I don't even go inside. After Ms. Moore dropped me off, I pedaled at top speed all the way from El Bueno Burrito, and my muscles are tired, but if I don't do this now, I'll lose my nerve. I lean my bike against the porch and run. The breeze feels good against my cheeks as I dodge tree branches and upturned roots, each step bringing me closer to the thing I fear the most.

I reach the stable in record time, racing against the sun that has already begun to set. No time for backing out. No time for dawdling. I don't want to be riding through the woods at night. That's too dangerous when you're alone. I won't go far. I'll just saddle him up and see what happens.

I open the door, and panic floods through my veins.

I can't do this. This is a mistake.

But I can't get Ms. Moore's words out of my head. Does she really believe I'm not afraid of anything? Or did she say it to spur me on because she suspects the truth? I think about the papers shoved into my bag and how much we've all changed. After her mother died, Christine gave up on God because the world seemed too cruel to have a creator, but now her family is making a new life together. Riley learned that even though God loves her to the moon and back, she's not invincible. Even Ana realized that only the truth would set her free.

I force myself to turn back around and face my fears. I go through all the steps to get Alfalfa saddled up: bridle, blanket, saddle, adjustments. My hands work quickly, and in what feels like the blink of an eye, he's ready to go. I take a deep breath and lead him out into the fading sunlight, then pray for courage.

"Hey there, buddy. Did you miss me?" I rub my hand gently along his nose. It's soft and warm and solid. "Want to go for a short ride? Hmm?" I touch his mane and remember how in middle school I would braid it with ribbons and flowers. I used to spend every waking moment out in the stable with Alfalfa. He was my first true friend.

I catch his eye and swear for a moment I see a glimmer of something, of understanding and compassion.

"Okay, buddy. Here we go," I whisper.

I walk around to his left side, keeping a hand on his body at all times so that he doesn't get spooked. I grab the saddle horn with my left hand, put my left sneaker in the stirrup, and swing myself up in one easy movement.

"Ahg!" A small inscrutable sound escapes my lips. I grab the saddle and remind myself not to squeeze his sides. That's the signal to go, and going is about the last thing I need right now. I shut my eyes and focus on slowing my breathing. *Be calm. Good horse. Be quiet and still. You're a good horse.*

After a few minutes, I dare to open one eye, then, slowly, the other, and find the world unchanged. Everywhere I look, things are exactly as they were a few minutes ago: the trees are blowing in the gusty March winds, the grass is still shriveled and brittle, the stable is standing right where it always was.

I take a deep breath and let my shoulders relax a little. I'm a lot taller than I was last time, and I wiggle around in the saddle a little bit, trying to get used to the new fit. Alfalfa waits patiently as I get settled. I find the reins with my right hand, keeping an eye on Alfalfa's ears. A horse shows you exactly how he's feeling with his ears. If they're facing forward, all is well, but if they're facing back, watch out.

Alfalfa's velvety ears are facing forward now, and there's a sense of calmness about him. I let out a breath and try to relax. Maybe we can go on the ten-minute loop. Ed cleared it ages ago for the riding school he wanted to start, and we've always used it to give the horses a little exercise. I know it like the back of my hand.

I lean over a little and whisper, "Are you ready? Promise to go slow?"

Obviously Alfalfa doesn't say anything, but he doesn't have to. He always had this way of knowing. He knew what I wanted him to do with the smallest gesture, without so much as a word. I give him a gentle squeeze with my legs, and he eases forward. He breathes slowly and evenly, and soon I let my body sway in time with the gentle bobbing of his gait.

I feel a familiar tightening in my cheeks and realize I'm smiling. I never thought I would ride a horse again, but it feels so good to be here. I throw back my head and let the last rays of the setting sun warm my face, and I smile bigger and bigger until a few tears run down my face. Who would have thought I'd be here again?

But of course, Ms. Moore knew I could do it. As Alfalfa steps into the clearing, I whisper a prayer of thanks.

36

By the time I return Alfalfa to his stall and get him settled in for the night, it's already six o'clock. I should go in and tell Dreamy all about what I've accomplished, but adrenaline is coursing through my veins, and there's still more to do.

I pull out my phone and start making calls to the Miracle Girls. They can't flake out on me now. Everything comes down to this.

♡

"Are you going to tell us what we're doing here?" Riley yawns, leans back on the floral couch, and stretches her feet out in front of her. It's 7:30 now. We lost precious time getting organized.

Christine's stepsister, Emma, is in the house, watching some new dance music video again and again, trying to teach herself the moves, so we're in the old painting studio in the backyard. It's better this way. Fewer people will be in on the secret.

"Yeah, what's the deal?" Ana plops down next to Christine on the couch and wrinkles up her nose at the musty smell. For some reason Christine loves this old thing, even though it looks like it should have been dragged to the dump years ago.

"We're finally going to do it. We're saving Ms. Moore. Tonight." I start pacing, but I don't miss the look the other girls exchange. I know I sound crazy, but I figured out exactly how we're going to fix this, and I need to get the other girls on board. I can't make this happen by myself. "So what we need now are your poster paints. Where are they?"

"In there?" Christine points to a closet across the room, raising an eyebrow.

"We're going to paint Ms. Moore into a job?" Ana shakes her head, watching me.

I stop pacing and open the closet door, and I start digging around on the shelves. There's all kinds of stuff in here—brushes, canvases, bottles, tubes, and jars.

"What are we going to do with poster paints?" Riley pushes herself up and comes over to the closet to help me poke around.

"Ms. Moore got a job interview at some private school for rich kids in Boston, and she's thinking of taking it. She's flying out for an interview. She's slipping away from us, and we've got to stop her." I take a few breaths. "The school board wants to hush up the court case and make it go away, so she thinks there's no point in staying. Plus, without Ashley to testify against her father, there's no way for the school board to win the case."

"What?" Ana sits straight up. "But I thought they voted to reinstate her?"

"Only if she won the case."

Riley chews on her lip and takes a deep breath. "Zoe, we all love her, but I don't really know what else we can do."

My eyes go wide. "I do." I yank a bag off a shelf and look

inside. Watercolors. I toss it on the floor. "We can't give up. Don't you see? She never let us give up on ourselves." I nudge Riley. "When we first met you, we couldn't see who you really were. It was Ms. Moore who stuck up for you and challenged us to get to know the girl behind the cheerleading skirt."

Christine laughs a little, and Riley lets a hint of a smile creep across her face.

"And Christine." I shove aside a box brimming over with crumpled-up newspapers. "Without Ms. Moore, I don't think you would have made it through last year." Christine's eyes water a little, and she bows her head to hide it. "No one else would have yelled at your dad, and that's exactly what he needed."

Christine stares at the floor. I'm not worried about those two. They're usually up for anything, and even though this is very definitely against school rules, for some reason I suspect that will only make this more appealing to them. It's Ana I'm not sure about. She is so good, so driven.

"Zoe's right," Ana says quietly. "Ms. Moore always told me to stay on my parents and not give up hope that someday we'd reach a compromise. And she was right." Christine peeks up at her. "I mean, they're still crazy, but things are better."

"Aha!" I pull out a plastic grocery bag full of poster paints and hold it up triumphantly. "You guys—" I take a deep breath. They're all staring at me. "Even if she's given up on herself, we can't give up on her."

Christine walks slowly toward me. She takes the bag out of my hand and reaches into the closet to pull out a coffee can full of brushes.

"So what's the plan, Red?"

♡

"Oh thank goodness," I say as Ashley Anderson and Riley emerge from Jordan Fletcher's party. Only Riley was brave enough to go in there and get her. Two football players stagger back and forth on the lawn, their arms slung over each other's shoulders. Riley opens the backseat door and motions to Ashley to get in.

"Sorry to, uh, tear you away," Christine says from behind the wheel. I smile at her from the passenger seat.

Ashley hesitates as she takes in the handmade posters, the boxes stuffed with flyers, and the rolls of duct tape at my feet. She turns back to Riley, who shrugs and smiles sheepishly.

"You guys have been busy." Ashley takes the middle seat and leaves Riley the one behind me. Ana scoots over to make room and nods at Ashley. Ana stunned us all with her idea to include our ultimate frienemy in our plan, but once she suggested it, we knew it was the right thing to do.

"Buckle up. We're on a mission!" Christine acts like she's going to peel out, but instead she looks up and down the streets of Jordan's otherwise sleepy subdivision and then eases forward, driving like a grandma.

As we slip through the nearly silent streets toward the school, we fill Ashley in on Ms. Moore's upcoming move and our little plan. She's excited, which is good because we didn't really give her a choice. It's midnight now, and I try to rub the tiredness out of my eyes. This morning seems like it was a month ago, but it feels good to finally be taking action in my life. No more sitting around, whining about how it's all playing out.

"So we're going to paper the school with flyers?" Ashley claps her hands. "What do they say?"

"Um . . ." I blink, trying to make my brain work at this late hour. I can't really even remember. There's one about justice being served. Another about having a say in our futures. I can remember one about being innocent until proven guilty. "A bunch of protest messages. We're going to put them everywhere." I point behind me.

Christine rounds the final corner and points her car toward school. In the distance the shadowy walls are dark and still. She slows down to a crawl in the school zone.

"Have you figured out how we're actually getting all this stuff into the school? They padlock the fence around the school after hours." A huge streetlight illuminates the truth of Ashley's statement. We forgot about the huge fence around the perimeter because we see it every day. "How much do you have to carry?"

"Great." Christine bumps her head on the back of the seat. "It's hardly going to be a covert operation if we have to hop a fence with this stuff."

"Go around back." I point to the end of the block. "I know the code to the lock on the gate by the band room."

"Really?" Ana's face breaks into a smile as Christine executes a very cautious U-turn and heads toward the side street that leads to the back of the school. For once in my life being a band geek has paid off.

"Yeah, we always have competitions and parades on the weekend, and Mr. Parker knows the code. That way they don't have to send someone out to unlock it every time." I shrug. "He, uh, let it slip one time."

"Zoe, you are a genius," Riley whispers, and a moment later Christine pulls her car into the small parking lot by the band room, then steers over to the edge of the main lot, right next to the front office.

We all tumble out of the car in silence. The moon casts a silvery light on the old, crumbling roof of Marina Vista High, and the entire school looks like some abandoned ghost town from long ago. I pick out my math classroom and find myself mesmerized by how different it all seems at night—empty, quiet.

"Okay, the best strategy is to split up." Ashley holds out her hand, and Christine gives her car keys as if it's the most natural thing in the world. She opens the trunk and rubs her hands together greedily. "Good job on this." Ashley opens one of the huge boxes of flyers that we printed up at the 24-hour FedEx Office store. "Let's all take a part of the school we're familiar with." She hands me a stack. "Zoe, band room and the surrounding area. Obviously you won't be able to get in the classrooms, but the breezeways are fair game. Slide a bunch under the classroom doors if you can. Put a flyer in every locker, every nook, and every cranny. The more creative you can be, the better."

She assigns the rest of the girls different sections of the school, and then checks her watch. "Let's meet back here in exactly thirty minutes. Then we'll go in groups to hang the posters."

We all nod, and I realize that I was right about Ashley. She may have wronged us in the past, and she may still have some very serious character flaws, but she sincerely loves Ms. Moore. And that makes her a little bit like us.

"The key is we can't make this easy for them. The teachers and administrators get here first, so we don't want them to have time to clean it up." She makes eye contact with each of us. Her stare fills me with confidence. "Got it?"

"Got it." Ana gives her a high five before she turns and runs toward the English classrooms, laughing.

37

Dreamy, Nick, and I shivered through the service at Church of the Redwoods this morning. After last night I could barely drag myself out of bed, but I was glad I went. Pastor Levi's talk was about Jesus the Radical, the man who overturned tables in the temple and said, "Give to Caesar what is Caesar's," and I felt a great calm come over me. Being a Christian isn't about being "good." It's about walking the path of truth and light, and when something isn't right, not being afraid to stand up and say, "Not today, not if I can help it, not without a fight."

A part of me still can't believe we did it, but mostly, I'm proud. It was irrational and over the top, but we did the only thing we could, and that feels good. But once I got home from church and spent the afternoon staring at my phone, willing it to ring, I realized that it was too early to celebrate the new and improved Zoe Fairchild. I have one more thing to do. I want him to be mine, and I'm going to tell him.

I IM the girls to say I'll miss youth group tonight, then hop in the shower and blow my hair straight. I carefully apply a thin layer of pressed powder and smooth on a coat of lipstick. I slip on my best jeans and a shirt that's just tight enough but not too revealing. Then I call him. I call him because I want to, because I like him and I'm ready to admit that now. Marcus and I are over, and he broke up with Grace to be with me. There's no reason we shouldn't be together, and I'm not afraid anymore.

He promises to meet me downtown in half an hour.

When Dean drives up in his boxy brown Toyota from the eighties, I'm waiting on a bench outside Half Moon Bay Coffee Company watching the last bit of the afternoon sun fade away. I've been picturing his face in my mind for so long it's almost weird to see it in person. He's even cuter than I remembered.

"Hey." Dean's wearing dark blue jeans and a white T-shirt with some sort of Chinese character on it that stretches across his chest a little. "Wanna go?"

I try to make my mouth work. "Huh?" How is it that the moment I see him I lose all train of thought? I wanted to see him, but now that he's here I'm not sure what to do with myself or how to say that. I can't say, "Will you be my boyfriend?" Or wait, can I? I should have called Riley first. But he's already back inside his car, so I decide to embrace the new me and just go with it.

The worn leather gives off a sweet smell as I slide into the passenger seat. He turns on the engine, tunes the radio to the local college station, and pulls onto Main Street. My mind wanders as the cookie-cutter houses of our little town zip past the window. What happened to me this weekend? It feels like everything has changed, like I'm a totally different person.

I lean forward and turn the radio down. "Where are we going? Are we running from the law?"

"I want to show you my mom's Christmas present." He smiles at me as if that explains everything, and I roll my eyes.

Still, I settle back against the cushion and feel strangely content. Empty fields whiz past my window as darkness grows, and we drive farther north.

Eventually Dean turns right off the highway and takes a left at the underpass. I sit up in my seat and crane my neck to look around, but the seat belt catches and pinches my throat. If we were just going north on Highway 1, that means we're now barreling toward the Pacific Ocean. I try to make out some hint of where we're headed in the dark night. He comes to a small winding road that traces the coast and takes a right to follow it.

"Do you even know where we're going?" I try to catch Dean's eye, but he keeps his face turned toward the road ahead of us.

"Don't you trust me, Zoe?"

I study his profile. Do I trust him? I don't really know. I want to trust him with my heart, but he's so unpredictable. Then again, maybe not knowing is part of the thrill. I don't answer him.

The ocean is on his side of the car as we pass lonely, decrepit piers with fishing boats, the occasional surf shack, and fish-n-chips places. I roll down my window and allow the saturated salty air in the car. I take a deep breath, then search the sky for the moon, but all I see are stars in the clear sky. Tonight must be a new moon.

Dean rolls into a deserted parking lot, and the tires crunch on the oyster shells that form makeshift gravel. He turns off the car and smiles at me. "You ready?"

"I guess." I slam the door shut and follow him. There's a hand-painted wooden sign that says Pillar Point Harbor. "Hey, this is where people park their boats."

Dean puts out an arm to stop me from walking, looks up and down the windy back road, and then hurries me across it. "Berth."

"Huh?"

He strides out on a long pier with many wooden arms shooting off it. It smells briny and almost tangy, and the air is softer here, laced with a little bit of moisture.

"People *berth* their boats here. That's what it's called."

"Ohhhh. Sorry, Popeye."

I hear him laugh, but he's focused on reading cryptic numbers marking each pier. Finally he seems to find the one he wants and takes a left. He pulls a key from his pocket, unlocks the gate that leads down the pier, and pushes it open.

Around us hundreds of sailboat poles sway back and forth as the gentle lap, lap, lap of the Pacific tickles the hulls. I focus on dodging coils of rope that have become unwound, splintering boards warped from the sun, and rusty nails sticking up at haphazard angles. We stop in front of a funny-looking boat.

"What's this?"

Dean takes a long stride onto the boat and lands easily on the tarp. My eyes go wide. He smiles at me and holds his arms out by his sides. "This," he says, gesturing around, "is my mom's Christmas present."

It's definitely a sailboat. That much I can figure out by the huge, uh, pole thingy in the middle. Mast. Yeah, it's called a mast, I think. But this sailboat does not have a little house in the belly. Instead it's some kind of sportier version. It has two long, uh, floaty arm thingies and a tarp stretched between them.

"It's only a basic cat, but Mom said she didn't want to fool around with all the upkeep anymore." Dean grabs ahold of the mast and beams at me.

"Some cat. Is it house-trained?" The boat sways beneath him as it adjusts to his weight.

"*Catamaran*. That means it has two hulls." He points down at the floaty arm thingies. "Time's a wastin', matey. Climb aboard."

I start to back away slowly. This is not exactly how I pictured our first official date.

"C'mon. What are you afraid of?"

I hold up a finger. "One, my parents finding my body on the bottom of the ocean." I take a few more steps backward and hold up another. "Two, ending up in Bora Bora. Three, puking my guts out all night." The one I don't mention is the thing I'm probably most worried about: being alone on a boat with Dean.

"I'm not suggesting we sail it." Dean flops down and pats the space next to him on the tarp. "Just a little innocent stargazing."

I glance up at the sky and see a thousand tiny pinpricks twinkling back at me. A new moon is the best time for looking at the heavens. Ed used to love to go out on the back deck with his old telescope and point out constellations to me.

"You swear we won't go anywhere?"

Dean draws an *x* over his heart, and I can't help but notice the subtle outline of his chest through the beat-up old sweater he threw on.

I gulp and take a few steps forward. Really, it's not fair to do this to a girl. The stars, the sound of the water lapping against the boat . . . he knows what he's doing to me. He knows I can't say no, even if he did convince me to sail to Bora Bora with him, which is kind of scary and kind of thrilling all at once.

"Okay, but if you make any sudden, nautical movements, I'm out of here." I can't be afraid of love. It's dangerous, it's reckless, but it's everything. I have to go for it. No chickening out now.

I sit down on the edge of the dock and grip the boards tightly. The boat has drifted away a little, so I'm going to have to make a leap for it.

Dean holds out his hand and raises an eyebrow. "Avast, ye've come to yer senses."

I slowly reach out for him, and his hand is cool to the touch. Suddenly all my troubles with Dreamy and Ed, Marcus, and Ms. Moore feel so far away.

Dean eases me onto the boat, and it instantly starts rocking under my land-loving feet.

"EEEK!" I double over and grab the spongy tarp with my hands, wrapping my fingers around the lacing.

"Eeek? There's no eeek at sea." Dean laughs and plops down without any trouble, even though I'm rocking the boat. "Pop a squat and you'll be fine."

I grip the lacing even tighter and slowly lower my butt down. The instant it reaches the tarp, the rocking slows down.

"I take it you never got your junior skipper's license?" A small cloud of air puffs out of his lips when he speaks.

I blow into my hands. It's colder down here on the boat.

"Oh." Dean opens his messenger bag and pulls out the blanket. "Here."

"Thanks." I wrap it over my shoulders and hesitate. Am I supposed to share this with him? But I can't. That's . . . too personal. On the other hand, it is cold. Is it up to me to offer it? No, he's going to have to ask for it. I can't bear to offer it to him or even draw any attention at all to the blanket. I pull it tighter around my body.

Dean leans back on the tarp and pats the space next to him. "New rule. You're not allowed to hog the blanket *and* sit clear across the boat from me."

I pull the blanket tighter around my shoulders. I'm not used to a guy who says what he wants. With Marcus I had to read his subtle clues and figure out what they meant.

"Zoe, I'm not going to bite you." He props himself up on his elbows. "Come share the tarp with me. The blanket can be all yours, I promise."

"It's no big deal," I say, and he smirks. I scoot over to his side of the boat and lie next to him with the blanket wrapped tightly around me. I inhale a little, and it smells like salt and Dean, an earthy aroma mixed with some kind of clean-scented cologne.

Dean laces his fingers behind his head so that I'm eye level with his chest. I watch it rise and fall for a moment, then inch my body closer.

"You shouldn't tell anyone else you have a sailboat." I meant it to come off as a joke, but instead my voice got choked up and I whispered it, giving my words a gravity I didn't intend. The whole world seems to have faded away and all that matters is Dean, and me, and the deep blue sea.

"Why?" He touches my hair lightly and whispers back.

"So not rock and roll." I slide over on my side and prop my head in my hand. He rolls over too, and we stare at each other. No one says anything, and somewhere, far off in the distance, I hear a foghorn blowing.

"It's amazing, isn't it?" Dean turns his head and looks up at the sky. "Once you get away from the city lights, there are all these stars you can't see otherwise."

I nod and try to remember not to stare at him. But up close, his face is so beautiful that I have to fight the urge to study its every contour and shape.

"I've always wanted to take my camera and shoot a film down here," he says, smiling.

My throat is dry, and I can't seem to peel my eyes from his. I want to reach out and touch his hand, but I can't be the one who crosses the chasm between us. Even though with every beat my heart is saying, "Do it, do it, do it," I stay still.

"So? Things are good?" Dean says quietly.

I don't know what he's really asking, so I shrug. "Ed's been picking up a few jobs. And Dreamy's thinking of enrolling in night school, which kind of scares me. Like she's really moving on now." I try to make my voice sound normal, as though we're just two people having a conversation together.

He studies my face, running his eyes from my hair, to my eyes, to my lips, to my quivering chin.

"It's a good thing, you know?" He stares at my lips, and I roll them in self-consciously. "No matter what happens with your parents, it'll be good for her."

I nod slowly. "She thinks she wants to become a paralegal." I look up and my eyes rest on a star not twinkling like the others. Ed once said that meant it was a planet. "That's what's so sick about the whole thing. All this . . ." I take a deep breath. I still can't say the *d* word without bursting into tears, "legal stuff has made her realize she's good with documents and contracts and laws. Have you ever heard anything more perverse in your life?" I laugh bitterly, not sounding like myself at all. I sound like an adult, someone who has seen things and been places.

"Yeah, I have." Dean moves closer, grabs the edge of the blanket, and pulls it over him. My arm becomes aware of itself, the skin going wild with longing. His arm must be only a few inches from me under the blanket. He could reach out and touch me if he wanted to. Dean leans his face close to mine, and we are just inches from each other, too close to really focus. He brings his lips to my ear, and I study the stubble on his cheek. "Growing up, the only thing I ever wanted was my own room . . . and then one day I got it." His voice breaks with an aching sadness at the end.

He stays where he is, his warm breath soothing my cold ear. Here we are, two sad, broken people who have seen and lived through horrible, life-altering events, wishing we could take things back, return to simpler times. But we can't, and life is still rolling forward, and together, it's beautiful again.

I find myself breathing in rhythm with him, unable to resist the urge to be in sync with his every move.

"Zoe," he says, with something like longing in his voice.

I move my head, shut my eyes, and lean toward him.

"I'm still with Grace," he whispers.

It takes a second for his words to break through the fog surrounding my brain.

"What?!" I bolt up, and the sailboat rocks wildly.

"Please. Stop." He reaches for my hand but I jerk it away.

I grab at the mast desperately as the blanket drops around my feet. This whole time he's been with Grace?

Dean helps steady me. "Please listen for a second."

Not only did he lead me on, but now I'm complicit in hurting her. I'm the other woman.

"Look, it's simple." I cling to the mast with one hand and reach for the dock with the other. "Are you with her? Yes or no?"

"Well, yes, but . . ." He grabs my waist to help me as I let go of the pole and reach for the dock's edge.

Somehow, sheer adrenaline probably, I grab the dock and pull myself up. Tears begin to sting my eyes. Didn't he feel this too? Doesn't he see that this doesn't happen every day? It's special and rare.

"Zoe, wait up." Dean hustles back to grab the blanket. "I'll give you a ride home."

"Don't bother." I hear his footsteps behind me, but I don't look back as I scurry through the maze of piers. I can't believe I don't have a stupid car. I need to start saving double time. I pull out my phone and call Riley. She promises to be here as fast as the speed limit will allow.

38

ook at this one. It was taped underneath my table at lunch!" Emily Mack unrolls one of my flyers and shows it to Ben Nayar. He reads it, and his eyes go wide while I sink lower in my seat.

"There was one taped above every urinal in the guys' bathroom." Ben laughs and shakes his head. "Lovchuck didn't think to look in there."

I bore my eyes into my desk and focus hard on disappearing. Lovchuck and the other teachers got most of the posters down before the students arrived, but I never really stopped to think how I would feel once people started finding our flyers tucked into every corner of the school. Thankfully, no one knows who's responsible. This whole thing will blow over soon, and then Ms. Moore will be back at Marina Vista, and it will have all been worth it.

"What is wrong with you guys today?" Mrs. Narveson shakes her head. We're divided into small groups, working on the latest project, which is an in-class game about turn-of-the-century imperialism. It's basically like a running game of Risk, only you get armies by scoring well on quizzes, and everyone has the same goal: take over as many territories as you can to make your country the biggest. "Normally you're quietly trying to take over the world. Today you won't stop gossiping like a bunch of busybodies."

I glance at Dean and Kayleen, hunched over the continent of Asia and plotting some sort of move for their army, and say a silent prayer of thanks that I didn't mention anything to him about the school break-in last night. I obviously can't trust him.

The classroom door bangs open, and we all swivel at the sound. Ms. Lovchuck is standing in the doorway, her face beet red.

"Zoe Fairchild and Christine Lee." She scans the room with her reading glasses perched on the end of her nose. When she sees me, she rips them off and lets the chain around her neck catch them. "Let's go."

A few people "woo" and snicker.

Christine starts packing up, but I feel frozen in place as my heart races in my chest. I'm being called out of class? Is this actually happening? Maybe it's not about . . . but why would she need Christine too?

"Now!" Ms. Lovchuck glares at me. "And get your things, Miss Fairchild. You won't be coming back."

I swallow and will my hands to move. My fingers are numb, my hands are shaky, and the whole world is blurry. I knock my pencil off my desk as I try to stuff things into my backpack, and I decide to leave it behind. Everyone in the class is watching us. Christine holds her head high, puts a smirk on her face, and stalks over to the door as if leaving in the middle of history class was all her idea, come to think of it.

Somehow I get everything in my bag, even as the whispers

grow. Dean crosses his arms over his chest and smiles as I walk past him, but I pretend I don't notice.

Once outside the classroom, we follow behind Lovchuck. We don't dare utter even a syllable to each other, and I keep my eyes on the cement. Maybe this is all a bad dream.

But when I walk into the front office and see both of my parents, sitting together, I know that this is very real. Neither of them says a word as I sit down next to Ed.

"Christine!" I turn at the sound of Candace's voice as she rushes in the front office door. The round mound of her belly bulges out in front of her. "It's okay. I'm here." She grabs Christine in a hug, and Christine screws up her face, but she goes along with it, if a bit stiffly.

I crane my neck and try to spot Ms. Lovchuck. After depositing us in the waiting area she disappeared down a long hallway, no doubt to cackle in delight that she caught us. But how? Ashley? She wouldn't, would she?

"You weren't thinking." Mrs. Dominguez's voice raises above the thrum in the lobby. She and Ana are huddled by the counter, and Mrs. Dominguez is shaking her head and flaring her nostrils. "That's the problem. Do you realize this will go on your permanent record?"

"Mom, I'm sure nothing is going on—" Ana's voice stops short. I turn to see what startled her.

Ashley and Dr. Anderson appear in the doorway. Ashley lifts her chin a little higher and walks away from her father. He chases after her, hissing under his breath.

"I can't believe you did this to me." Dr. Anderson grabs her arms. Ashley shirks away and gives him a withering look.

The others don't seem to notice. Riley and her mom sit with their arms crossed in the exact same way, ignoring one another. Ana and Mrs. Dominguez are locked in a hushed argument. Christine reaches out and silently hands her iPhone over to Candace.

"Maybe I'm not like you. Did you ever think of that?" Ashley makes a point to level her eyes at her father. "*I* know right from wrong, and *I'm* not afraid to stand up for what's right."

"Okay." Ms. Lovchuck reappears out of thin air. "I'll meet with each family, one by one. We'll start with the Fairchilds." Dreamy clenches her jaw, then smiles from ear to ear. "Please, follow me."

"Stand firm, Zoe," Ashley yells as I stand up. Her dad glowers at her, but Christine gives me a thumbs-up just before I step into the hallway. Ed's work boots sound on the tile floor, but no one says anything until we get to the big office at the very end. Ms. Lovchuck walks in and sits behind her huge desk, then motions at the three chairs in front of her. Even my parents seem a little intimidated by her sharp nose and scowling and pinched face.

She takes a deep breath and then exhales. "Zoe, did you think the school didn't have security cameras?" I keep my eyes on the gurgling fish tank in the corner.

"I . . ." My face flushes, and my ears begin to burn. I don't *think* the school doesn't have any security cameras. I *know* it doesn't. I have never, ever seen one. "I've never seen any."

"They're in the light fixtures." Ms. Lovchuck grabs the reading glasses from around her neck, puts them on the end of her nose, and opens a manila folder with my name on the tab. "We had them installed last summer after some"—she clears her throat—"problems with vandalism."

The light fixtures! Marina Vista has chemistry lab equipment left over from the Cold War and serves government cheese on its tacos. There's no way we have state-of-the-art security cameras. But then how else would they have known? It's just like *1984*, that weird book Ms. Moore made us read where "Big Brother" was always watching you.

"Now, Zoe has always been an exemplary student," Ms. Lovchuck says.

"She's never been in trouble before," Dreamy says, nodding.

"And I must say, Mrs. Fairchild—"

"Dreamy." She gives old Lovchuck a big smile, the one she uses when she's trying to win people over.

"Dreamy, then." She leans back in her high-backed, executive-style office chair. "I was shocked to see Zoe on the tape."

"We are as shocked as you are," Ed says, but I see the corner of his lips turning up a bit.

"You understand that this is a very serious offense."

I kick my feet under my seat. How did this happen? I only wanted to help, and now I've gone and gotten everyone I care about in trouble.

"We understand," Dreamy says quickly. "You can rest assured she will be punished." My ears prick. They've been using the singular for so long that "we" sounds a little funny. "At home."

Ms. Lovchuck finally peers over the edge of the folder and bores her steely gray eyes into Dreamy's.

"Home." Lovchuck studies Dreamy's face, then Ed's. "Actually, I wondered if that was part of the problem." She holds up the manila folder and shakes it a little. "I have access to Zoe's school records since kindergarten, and I'm sure I don't need to tell you they're flawless."

"She's always been very dedicated to her studies," Dreamy says, even though we all know this isn't true. I'm an average student on my best days. Still, Ed nods in agreement. I think it may be the first time I've seen them agree on anything in months.

"Usually when a child begins to act out very suddenly, it means there's trouble at home."

Dreamy shifts uncomfortably in her chair. "Listen, I—"

Ms. Lovchuck stands, interrupting her. "I have decided that all the girls will be suspended from school for one week and must do three months of community service. And I warn you that the police may get involved."

"What?!" I choke out. Suspension goes on my permanent record! Not to sound like Mrs. Dominguez here, but that's pretty serious. And the police? What does she mean by that?

"Miss Fairchild." Ms. Lovchuck puts her hands on her desk and leans across it. I angle backward to dodge her piercing stare. "What you did was very serious. Breaking and entering. Defacement of school property." She pulls her lips into a tight thread on her face. "Someone could have been seriously injured . . ."

"But no one was," Dreamy says quickly.

". . . And the entire act shows a distinct lack of respect for authority. The fact of the matter is, our hands are tied." She pantomimes tying a knot. "We valued Ms. Moore too, Zoe, both as a teacher and a friend." Ms. Lovchuck's voice softens a little. "But unless"—she clears her throat and raises her eyebrows—"the plaintiff drops the case, we can't change anything."

Dreamy and Ed don't move. They exchange a glance, and Ed sighs as if he's exhausted.

"We understand," he says finally.

Ms. Lovchuck walks across her large, cold, orderly office and opens the door. "Thank you for your time."

I glance back to see if Dreamy and Ed are following me, but they're still sitting in their chairs. Dreamy's head is bowed, and Ed puts his hands around her shoulders to help her up.

"We'll be in touch," Ms. Lovchuck says in a darkly chipper tone.

39

avid Copperfield dangles above my head, balanced on the balls of my feet. Not David Copperfield the magician, but the horrible, snoozerific book by Charles Dickens. Mrs. Dietrich is really ramping up her torture techniques, and I'm not even at school. As of today, I wish I were.

Sometimes being punished helps you feel better. It makes you feel like you're doing something to right your wrong. But this week hasn't done a whole lot for me. I'm not exactly sorry about what I did, so my suspension is more like an annoying, imposed break from school. And the world, really. The worst part of this whole thing is that I'm on house arrest, which means Dreamy won't even let me use my phone or the computer or go outside except to help with the horses and go to work. I have no idea what's going on with the Miracle Girls.

The only good thing is our story made the paper. In a town like Half Moon Bay, what we did is pretty big news, and every day there've been more articles and editorials about Ms. Moore's case.

I roll my head to the side and see that it's almost three, meaning that another day of school is officially over. Whew. I only have to live through Thursday and Friday, and then I'll be allowed to go back to class next week. I'm actually looking forward to our community service so I can talk to the Miracle Girls.

With just a little more concentration I can pass the book . . . from . . . one foot to . . .

The doorbell sounds from downstairs, and I launch *David Copperfield* across the room. "I got it," I yell over the upstairs railing and pound down the steps. Someone from the outside world! Yesterday when the UPS guy came to our house I opened the door with such gusto that he almost jumped out of his skin.

"Hello?" I yank open the door, but then stop short.

Dean laughs a little at me. I realize I'm wearing a T-shirt with a bank logo on it and old purple shorts that are now way too short. "Nice to see you too."

I glance back inside my house, then shut the door behind me and take a few steps forward, forcing him off my porch.

"What are you doing here?" A few months ago, I would have never spoken to anyone this way. I guess I've been hardened by my life of crime.

Dean gives me a lopsided grin. "Absence hasn't made your heart grow fonder?"

I cross my arms over my chest. He is not going to charm his way out of this mess, not this time. Not ever again.

"No. What do you want?"

"That was pretty cool, what you guys did at school."

I cock an eyebrow. "Is that what you came here to tell me?"

"No." Dean takes a step closer. "Listen, Zoe, I'm sorry about what happened, but there is an explanation."

"I'm listening." I let my hands rest on the porch railing and trace my eyes along his cheekbone. Even now, even though he's hurt me, I don't want to look away.

"I guess I just wanted to say . . ." He clears his throat, as if to buy time, and I realize that he's lost his train of thought. I suppress a smile. "I've been trying to break up with Grace for a while. We never should have been dating in the first place."

Goose bumps raise on my legs. It's March, but it's still cool in the hazy afternoon sunshine. So far it's only faintly drizzled twice this spring, and the drought rages on like an ugly curse.

"She liked me, and I tried to be into it too. Plus, the girl I actually liked was with someone else, so . . ." He peeks at me shyly, and I roll my eyes.

That night on the sailboat comes back to me. We were practically kissing. But he was dating another girl—a girl he intentionally led me to believe he was not with anymore. How can I trust him after a thing like that? If he did it to her, he'll do it to me too. Maybe not today, but someday.

"You should have thought about that before you hurt both of us then." I take a few steps backward and clutch the doorknob. I need to get out of here before my resolve wavers.

"Zoe," he says, staring at me with desperation. "Grace's grandmother has been sick. She had a stroke and slipped into a coma." He rubs a hand over his face like he has a headache. "You don't dump someone when all of that is going on."

"You still let it get too far." My cheeks burn when I realize how awful Grace would feel if she knew what had happened that night under the starry sky. "You should have done something earlier."

But even as the words come out of my mouth, I hear the hypocrisy in them. Isn't that exactly what I did to Marcus? I stayed with him for far longer than I should have, for so many reasons, but mostly because it's very hard to hurt someone who has done nothing to deserve it. I feel a dull ache in the back of my throat and clench my jaw shut.

"I couldn't." He reaches out a hand to touch mine. "I wanted to, but you're too hard to resist." His cool blue eyes are pleading with me. I make myself look away so I can think straight.

"You . . ." I try to make my words make sense. "It wasn't right." I feel tears welling up. I'm not even sure I'm talking about Dean anymore.

"I broke up with her last night."

I take a step back toward the door.

"Zoe, wait."

I reach for the knob and step inside, slamming the door behind me. He just . . . I did . . . I run upstairs, my footsteps shaking the narrow staircase, tears streaming down my face.

40

My eyes are almost swollen shut. I force them open, one lid at a time. My room is dark as I sit up. What am I doing here? What time is it? It takes me a minute, but the familiar shapes in my room begin to emerge from the shadows. My alarm clock reads 10:20. It must mean p.m. And then it all comes rushing back.

I close my eyes again, hoping to lose myself in the blessed amnesia of sleep, but my stomach grumbles, and I realize I haven't eaten anything since lunch. Stupid, annoying basic needs of the body. I flip on the light and push myself out of bed. I'll just run down to the kitchen, cram something into my mouth, and then go back to bed. Sleep is the best way to put off the pain.

I hear low voices coming from the kitchen as I make my way down the stairs. I make out Dreamy's raspy tones right away, but I don't recognize the second voice as Ed's until I'm almost there.

I freeze, then duck into the living room. If they're talking about legal stuff, I'll turn around and go back up. I'd rather starve to death than listen to my parents work out the details of their divorce on top of everything else today. I hold my breath and try to stay silent, but Dreamy's next comment catches me off guard.

"I don't know." Her voice is low and soothing, the voice she often uses to comfort me. It sounds a little like honey oozing. "Maybe that's too harsh. All they did was hang up a few posters. It's not like anybody got hurt, and the school is punishing her plenty already."

"But she needs to learn. Civil disobedience is one thing. Breaking and entering is another." Ed sighs and shifts around in his favorite chair, making a familiar squeaking noise. "We have to teach her the difference between good protests and bad protests. And bad protests come with repercussions."

I pause and take a step toward the wall that separates the living room from the kitchen. The lights are on, casting a yellow glow over the kitchen, but Dreamy and Ed must be sitting at the table, just out of my view.

"But a whole year?" I inch forward. This can't be good. "She's been working so hard to save up for that car."

Uh-oh. I feel my heart sink. They're not going to let me get a car for a whole year? I'll practically be graduating by then.

"Maybe six months," Ed says, and I silently let out a breath. He always was a softie. I don't think I'll be able to afford a car before then anyway.

"That sounds better," Dreamy says. I hear ice cubes clink against the edge of a glass. "I'm afraid she hasn't been able to save much anyway. I've been cashing her checks, and she's insisted I keep a big chunk each time. She's been helping with the groceries and gas for months now, more than she probably lets on to you."

"I suspected," Ed says quietly. "And I'm sorry about that, but the work is really picking up. If it ever rains and the landscaping gets going again, I'll have more work than I know what to do with." He chuckles a little, but it's a sad sound.

I wait, but all I hear is a faint rustling. I take another step and lean forward so that I can barely see around the wall now. Dreamy and Ed are sitting across from each other at the table, staring into each other's eyes. I watch as Ed moves his hand, slowly, and lays it on top of hers, and Dreamy jumps a little but doesn't pull it away.

"Do you remember that old Volkswagen van we had in '75? I found a picture of it in one of my books the other day." Ed laughs a little under his breath. "Now that was a car."

"The cheese mobile." Dreamy shakes her head. "That hideous yellow, and those awful squeaky brakes. You rigged it with that 8-track and played 'Yellow Submarine' over and over."

"Too bad we don't still have that thing. Zoe would look real cool driving to high school in that old heap."

"Thank goodness for small mercies." Dreamy tilts her head to the left and then the right, stretching her neck, but carefully keeps her hand in Ed's. "The poor girl has been through enough."

Suddenly it hits me how much of their marriage, of their lives really, happened before I came along. Somehow I always imagined my parents' lives as two long chains of events leading up to me. I guess I thought of my birth as the point they were building toward the whole time. And I never considered what it will be like for them after I move out and move on, when it's just the two of them again.

Ed rubs his thumb across the back of Dreamy's hand and smiles at her. The dishwasher shuts off, and for a minute neither one of them says anything. I lean into the wall, resting my shoulder against the smooth white plaster.

"Our little radical."

"You would have been disappointed if she'd been anything but," Ed says, laughing quietly.

"Nah." Dreamy smiles. "I would have loved her no matter what." She lifts her eyes to Ed's, and I shrink back a little. "But I am glad to see she inherited some of my genes after all."

"She did at that." Ed runs his free hand through his hair. "Breaking into the school to put up flyers. That's a signature Danielle Horowitz move if I ever saw one."

My eyes go wide at Dreamy's real name. I mean, yeah, I knew that she legally changed it from Danielle a long time ago, but I haven't heard that name in so long. Dreamy flips her palm over and gives Ed's hand a squeeze.

"She turned out good, didn't she?"

"Yeah." Dreamy nods. "Better than good. She's a . . . a miracle."

I feel my cheeks flush, but I can't help but think maybe this whole stupid thing has done some good after all.

41

For once I'm almost dreading getting off work. I'm bored out of my mind at home so being at El Bueno Burrito is kind of fun. Plus, it's payday, which is always a good thing.

Gus waves as I step out into the night and head toward my bike, but I freeze when I see a shadowy figure sitting on the rack. I squint. It wouldn't be . . . and it's too small to be him anyway. I wait a second as my eyes adjust to the dark.

"It's just me, Zo." Riley. I walk toward her, my heart quickening. "It takes you guys forever to close up, you know that?" She laughs a little, but it sounds kind of forced.

"You were waiting for me?"

She nods and pushes herself off the metal rack. "Let's go somewhere else."

I follow behind her on the sidewalk. "Your parents let you out?"

She points to her mom's minivan in the parking lot. Christine lovingly dubbed it the RealMobile because magnetic real estate ads featuring Mrs. McGee's smiling face are plastered on the sides.

"We ran out of milk, and Michael only eats cereal for breakfast." She passes the RealMobile and keeps going. "They were desperate. And I had to talk to someone." She shakes her head. "I knew you'd be here."

We walk in silence away from the harsh lights of the parking lot, toward the shadowy corner of the strip mall, where there's an opening to the back of the stores. Riley plops down on the edge of the loading dock behind the supermarket.

"So what's up?" I sit on the edge of the slab of concrete and let my feet dangle over the side.

"Tom's being so weird." Riley sighs.

I close my eyes for a second. I know the long-distance thing has been hard on them, but if they break up too, I don't know what I'll do. There's too much sorrow in my world lately.

"Did he break up with you?" I ask quietly, barely able to get the words out.

"It's . . . I don't know." Riley pulls her feet up and sits cross-legged on the slab. "Maybe he will. I just think college is really different. I know he still cares about me, but things have been weird." She waits for a second. "It's not only the distance, though that doesn't help. It's that all his friends are older, and interested in other things, and I don't know them, and . . . I don't know. I don't really fit into his world anymore."

I try to put myself inside Tom's head. College seems like a foreign universe. What would it be like to live in a dorm hundreds of miles from your family and have to make completely new friends? What's it like to have to start all over again? I can't even picture it or see how a long-distance girlfriend in high school would factor into it.

"I got this weird e-mail from him tonight, saying he's going to study in Mexico for the summer, and, I don't know, he didn't even seem that sad about it. About not seeing me." She takes a deep breath and lets it out slowly. "And I'm trying to figure out what to do about it."

"What do you mean?" Heather Boyd flashes into my mind. "Are you going to make some crazy gesture to try to win him back? Like drive down to Santa Barbara tonight in the Real-Mobile?" I picture the two of us racing down the freeway in the dark.

Riley shakes her head. "I don't think that would really solve anything."

It's strangely quiet now. The parking lot is on the other side of the stores, and the road is just beyond that, but back here the only noise is from someone throwing boxes out the back of the video store.

"I don't know if I should break it off or wait for him to do it himself."

She says it so calmly, so matter-of-factly, that I almost don't catch the pain in her voice, but Riley is practically my sister. I know this is killing her.

"You really think those are your only options?" I pull my knees up and wrap my arms around them. "What about fighting for him?"

Riley's face is pale in the moonlight, and she's biting her lip. "I think it's too late for that."

I watch her for a second and consider pulling her into a hug, but something in her face is cold and determined.

"Have you talked to Ana about this?" I let out a slow breath. "You know, because of Dave?"

Riley nods. "I think she was surprised by how hard it was to break up with Dave. She didn't really expect that kind of pain, you know?" Riley runs the cuff of her sleeve under her nose. "She thought I should stay with him, to do anything to avoid that kind of pain."

I sigh. I love Ana, and just a little while ago, I probably would have agreed, but now I'm not so sure. "If there's one thing I've learned this year, it's that you shouldn't wait for him to do it." I try to sound confident, but there's something unnerving about giving guy advice to Riley. "If it's over, the best thing to do is let him know, honestly and fairly."

Riley nods, her eyes focused on the fence at the other side of the alleyway.

"That's what I thought too."

42

"Could they have made these things any more unflattering?" Ashley pulls at her fluorescent orange vest. They're making us wear the hideous thing over our clothes so drivers can see us as they're cruising down the highway, though how they could miss five girls picking up trash along the side of the road is beyond me.

"Don't give them any ideas." Ana nods toward our jailers, otherwise know as James and John from the county correctional office. They're "supervising" our community service, which so far seems to include driving us out to this stretch of highway and relaxing inside the van. They've got the radio tuned to a country station, blaring the music out the open windows.

"I don't know. I was thinking of wearing it to the prom." Riley pulls the vest so it makes a sort of lopsided V-neck. "What do you think? Is it my color?" A truck zooms by, spewing out exhaust fumes, and she coughs and waves her hands in front of her face.

"Well, you wouldn't have to worry about anyone else showing up in the same dress." Christine rolls her eyes.

"The sick part is, it kind of does look good on you," Ana says as she reaches down and shoves another piece of paper into her trash bag. "Maybe prisoner-orange will be showing up on the runways this fall."

Riley throws a balled-up piece of paper toward Christine, who holds out her trash bag and catches it deftly.

"How many times do we have to do this?" Christine pretends to put a gun to her head, but she's smiling, and I suspect she's having more fun than she lets on.

"Every Saturday," Ashley says, "for the rest of the school year."

When I broke the news to Gus that I could no longer work Saturdays, he was none too happy about it, and more than a little shocked. He thinks of me as Comrade Zoe, his dependable little worker who never, ever calls in sick and always remembers to mop *under* the tables. Now I have to close on Saturday nights, meaning that I'm doing manual labor from ten in the morning till ten at night, which gives me ample time to think about what I did wrong. But at least I'll have less time to sit around and think about what a mess I've made of everything.

"This is going to be the cleanest stretch of highway known to man." Christine yawns. Ashley picks up a six-pack ring and swings it around in the air on the end of her finger, then tosses it in Christine's bag.

My phone buzzes in my pocket. I don't even have to look at it before I hit the button to send it straight to voice mail. When Dreamy gave me my phone back, I had five messages from Dean and about fifty text messages.

"I wouldn't mind so much if it had worked." Ana shakes her head.

"At least it got our cause out there." I'm trying to stay posi- tive about all this. It ain't over till the tofu crumbles, or some- thing. "There were those articles in the paper." There have been several editorials this week, including one written by Christine's father, pressuring the school district to fight for such a valued teacher.

"Yeah, but is it going to be enough?" Riley squints into the sun to look at me. "I just wish there was something more we could do."

"I'd get in trouble all over again if it would help." Ana swipes the back of her wrist across her face. "But we got the case the attention it needed. At this point, there's really not much we could do. Besides, you know that school in Boston is going to fall all over themselves to hire Ms. Moore."

"You don't know that." I reach for a bottle cap, glinting in the spring sunshine. I dig it out of the dry, dusty grass. "After all this publicity, the school would probably welcome her back like a hero if they could. She might come back and teach at Marina Vista if they drop the case." I shake my head. We all know who "they" is.

"Yeah," Ashley says quietly. She bends over to pick up a plastic grocery bag, and when she stands up again, I could swear there are tears in her eyes.

♡

The dopes from the correctional office dropped us back at the headquarters downtown about an hour ago, but none of us is in a hurry to get home. Ashley took off in her tank of a car, but the rest of us are sprawled out on metal chairs outside Half Moon Bay Coffee Company, trying to enjoy the warm spring air and a small moment of freedom before it's back to our jail cells, I mean, houses. Besides, I've got to report to El Bueno Burrito soon.

Christine's phone buzzes, and she picks it up and starts texting without a word.

"What's going on, freak?" Ana asks, shading her eyes with her arm.

"It's nothing." She shakes her head as her fingers fly over the screen.

"You're typing pretty fast for it to be nothing."

"Tyler's trying to get me to go to prom with him." She rolls her eyes and puts her phone back in her pocket.

"Ooh. So you're going, right?" Riley plays with the empty paper cup in front of her. She glares at Christine, but Christine shrugs.

"Probably not."

"What do you mean probably not?" Ana sits up straight. "You have to go. Tyler's a senior. This is his last chance to take cheesy prom pictures."

"Not my style." Christine tilts her cup up, trying to drain every last ounce of her mocha.

"Christine." Ana reaches over and lifts Christine's sunglasses off her face.

"Hey!" Christine reaches for the glasses, but Ana holds them out of her reach.

"You have to go."

"No I don't." Christine tries to grab the glasses again, but Ana folds them and puts them neatly into her bag. "Are you going?" Christine asks.

Ana points at her. "The difference is that *you* have a date."

"You can go with Tyler instead."

"And you're going with the Rebel without a Cause, right?" Ana jabs her thumb at me.

I shake my head. "I don't know anyone by that name."

"I'm going." We all turn toward Riley.

"With who?" Ana's eyes are wide. Riley made the split with Tom official two nights ago, and she seems to be holding up well. But she might have found a new date in that short period of time. She could point at a guy in the hall and inform him of her decision, and he would count it as the luckiest day of his life.

"With you guys." Riley smiles and blushes a little. "It would be perfect. This way we don't have to worry about all that date stuff. We can get dressed up and have a good time, just the four of us." She shoots a sly smile at Christine. "And Tyler. Just the five of us."

"I'm telling you, one of you guys should take Tyler. I don't even want to go."

Ana seems to consider the idea for a moment and then shakes her head.

"Come on. How fun would that be? We can go to a fancy dinner and dance the night away." Riley cranes her neck to look at each of us. "It's the first year we can all go to prom. We can't miss it. It's a high school milestone or whatever."

The way she's talking it up, it does sound like it could be fun. The truth is, I hadn't really given much thought to prom. Both juniors and seniors go at Marina Vista, but I had assumed Marcus would be my guest. And then, if Dean—my heartbeat speeds up—but then, he's made it pretty clear that it's not his scene, and I don't want to go with him now anyway.

"You don't want to go with one of the football players or something?" Christine eyes Riley skeptically.

"Yeah right." Riley snorts. Even though she was always rumored to be with different football players freshman year, I don't think she ever really was. Now that I really know her, now that I stop and think about it, there's only ever been Tom.

I study her face, and she's biting her lip. I wonder how much goes on in her head that we never see. What are the thoughts and fears and dreams of America's Most Beautiful Teenager? Suddenly I feel certain that the breakup with Tom is affecting her more than she's letting on. Maybe this is her way of dealing with it.

"Ana?" I watch her. She hardly ever mentions Dave at all anymore, but I know she still thinks about him.

"I'm in." She shrugs.

"What about you?" Riley nudges me with her elbow. "You're really not going with Mr. New York?"

I shake my head. "Dean is history."

"Which, incidentally, has a way of repeating itself," Christine says. I lunge at her, but she's too fast for me to catch her.

43

O kay, there's Harvard and MIT, but what else? I might not get into those." Riley keeps her eyes trained on the road as she drives us to San Francisco International Airport on Sunday afternoon.

No one is in a big hurry to see Ms. Moore off, and we've been silent for most of the ride. I tried to ask about her interview in Boston, but she was kind of evasive and she laughed when Ana asked if she was going to call her ex-fiancé. Christine simply stares out the side window, pretending she can't hear anything.

"If I can get into school up there, we can hang out." Riley is doing her best to keep things in the van chipper, proving that she is her mother's daughter after all.

"There's also Emerson, Boston College, and Boston University." Ms. Moore ticks them off on her fingers in the front seat of the RealMobile. "Tufts. Some art schools."

I have to fight the urge to ask them to shut up. The whole idea makes me depressed. I can't lose Riley too, but I remind myself that this is merely one of those things people say when someone is leaving, like when my best friend from middle school moved away. We said we'd keep in touch, but we never did.

I'm not so sure seeing her off was a good idea. The car goes silent as we approach the parking garage, and Riley winds her way up the circular ramp to the top level. She picks a spot a few rows over from the doorway to the terminal, and we all climb out of the van in slow motion.

It's another clear, cloudless day. Normally the dusty golden hills of South San Francisco would be turning a bright emerald green from spring rain, but not this year.

"I am going to miss this." Ms. Moore looks out across the surrounding hillsides toward downtown. "There's no city with views like this."

San Francisco is pretty, but the area around the airport is mostly lined with freeways and choked by ugly buildings. I guess she's feeling sentimental. Riley sticks her key in the back door, opens the hatch, and unloads Ms. Moore's suitcase. Riley, Ana, and Christine all make their way toward the stairs to the airport, but I stay back with Ms. Moore.

"Try not to wow them too much," I say, biting my lip. "Things are going to clear up here, and you're going to have a teaching job waiting for you this fall."

"I hope you're right, Zoe," Ms. Moore says, but I don't know whether she means it. She takes a deep breath. "The air smells different there. That's what always strikes me when I get off the plane here, how different the air smells at home."

Ms. Moore always has this weird way of going off on tangents, but I've learned that she usually brings them back around to something important, so I let her talk.

"It's funny how much it affects you, isn't it? Where you came from, I mean. There are all kinds of little things—like the way the air smells—that you don't really notice until you go away." She inhales another long, deep breath. "The place

you grew up is such a huge part of your history, and the people . . ." She lets her voice trail off. "Your family is so much a
part of who you end up being."

I'm not sure I'm following, but I nod as if I understand.

"You're going to be fine." Ms. Moore slides her arm around
my shoulder and pulls me in for a second. "I guess that's what
I'm trying to say. Even though things are rough right now, your
family is strong enough to make it. And"—she gestures to the
girls gathered around the door waiting for us—"you have your
other family. What you girls have is special. Never forget that."
I nod, and she lets out a long breath. "It's time for me to go
back to my home and my family. It's been too long."

Ms. Moore smiles at me, then drops her arm and starts
to walk toward the door. A minute later we're inside the
cool, dark airport. Ms. Moore puts her arm over Christine's
shoulder as we ride in the dank elevator, and the two of them
hang back as we make our way down the long tunnel to the
terminal.

Ana stands with Ms. Moore in the check-in line while the
rest of us lean on a low bench by the glass wall across from
the counter. And then, as we walk her to the security line, Ms.
Moore pulls Riley aside. The rest of us pretend not to notice.

I keep waiting for something to happen. If this were a
movie, there would be a dramatic phone call right now with
news that Mr. Anderson dropped the charges. Or some dash-
ing young man would arrive with a dozen roses and beg Ms.
Moore not to leave. Something, anything, to prevent her from
actually getting on that plane. But instead, we just walk in an
awkward clump through the crowded terminal.

Everything about this feels wrong. The middle of an airport is no place to say good-bye to someone. It feels so public, so anticlimactic.

"It's only an interview," Ms. Moore says, a little too loudly. She leans in and gives us each a hug. I can't help but feel like there must be something more we're supposed to say, but none of us does anything. Ms. Moore turns, gives us a smile, hikes her bag up over her shoulder, and gets in line.

We stand there, watching her, until she makes it through security. She turns and waves, then keeps walking and disappears into the terminal.

I don't know what the others are thinking, but I suspect I have a pretty good idea. She says she's just going for an interview, but they'll offer her the job. Who wouldn't hire Ms. Moore? And once she's there, she won't want to leave her family again to come back. But there's also something else, something that none of us wants to say out loud: we failed.

The Miracle Girls could not save Ms. Moore.

44

"Oh no. No, no, no."

There are boxes littering the living room, stacked at odd angles.

"Nick?" I drop my bag at the bottom of the stairs and run to his room. His radio is blasting some alternative country music, and his stuff is in piles all over the floor. "What do you think you're doing?"

I don't mean for it to sound accusatory, but . . . well, okay, maybe I do. He can't leave. He just got here. I'm finally getting used to having my brother around, and now he's . . .

"Packing." He shrugs and lifts a stack of books off his bookshelf and settles them into the cardboard box.

I stare at him, my mouth hanging open. I never asked Nick to waltz back into my life. Hey, I had been perfectly happy seeing him at holidays, going to visit him occasionally on the ranch. But he did come back, and in the past seven months, I've finally gotten to know my brother, know his hurts and his dreams and his secrets. He's been a part of my life, a part of this family, and now he's . . . now everything is falling apart.

"You want to hand me that?" He points to the black hoodie on the dresser behind me.

And suddenly, I'm angry. Before I can even process what I'm doing, I grab the hoodie off his dresser and launch it at him. It smacks him in the face, and he looks up, bewildered, but I'm only getting started. I storm into his room and reach behind his stereo and pull the power cord, then I kick at the box he's packing for good measure.

"Zoe?" He stares at me, shrinking back a little. To be honest, I'm almost as surprised as he is by my reaction.

"Fine." I flop down on the edge of his bed. "Move back to Colorado. And take all your junk with you." I yank the pillow off his bed and toss it into the box too. "I don't even care."

"Zoe, I'm not—"

"This family is falling apart, and if you leave, there's going to be no one left." He starts to speak again, but I don't even give him the chance. "But, hey, that's okay. Maybe I can be raised by wolves or something."

Nick waits, watching me, until he's sure I'm done. "Zoe?" He says my name tentatively. When I don't cut him off, he pushes himself up and sits down on the bed next to me. "What's going on?" He drapes his arm over my shoulder awkwardly, and I feel the anger begin to drain away.

The tears spring to my eyes before I can stop them. He pulls me closer, and I almost feel like a little girl again, safe with my big brother. I used to think he could do anything. It's been hard to learn that he's not perfect after all, but somehow during the past few months I've learned to love him, flaws and all. Maybe I'm crying because he represents the last semblance of structure left in this broken-down family. Maybe I'm just at the breaking point.

"Why does everybody have to leave?" I whisper.

He rubs my shoulder.

"First Ed, then Ms. Moore." I sniff and wipe away a tear

with the back of my hand. Another person comes to my mind, but I don't dare say his name. "And now you."

He lets me cry for a minute without saying anything.

"Zoe," he finally says, so quietly I almost don't hear him.

I nod.

"I'm only moving across town."

I sniff, trying to process what he's saying.

"What?"

He nods. "I got a job in Mountain View, so I'm going to stick around Half Moon Bay." I pull away and narrow my eyes at him. "I left the ranch . . . very suddenly, overnight, and I didn't know where to go or what to do so I came here." He looks around and sighs deeply. "Then I got here, and everything was a mess. I thought maybe I could help, so I decided to do an extended vacation kind of thing." He glances out the window at our quiet, go-nowhere town, and I think about his life at the ranch, with all the workers buzzing around. What a change all of this must be for him.

"I started picking up freelance work, building Web pages."

I glance at his silver MacBook Pro, shining from across the room. Though he never told me that's what he's been doing, I think I figured it out somewhere along the way. Not even Nick could play that many video games, and somebody had to be keeping this family afloat.

"And then something weird happened. I realized I'm happier than I've been in a long time, and after a lot of searching Half Moon Bay feels like home again." He scratches his stubble. "I'm having them ship all my stuff out from the ranch, and I'm moving into my own place. But I'll be over here to feed the horses all the time."

"Really?" I feel dense, but I can't quite bring myself to believe what he's saying.

"You know, a bachelor pad. To give you all some space. Let you enjoy high school without your dorky older brother hanging around all the time." He chuckles. "Plus, no one wants to date a guy who lives with his parents."

I snort.

"What?" Nick asks, pulling me into a side hug. "What's so funny?"

"The idea that some woman would want to go out with you, no matter where you live." I wipe my nose on the edge of my sleeve.

"Hey!" He pretends he's going to punch me, but I get out of the way.

We laugh for a moment, then fall quiet again. The relief that he's not moving finally sweeps over me.

"So you're okay?"

Nick studies me, his face serious again. I nod sheepishly. Did I really kick his box? No wonder Nick still thinks of me as his bratty little sister. Maybe I've still got some growing up to do.

"As long as you don't try to leave us again, we'll be okay."

45

E d's asleep on the couch when I come down the stairs Saturday morning. He and Dreamy were up late talking last night, but he's never stayed over before, not since he moved out, and it's strange to see him there. I watch his chest rise and fall under the crocheted blanket, and for a minute I feel like the parent, studying a sleeping newborn baby as if it's the most amazing wonder in the world. He rolls over, letting out a sigh. The old couch sags under him. I tiptoe toward the door and step out into the cool, dry morning.

The lights are on at Marcus's house. I say a quick prayer that he and his family will be well. I take my bike from the open garage, sling my leg over the seat, and give my head a little shake. Before my community service, I'm going to try to run a very important errand.

♡

I make it to the bank just as the manager unlocks the door. I chain my bike to the little bench out front and dash inside. Dreamy and Ed have had their accounts here for years, and though I've always had a small savings account with their names on it, it's time to open up my own bank account.

I step up to the counter and pull out Ed's old leather wallet. The teller's eyes widen at how thick it is.

"I'd like to open an account please."

"My goodness," she says, patting her teased hair. "Don't tell me you've had all that stashed under your mattress." Her name tag says *Brenda Bonilla, Here to Help.*

"My underwear drawer." It's mostly tens and twenties, so it looks much more impressive than it really is, but it's every penny I've managed to squirrel away from my paycheck. What hasn't gone toward groceries or gas has gone here. I lay the final bills on the counter and push the stack toward her.

She laughs and holds up one finger, telling me to wait, then she opens a drawer and pulls out a couple pieces of paper.

"So you decided to keep it somewhere safer." She nods as she shoves the papers across the counter toward me.

"Something like that." The truth is, I didn't really know I'd amassed this much, and once I counted it—it's a little more than $700—it seemed silly to have it just sitting there. Child-ish. Adults save money in banks, not drawers. And if I'm ever going to be able to save enough for a car, I knew I had to do it like an adult. This way I can cash my own checks, without waiting for Dreamy. It's time to grow up.

"If you could please fill this out, I'll start verifying the amount." She eyes the pile of money suspiciously, but I reach for the pen on the little chain and begin to fill in my informa-tion on the forms.

It takes Brenda Here to Help almost fifteen minutes to count up the stacks of bills, then she hands me a temporary ATM card.

"And are you depositing all of your money today, ma'am?" She pushes her glasses up on her nose and reaches for a deposit slip.

"Actually," I look down at the paper where she's listed my total. "No. I . . ." I pull my lower lip in. It feels so silly, after all those hours of work, and when there are so many things my parents could use the money for, and yet—"I'd like to keep a hundred," I say as confidently as I can. "There's . . . there's something I need to buy."

Brenda nods and writes the new total on the deposit slip, then hands me five crisp twenty-dollar bills.

"Thank you for doing business with us, Ms. Fairchild," she says, and I smile as I slip my money into Ed's old wallet. That *Ms. Fairchild* thing. That felt nice.

♡

Dean is sprawled out at one of the booths when I walk into El Bueno Burrito, reading *Screenplay* by Syd Field. He jumps up and starts to walk toward me.

"He's been here all day waiting for you," Gus says by way of a greeting. Dean grins at me, but I pretend I don't see him and make my way to the back. "This guy must be *muy loco* for you." Gus wiggles his eyebrows and smiles from ear to ear, thrilled at his own ability to speak basic rudimentary Spanish.

"Zoe, just give me a minute," Dean says, reaching out toward me. "I need to talk to you."

"I have to work." I shake my head and storm into the back.

"I'll be here when you come back out," Dean says, but I ignore him and grab a clean apron from the stack. I hear Gus's voice and lean in to listen.

"That's it, *amigo*."

"If you'd let me talk to her for a moment, I promise I'll leave and not come back."

I tie a knot behind my back and edge closer to the wall, pressing my body to it.

"Comrade Zoe is the boss around here," my actual boss says. It's funny. A weird kind of friendship has developed between me and Gus. "She doesn't want to see you, so you have to go."

"But I—"

"You have to go now, *amigo*." I hear a few steps and then the sound of Dean sighing.

I roll over, press my back to the wall, and stare up at the ceiling. Maybe I should have listened to him.

46

What are you doing?" Ana screws up her face at Christine, who's doing some kind of weird dance in front of a rack of sequined dresses.

"I'm making a music video for the security guards." Christine waves up at the tiny security camera stuck to the ceiling and continues to twirl her arms around in front of her. "You can be one of my backup dancers." She starts making beat box noises with her mouth, and Ana shakes her head.

"Zoe, what about this one?" Riley holds up a gorgeous shimmery chocolate-brown gown. It has a fitted bodice and a smooth satin skirt. It's perfect.

"How much?"

Riley shrugs and shoves it out toward me. "Just try it on."

I take it from her and try to ignore the silky feel of the fabric while I dig for the price tag. I've learned not to fall in love too easily. Prom dresses, like guys, are fickle, and all the good ones are out of my league.

"Two hundred and eighty dollars?!" I shove it back at her. "Riley, that's not even in the right ballpark."

"Lucky we're not playing baseball." She shrugs and hangs it back on the rack. "I just think you need to try a few things on so you can get a sense for what looks good."

"And I think you should stop being ridiculous and try to help me."

For the record, a hundred dollars is not enough to buy a dress you'd actually want to wear to the prom. You can get something cheesy, or some leftover in size extra-, extra-large, but after hours of perusing the shelves, I'm ready to give up. And I didn't even factor in shoes, or accessories, or whatever kind of weird push-up bra you need to hold these things up. My bank withdrawal is looking more and more pathetic by the hour.

"How about these?" Ana comes back with a handful of plain black dresses. She holds them up, one at a time, and I examine them. They're not particularly exciting, but they're closer to the right price range anyway. She's trying, which is more than I can say for Christine, who's currently perfecting her moonwalk.

The other girls have it so easy. Ana's mom is taking her to some boutique in San Francisco next weekend, but then for Ana, price is never a concern. Christine is threatening to go in jeans, a T-shirt, and a pair of Chucks, and Riley's been Homecoming Princess every year, so she already has dozens of dresses in the closet. Even if I had something I'd want to wear again, I don't fit into anything I bought before last summer.

"You guys, maybe this was a bad idea." I take the dresses from Ana and fold them over my arm. "You should just go without me."

"Don't even think about it, Red. If I'm going, you're going," Christine calls without looking away from the camera.

"We'll find something, Zoe," Riley says, waving my concern away. "Don't you dare try to back out of this. You're going to the prom, Cinderella."

♡

The house is dark when I get home, and as soon as I step inside, I can see that the only light is coming from the kitchen. Nick doesn't officially move out until this weekend, but he started his new job this week, so he's hardly been around. It must be Dreamy. I kick off my shoes and walk toward the back of the house.

Dreamy has papers spread all over the table. "Hey Zo," she calls as I walk into the room. She takes off her reading glasses and presses the tips of her fingers to the bridge of her nose.

"Hey." I plop down on one of the kitchen chairs and smile at her. "What's all this?"

She sighs. "My application for City College." She spreads out some of the papers. "If it's this challenging to apply, I can't imagine what the actual classes are going to be like."

"Wow." I prop my feet up on the chair next to me. "That's so cool. You're actually doing it."

"I'm trying, anyway."

"I'm glad." My heart swells with pride. This is a huge opportunity for her.

"While you were out, some boy called for you." She levels her eyes at me. "I think his name was Dean? He asked me if I could have you call him back."

"Ugh." When Nick was growing up, girls would call the house for him all the time, but that was before cell phones. It may be lost on Dreamy, but Dean is getting pretty desperate to call our landline. I push myself up, and my chair scrapes along the floor. I walk over to the cabinet and grab a glass, then pour myself some water from the pitcher in the refrigerator. "Did you ask him how he got this number?"

"I did not. There's this thing called the phone book, you know." Dreamy watches me, eyebrows raised, as I take a sip. "But it did make me realize that I haven't heard from Marcus in a while."

"Yeah." I take a long, cool gulp.

"It must be a couple of months since he's been over here." Dreamy stares at me, and I turn away. Has it been that long since we've really talked? She waits. I refill my glass and sigh. It's going to have to come out sooner or later.

"Marcus and I broke up." I flop back onto the chair and put my glass on the table. "A while ago. I'm not really sure what happened."

"Was it a mutual thing?"

I shake my head. "I don't know. Not really." I slide a coaster under my glass. "I kind of made him do it, which I thought would be easier, but . . ."

"I'm sorry, honey." Dreamy shakes her head and seems to be lost in her own thoughts for a moment. "You don't seem that upset about it though."

I trace my finger along the cool fog on the glass, making a Z.

"I am. Or was." I bite my lip, picturing his sad face on that day. "Am."

Dreamy taps the end of her pen on the table. "Zoe, do you want to be with Marcus?"

I move onto an O, sliding my finger along the smooth surface of the glass, trying to make a perfect circle. I feel like I'm
being cross-examined.

"No." I shake my head. "I guess not."

"I didn't think so."

"Huh?"

"Honey." Dreamy laughs. "I'm your mother. I know you
pretty well." She clears her throat.

I look back down at the table. She couldn't mean . . . I
feel my cheeks flush. All those nights on the porch, when I
thought everyone was asleep.

"I wait up for you, Zoe." She shushes me before I have a
chance to get indignant. "I don't mean to. It's not like that.
But I'm a mother, and I can't fall asleep until I know you're
safe at home. So I knew there was someone new."

There's really not enough room on my glass for an E, but I
try to squeeze it in anyway.

"There's nothing wrong with it. You've changed. You've
grown up. And Marcus." She collects her papers into a neat
stack. "Well, Marcus is young. He's a good guy, and you got
lucky to have him as your first boyfriend, but—"

I underline the whole name and accidentally wipe out the
bottom rung of the E. "I did really like him. I'm not one of
those girls who—"

"I know you did." Dreamy's voice is low and soothing. "But
that doesn't mean you had to stay together forever once you
stopped caring about him."

"But he's so nice. He never, ever did anything wrong," I say
before I can stop myself. "I tried to stay with him. I didn't
want to hurt him."

"And that probably ended up hurting him more in the end," she says quietly. I nod. She puts her pen down and leans forward a bit.

"You guys are teenagers. Some people get it right on their first try, but most don't, and that's okay."

I don't answer.

"Zoe, look at me."

I peer up at her, clutching my cool glass.

"I have no idea who you'll end up with or how you'll get there, honey. But I can tell you one thing. You'll know. When the right person comes along, you won't have to ask yourself whether it's right. We were made to love, designed for it. That's part of how God put us together. And when you find the right person, every cell in your body will know it."

She stares into my eyes so intensely I have to look away. I wipe out my whole name with my balled-up fist.

"But relationships fall apart all the time." I start to choke up, but I force myself to get the words out. "Even when people 'know' and promise to stay together forever, sometimes they end up screwing the whole thing up."

Dreamy takes several deep breaths before she opens her mouth, but even then she stumbles over her words.

"Marriage is hard, Zoe, and it's . . . it's a lifelong commitment. And sometimes, it doesn't work out the way you'd hope. But sometimes it does. Your father and I . . ." She waits so long I'm almost afraid she's not going to go on, but then quietly she does. I hold my breath. "We really, really love each other."

My hopes soar, just a little.

"We're going to try." She picks up her pen again and starts

drawing square, even boxes on her paper. "I don't know what it's going to look like, but we're going to try to make it work again. I know you were fighting for this."

"I—"

"I knew what you were doing, and I appreciate it." She reaches across the table and puts her hand under my chin. She tilts my head up, forcing me to look into her eyes. "Without you trying to make us keep going, we would never be giving it one more shot."

"What about the divorce?"

"It may still happen. But your father, your sweet, stubborn father, never signed the papers." She shakes her head as tears spring to her eyes. "We all want it to work out, but there are no guarantees. I need you to keep fighting for us."

I nod. The ticking of the kitchen clock is the only sound for a few minutes.

"But you and Marcus, that's different. It didn't work out, and that's okay. You've got plenty more shots at love in your future." She reaches for my hand. "Maybe it's time you forgive yourself."

I let her words sink in for a moment. Maybe she's right. I need to forgive myself and I need to . . . oh my. How have I not done that yet? I think about Marcus, how heartbroken he looked that day I chose Dean in the quad, and I know there's something else I need to do.

"So if Marcus is out of the picture, are you skipping the prom?" Dreamy stands up and puts her application papers into a manila envelope on the counter.

I put my head on the kitchen table for a moment and groan. "I don't know if I want to go. It seems like a waste of money."

"Maybe this other guy would want to go?"

I snort. "Trust me, you only say that because you have no idea." Dean would never go to the prom. He's made that abundantly clear—and I'm not going to the prom with him, for sure.

"You should go, Zo. You're only young once."

"Well." I sit up a little. "Riley wants the Miracle Girls to go together, but I can't find a dress that I like and now I'm kind of wondering if it's a sign I shouldn't go."

"I'll take you shopping. I might be able to help you find something."

I don't know how to respond. It's not that I don't want to go with her but, well, I don't want her to spend money on something like this.

"Maybe I can borrow something from Riley." I'm several inches taller than Riley, and she's more athletic, but it's all I can think of at the moment to get her off my trail.

Dreamy's eyes go glassy, and she looks like she's somewhere far away. Then it's like she comes to, and she stands up suddenly. "I don't know if this would interest you or not," she says, walking into the living room. I hear the stairs start to vibrate, and I realize she's headed up to the second floor. I don't know what else to do, so I follow her.

I find her digging in the back of her closet. I sit down on the edge of her water bed, and she comes out with a big cardboard box.

"Maybe these are way out of fashion now, I don't know. I think these are the kinds of things kids are wearing again." Oh no. Her old clothes. I brace myself for some hideous seventies psychedelic monstrosities. My mother has never kept up on fashion, even in current times. There's no way her old clothes from thirty-five years ago are going to work. "If you wanted to try them on, you're welcome to." She opens the box and begins pulling out dresses.

I hold up the first one and suck in my breath. It's actually cute. It's mod, with a wide band of fabric around the neck and a matching swath at the bottom of the short skirt. It's not formal enough for prom, but it's totally cool.

"You had this in the closet all this time?"

She keeps digging, pulling out layers and layers of old clothes. I lift up a light blue dress that drapes over the shoulders and a short tennis-style skirt.

"Aha." She reaches down to the bottom of the box and pulls out a long, soft bluish-green dress with a structured bodice and spaghetti straps. When she holds it up, it hangs beautifully, and it's so simple it's elegant. I take it from her and stand up, pressing it against my body.

"I know it's not what you'd find in the stores these days, but your grandmother made it for my prom."

"No, it's beautiful." I walk to the bedroom door and pull it shut, holding the dress up in front of me in the full-length mirror on the back of the door. It's not like the sparkly, bright dresses everyone else will be wearing, but it's beautiful fabric—it feels like silk—and it's gorgeous in its simplicity. "I love it." It smells like mothballs, but we can fix that.

"Let's see if it fits," Dreamy says, ushering me into the bathroom off her bedroom. I come out a few minutes later with the dress on, my bra straps peeking out of the top, and I look in the mirror. It fits like it was made for me, which I guess makes sense because it was made for my mom when she was my age.

"You're a little taller than I was, but I can let out the bottom a bit." Dreamy crosses her arms over her chest, but I can see that she's pleased too.

I run my fingers down the smooth silk. It feels kind of weird to be wearing her dress, but somehow wearing it makes me feel like I understand a little bit more of what made my mother into the woman she is. For some reason, that feels right.

47

've helped Nick pack up every last article of clothing he owns and drive it over to his new apartment. I've helped Dreamy vacuum and straighten up his room. I've slogged through all my homework, even double-checking my answers in trig. And then, when the sun starts slipping behind the ridge of the treetops, I know it's time. I've put it off for as long as I can.

The fastest way to get to the Farcus house is a path Marcus cut through the woods when he first moved in. He drove me crazy that first summer, always showing up at the most random times with some kind of flimsy excuse. He had to borrow a cup of sugar, or he found some new kind of insect he just had to show me, or he would like me to come and watch *Trekkies* with him. Eventually I couldn't remember what my life was like before he came along.

The April air is warm and dry, and it's already starting to feel like summer again around here. The path is a little overgrown, so I pick my way over it carefully, but I still make it to the hard-packed dirt road sooner than I want to. Twilight casts a purple glow over the forest, and as I get close to Marcus's house, I hear the sound of splashing water, just like I knew I would. Marcus is nothing if not consistent.

I break through the trees into the clearing around the house and lift the latch on the gate. Marcus is cutting through the shimmering surface of the water in smooth, even strokes. When he gets to the end of the pool, he executes a perfect flip turn and starts heading back the other way, a regular Michael Phelps in training. He turns his head to breathe every other stroke. I know he sees me, but I also know better than to think he's going to interrupt his workout. I sit down on one of the wrought-iron chairs placed around the outdoor table. I can wait.

The soft sound of the water lapping up around the edge is soothing in its regularity, its familiarity. I've missed lazy summer evenings by the pool. I watch as Marcus crisscrosses the water, slicing into its surface cleanly with each stroke.

I've only been waiting about ten minutes when Marcus slows his pace, does a few more leisurely laps, and touches the wall triumphantly. He stands up and lifts his goggles off his eyes, then drops them on the cement. Without a word, he steps out of the pool, wraps himself in a beach towel, slides his feet into flip-flops, and walks toward me.

Maybe I haven't really looked at him recently, or maybe he finally hit that magical growth spurt boys seem to stumble upon, but he's taller now, and not nearly as lanky. He's still Marcus, still thin and pale, but there are signs of change . . . particularly growing out of his chest. I look away, trying not to notice.

The chair scrapes against the pavement when he pulls it back, and he sits down and waits.

"Marcus." His hair is slicked back by the water, and there's something wiser around his eyes. I frown, realizing that I fed him his first bite of betrayal. "I'm sorry."

He lifts his chin and pulls his towel around his shoulders tightly.

"I never meant to hurt you, but I did, and I know it, and it was horrible of me. I—" I have the urge to reach out and touch him, but I'm afraid of having him pull away, so I leave my hands twisting awkwardly in my lap. "I care about you. But—" I'm digging myself into a hole here. "I'm sorry. I guess that's what I really came here to say."

Droplets of water are dripping off Marcus's swimming trunks and collecting in little puddles at the base of the chair.

"I know, Zoe." Marcus runs his hand through his hair, squeezing out the water. "I know you're a good person, and I know you were trying to do the right thing."

My breath catches in my throat. How could I have broken up with this guy, who is better to me than I ever deserved? I'm a fool to let him go. For one crazy instant, I have the urge to lean over and kiss him, right here and now, just to see. Maybe sparks would fly. Maybe I would discover that I love him with every cell of my body after all.

But before I can stop it, Dean's face pops into my head, and I understand with a certainty I could never explain that it's not going to work with Marcus. I may never find another guy like him, but it's over. I have to let him go.

"I just . . . I would do it all over again, if I could." I shake my head. What am I saying? "I would have done it better, and I would have been more honest, and I would have . . ."

Marcus's eyes are watering, and I don't think it's from the chlorine.

"I know, Zoe." He stands up suddenly and adjusts his towel on his shoulders, and before I know what's happening, he leans in and plants a light kiss on my cheek. Then, without a word, he turns and walks back around to the other side of the pool. His heels squeak against his wet flip-flops, and he leaves a trail of footprints across the cement as he makes his way toward the door. The glass door to his living room slides closed behind him, and I sit there for a few minutes, watching the lights from the house play across the glassy surface of the water before I head for home.

48

"ean, wait up!" I wave good-bye to Christine after class and jog after him. Now that I've apologized to Marcus, I can deal with this. I catch up to him, and he keeps his eyes on the exit of the hall.

"Hey, I need to talk to you." I poke his shoulder with my finger.

Dean scrunches his nose up a little. "I'm late for class." He makes a break for the door, but I chase after him.

"Listen." I catch his arm, and he stops. "I'm sorry about everything. I was upset, but I can see that you're sorry and that you get it now."

He turns back to me, his top lip in an ugly snarl. "You want to know why I was calling?"

I swallow, suddenly aware that it wasn't any of the reasons I had secretly hoped. He shakes his head at me. "I wanted to tell you you've been right from the beginning. I was wrong, and I shouldn't have treated you like that. Either of you."

A bit of my hair falls in front of my face, and I look up at him from under it. "Right, but I was kind of—"

"And I wanted to say that I get the message, and I'll stop." He takes a few strides into the morning light.

"No. Wait."

"Also, I'm emancipating the poor citizens of Zoeville." He pulls a stack of papers out of his bag and holds them up. It's our constitution. "No more serfs."

"What?"

"Forty acres and a mule for everyone." He rips the paper in half, hands me the scraps, and turns on his heel and walks off. He's almost to the corner before I manage to make my mouth work again.

"It was a democracy!" I yell. He doesn't turn around.

He always does this. He gets me so turned around I can't figure out what I was trying to say in the first place.

♡

"You know what I heard?" I can't take this silence anymore. I have to talk about something, even if it is the weather. "Ed called this morning and said it was supposed to rain . . . hard."

Christine shields the bright afternoon sun from her eyes and snorts. "I'll believe it when my trick knee starts acting up."

Around us people are cheering, slapping hands, and blaring music from their car stereos. School will be out in just a few weeks, and you can feel the excitement in the air. But even though everybody else is high on the promise of summer freedom, the Miracle Girls are shapeless lumps of self-pity—and I'm probably the biggest lump. I have nothing to look forward to but a hot summer of shoveling horse poop and marinating in meat fumes.

"It must be bad if we haven't heard anything yet," Riley says. No one has to ask what she's talking about. "Surely she's had her interview by now."

"Of course she has, and they've probably snatched her up already." Ana adjusts her sweatshirt. She's balled it up and is using it as a pillow against the windshield of Christine's car. "She has an Ivy League degree, and she's any administrator's dream come true. We might as well start getting used to the idea of not having her around anymore."

"Maybe she won't get the job. Maybe they'll hear about the case and be scared off." My feet rest on the front bumper.

"I'm not sure whether to hope you're right or not. Both options seem pretty disloyal." Christine blows a bubble with her chewing gum. Ana reaches out to pop it, but Christine sucks it in at the last second.

I let my eyes rest on the high gray walls of the gym at the other end of the lot. The student government has already started hanging decorations inside for the prom. It still doesn't feel real. Prom is one of those things you always dream about as a kid, but it never feels like it will actually happen.

"It didn't exactly turn out like we hoped, huh?" Riley says quietly. I'm not sure whether she means the Ms. Moore thing or the year in general. Both are true enough, I guess. I remember the four of us lying here on the first day of school, our heads filled with big dreams about what we were going to do this year. We were so sure we were going to save Ms. Moore. We were the Miracle Girls, and we could do anything.

No one answers her.

I let my eyes focus on the long chain-link fence that runs around the perimeter of the parking lot. What will Marina Vista look like now that she's gone? I try to imagine it, and it surprises me how easy it is. The thing is, Ms. Moore has been out of the classroom for a year now. We raised some attention for her cause at different points this year, but she's been away for a long time. We've moved on without her. We didn't want to do it, but we have learned to survive.

I'm so lost in my thoughts I don't even notice when the huge white Hummer pulls up next to us.

"Get in." Ashley doesn't even wait for the window to roll down all the way before she starts talking.

Christine props herself up on her elbows and squints at her. "Huh?"

"I'll explain on the way." Ashley pushes a button, and I hear the back doors unlock. "Just get in the car."

Ashley's hair is scraped back into a messy ponytail, and while she's not exactly what I would call calm even on her best days, she is very agitated now. I look around, but the other girls seem to be as confused as I am.

"Where are we going?" Ana says, shaking her head.

Ashley bites her lip. "Please. I need you guys."

Riley glances at me and raises her eyebrows. I lift my shoulders, just a little bit. I have no idea what to do either. Finally, Ana jumps off the hood.

"How much more trouble could we get in anyway?" She yanks open Ashley's back door. "They already threw the book at us." Ana's already in some serious trouble, and if I'm honest, it could be a lot worse, but if Ana's in, I'm in. That's the thing about being a Miracle Girl. We're not just all in this together. We've all been in this together from the beginning, even before we knew it.

Riley scrambes into the front seat. A second later, Christine is crawling into the backseat, and I'm right behind her. I've barely had a chance to close the door before Ashley guns the engine and takes off across the parking lot.

♡

I'm starting to understand the appeal of SUVs. They're still gas-guzzling monstrosities that are terrible for the environment, and Dreamy would never in a million years approve if she knew where I was right now, but man oh man is this leather soft. And even though there are five of us in this thing, there's tons of room for us to spread out.

Still, I can't relax until Ashley gives us some sort of hint about where we're headed, and even then, her answer isn't exactly comforting: San Francisco.

Dreamy and Ed are going to kill me.

She fills us in on the details as we zip around the steep mountain curves that lead out of town toward the big freeway. The way Ashley is taking these bends, I'm thankful this car is basically a tank.

She just discovered that her dad has to file the final papers to settle the case against the school board by five p.m. today. That gives us—I crane my neck to see the numbers on the stereo—an hour and a half to convince him to change his mind.

As we race up the freeway in the carpool lane, Riley tries to get as many answers as she can out of Ashley. No, her dad doesn't know we're coming. No, she didn't realize there was still time to make him change his mind until today, when she found some messages in his inbox. Yes, she logged into his e-mail. No, she didn't have a plan for what we would do once we got there.

But as the dry, rolling hills of the South Bay morph into the cityscape around us, there's still one question that stands out in my mind.

"Ashley?" My voice sounds thin and high-pitched, but Ashley navigates the snarling traffic with ease. We turn down California Street and the canyon-like walls of the buildings surround us. "What about us?" She swerves around a taxi stopped in the right lane, and I grab the door handle. "I mean, I'm thrilled, don't get me wrong, and it's awesome that you're finally going to stand up to your dad, but why did you need us to come?"

Ashley doesn't take her eyes off the road as she weaves through the jam-packed traffic. "You guys didn't tell anyone. Even when you could have, you didn't. If it had been the other way around, I don't know if I would have been as loyal."

She yanks the wheel to the left and barrels into the entrance to an underground parking garage. Seconds later we're careening down a ramp into the bowels of a big San Francisco office building.

"Maybe I just need someone there with me to make sure I go through with this," she finally finishes. "And I have this sense that whether I like it or not, we're all in this together."

Riley meets my eyes in the rearview mirror, and I nod. I guess we've probably all known that for a while. Somehow, in these past few months, Ashley has wound her way into the middle of everything and brought us together in a way we never would have predicted. She's not really one of us, but she's a part of it too.

Ashley whips the wheel to the right and pulls into a space much too narrow for her giant car. She stomps the brake, puts the car in park, and turns off the engine.

"Maybe, when it comes down to it," she says in the silence that follows, "I need a miracle too."

49

The elevator doors open on the fifth floor, and we walk into the waiting room. This place smells like flowers and antiseptic. The heavy-set woman at the front desk smiles at us, but Ashley doesn't stop; she walks right on by the patients waiting in plastic chairs, opens the door to the back of the office, and barrels down the hallway that branches off to the right. The receptionist calls after us, but we don't slow down. I turn and give an apologetic wave before we disappear around the corner.

There are exam rooms on our right, but Ashley walks past them, directly to the office at the end of the hallway, and steps inside. The rest of us fill in the doorway behind her. Dr. Anderson is wearing a white lab coat and sitting behind a heavy wooden desk. He looks up from the computer screen, his eyes wide.

"Hey there," he says, turning. "Good to see you. Uh . . ." He nods at the rest of us. "I don't know if this is the best time for a visit. I have a few patients waiting."

"Dad, I want you to drop the case," Ashley says, planting her hands on her hips. "I never wanted you to sue the school in the first place, but this has gone way too far."

Dr. Anderson rears back in his office chair, and the metal wheels roll back a few inches on the tile floor.

"I know you think I'm only a kid and don't know what's best for me, and I know you think you're out there righting wrongs or whatever, but I cared about Ms. Moore. She was the only one who ever listened to me, and now because of you she's gone."

Dr. Anderson waits for her to finish, then sits up slowly. He takes a pen out of the pocket of his lab coat and rolls it around in his fingers.

"Ashley, why didn't you say something before?" His brow wrinkles. "I thought . . ." He shakes his head. "You're the one who told me about it. You seemed so certain she was in the wrong."

"I know," Ashley says, letting out a breath. "I did, and I was wrong. I was angry about—well, about everything, and I thought this would be a way to make it better." She takes another step closer to his desk. "But I never expected her to get fired, or for this whole thing to go as far as it has. I should have said something to you a long time ago, I know, but I was afraid to—I was afraid of having you be mad at me and disappointing you, and now I know maybe it's too late, but I want you to stop."

Ashley stops to catch her breath after her tirade, and though I'm not sure I totally understood much of what she said, I'm proud of her. A month ago she was scared to death of telling her father the truth, and now she's managed to get it all out in one breath.

"We do too," Christine says.

Ashley's dad narrows his eyes at her. I brace myself, waiting for him to start screaming. He's been the maniacal bad guy in my mind for so long I hadn't envisioned any other possible reaction. But he's sitting here now, staring at his daughter, looking for all the world as if he's only trying to figure out how to make her happy.

"Would you excuse us?" Dr. Anderson says, gritting his teeth. He gestures at the four of us in the doorway. "My daughter and I need to have a little talk."

Ashley is chewing her lip, but she nods, and the rest of us step out of the way. A moment later, the office door slams.

"Would you care to wait in the reception area?" A woman in mint green scrubs appears behind us. She gestures toward the waiting room, her hand encased in a rubber glove. We take the hint and troop back into the lobby, falling into the overstuffed chairs arranged around a miniature coffee table. The receptionist offers us some coffee, then leaves us to page through magazines while we wait.

The others page through copies of *House Beautiful* and *Good Housekeeping*. Riley scores an old *People* with a smiling blond couple on the cover. The receptionist calls the other patients up to the desk one at a time and explains that Dr. Anderson has been unavoidably delayed.

Eventually, we all get so bored that I decide to get started on my history assignment. As part of our final project, Mrs. Narveson wants us to write about one movement in America that changed the course of history. I think she means for us to write about Abolition, or Civil Rights, or the fight for the 19th Amendment, which gave women the right to vote. But I'm going to do this my own way. I'm writing about the Jesus Movement and how it changed the direction of the Christian church, and, perhaps more important, how it changed the direction of my parents' lives. I don't think she'll mind. She's the one who told us that to understand a person you have to understand their past. If I really want to walk the long road that brought my parents to where they are, I need to start at the beginning.

I'm scratching out an outline on a pad of paper the receptionist gave me when the nurses leave for the day. I breathe a sigh of relief when I realize it's after five. Too late for anyone to be filing the papers. But it's another hour before Ashley and Dr. Anderson appear in the waiting room. Her eyes are red and her face is puffy and her hair is pressed up against her head in crazy angles, but she's smiling.

Dr. Anderson turns and gives her a long hug, holding her in his arms tightly. "I'll see you this weekend, sweetie," he says, his voice raspy. "I love you." He bites his lip and turns back toward his office, but not before I see that his eyes are rimmed in red too.

Ashley waits until he disappears down the hall.

"We did it," she says. She hasn't even finished saying the words before we've all thrown our arms around her.

50

took the girls out to celebrate our victory. One hundred dollars may not buy a very nice dress, but it can buy a whole lot of In-N-Out and some gas too. It seems like kind of a waste—that's more than twenty hours at El Bueno Burrito down the tubes—but for a new chapter for the Miracle Girls, well, somehow it doesn't even seem like quite enough.

We called Ms. Moore on the way to tell her the good news, but she warned us that she had a lot of thinking to do. She's been offered the job in Boston, and there's no guarantee Marina Vista would take her back after everything. We decide to ignore her pessimism. We moved mountains this year with just the tiniest bit of faith. We'll get her back.

Ashley drops us off at the school so the others can get their cars. I hop out too. I have something else I need to do. The early evening sky is dark and obscured by clouds, and the air feels electric, like victory, or like possibility. Maybe both.

"You sure, Zoe?" Ashley glances up at the threatening thunderheads. "It's going to start pouring any minute."

I look up at the heavens and smile as I say a quick prayer of thanks. It does look like rain. Maybe the tension is breaking at last. Maybe things can only stay bad for so long before the sky opens up and rains down a new promise.

"Thanks, Ash." I hold out my palm but don't feel any drops yet. "I'm sort of hoping to get caught in the rain."

Eventually they give up and resign themselves to the fact that I want to walk home in the downpour. Riley winks at me in a knowing way, proving that sometimes we can read each other's minds. I wait until they have piled into their cars and disappeared out the parking lot gate before I start walking.

The streets are quiet, the sky is heavy with clouds, and there's a devilish wind rustling the leaves on the trees. As I leave the school property behind, a huge clap of thunder peals through the air. I freeze, the hair standing up on my arms. Then I hear a patter, coming up fast behind me. I spin on my heels and see the storm coming toward me, the drops falling hard and leaving little divots in the dry, dusty earth. It sweeps over the PE fields and then drenches the J-wing. I bend my head back, shut my eyes, and stick out my tongue, and within moments the rain is pattering all around me, soaking my hair, my clothes, my bag. Tiny rivers run down my hair and onto my face. The rain tastes sweet and smells incredible, earthy and wet.

Something about the excitement of the storm, or the certainty of what I need to do, compels me forward. I begin to barrel toward his house, weaving through our little town like only a local can, ducking down back alleys, taking a shortcut through the park, enjoying the first serious soaker we've had in almost a year, splashing and laughing.

I'm at his house in no time. I walk right up to his yard. The rest of the house is dark and still, but the light in his room is on and the window is cracked.

I swallow. Why did I come here? What did I want to know? I see a shadow move across the wall in his room, and I stumble back on the step. The rain continues to pour, as if this whole year it had only been holding itself back, growing and gaining strength for the day when it would burst forth. I shut my eyes and hold my face up to the sky.

I came here for answers. Who is this guy who showed up from the other side of the country, headstrong and independent? What is he really? Is he the best thing that ever happened to me? Or is he bad news, someone who will only leave me with tears and heartbreak? Is he the grieving son of a loving family and an earnest musician, or is he just another teenage rebel and part-time rock star who will never amount to anything?

The rain drums loudly in my ear, but over it I can barely make out a sweet and mournful sound, beautiful notes that feel so right for this moment. I shake my head and squint through the sheets of rain. The sound is coming from his room. I take a few steps closer, and as I near the sound swells in my ears. The saxophone.

For a while I simply listen to him play, lost to the world as I stare up at his window. I stop thinking about all my fears and all the ups and downs we've been through this year, and I allow myself to just enjoy Dean. I picture his face in my mind, and watch his shadow on the wall, and listen to his music. His mother was right. It's a shame he gave it up.

The sound abruptly stops, and I lean in to make sure it's not the roar of the rain drowning it out. There's a shuffling in the room, and suddenly I realize that I'm standing on Dean's lawn like some sort of madwoman, soaked to the bone. I meant to walk right up, ring the doorbell, and have a nice long chat with him.

The front door unlocks, and I take off at a dash without thinking—but then stop a few feet away. I should apologize and try to explain to his mom so they don't think I'm crazy.

But it isn't his mom. I think I glimpse her in the background, but it's Dean at the door. We lock eyes. He steps out onto the porch and shuts the door.

I stay right where I am in the middle of the yard, my heart pounding. He said he was through with me. Why can't I take a hint? How much clearer could he be?

I can't read his face as he strides toward me. I want to turn and run away, but I can't make myself. The weight of the water on my clothes makes me feel hundreds of pounds heavier, frozen in place.

He walks over to me, grabs my face in both of his hands, and pulls me in for a kiss so deep and long that even though I am on another planet, happier than I ever thought possible, I still have time to come back to earth and relish it.

He stops and grabs me into a tight, tangled, desperate hug. In the middle, between our faces, we create a small cave where only the occasional raindrop falls. For a very long time we just listen to each other breathe short, gasping breaths of joy and relief and wonder. It may be the greatest pleasure I have ever known.

So this is love.

51

recognize the song from the first loud, brash notes. Some of the kids in the class roll their eyes when Mrs. Narveson starts playing the track, and it does seem a bit weird to end her lecture about the Vietnam War by playing a song used to protest against it. But I can't help smiling. "Revolution" is Ed's favorite Beatles song.

There are only two weeks of school left, and since next week will be taken up with testing and end-of-the-year stuff, this will be Mrs. Narveson's last lecture. I'm kind of impressed that we made it as far as we did in the textbook. No teacher in the history of teaching history has made it up to the present day, but we only missed it by a few decades.

As the familiar song blasts out across the quiet classroom, I close my eyes and try to imagine what it must have been like for my parents when this song first came out: storming the streets of Berkeley, standing up against an unjust war, fighting to make their voices heard. This song is all about challenging the people in power to build a better world. Now, more than ever before, I have an inkling of what that really means, and I know that I have big shoes to fill.

"Don't you know it's gonna *be* . . . all right," Mrs. Narveson sings, closing her eyes and grooving to the music. She repeats the words *all right* again and again, just like John Lennon, and then when the song ends, she waits for a minute with her eyes closed before she turns off the speakers on the iPod dock.

I peek at Christine, who has bags under her eyes and a wistful expression on her face. Her new brother, Ellis, was born late last night. Then I steal a glance at Dean, who winks at me, and I start to feel like maybe Mrs. Narveson is right. Things aren't perfect. The world isn't fair, or just, or kind, and there are no guarantees it's going to get better. But somehow, I do believe it's going to be all right.

Mrs. Narveson takes a few steps over to the window and spends a long moment staring out at the courtyard. I can hear the industrial wall clock's second hand tick in the silence.

"Every year I leave my students with one parting thought." She looks out at us, really looks at us, studying each and every student one by one. "There is so much I hope you learned this year, and it's not facts or battles or some long list of president names." She walks back to her podium and shakes her head, almost sadly. "I hope you've seen the human struggle played out on the stage of your minds. I hope you've felt connected to many cultures across time. I hope, in some small way, you've learned what it means to be American and what it means to be a citizen of the world." She points at the door and bites her lip. "Because this is your world, and when you walk out that door, you get to start making decisions about what kind of place it's going to be. You carry with you the stories of your past, of all of our pasts, but it's up to you what you do with this knowledge."

She locks eyes with me and smiles a little. I could swear she's tearing up. "Go out and make history. And make me proud."

52

The Miracle Girls are supposed to be here in fifteen minutes, but my hair won't lie down and be nice and straight like it's supposed to. It doesn't matter how many times I press it with my straightening iron, the curls still insist on poking out in weird ways.

I sort of assumed we would all get ready together, preferably at a house where people own things like eye shadow and hair spray, but Dreamy really wanted to see me all dolled up and for some reason Ana couldn't come get me any earlier, so here I am, struggling against the elements, on my own. Dreamy keeps running around handing me things like witch hazel and cold cream, and I don't have even the slightest idea what to do with them.

I'm giving my hair one last attempt. If it decides not to cooperate this time I will succumb to the inevitable. I wrap a front section around the base of the straightening iron and study my reflection in the mirror. The dress is gorgeous, and it skims my hips a little before falling in a straight line to my feet. I can't stop looking at it.

Ed pokes his head around the wall and snaps a picture. He's been doing this all evening. Normally it would be driving me crazy, but I still can't help but marvel at his very presence around here. Every silly thing he does makes me want to sweep him into a big hug.

I let the section go and it's straight, sort of, so I give up. I unplug the stupid thing and flip off the bathroom light, then the doorbell rings. I hold the hem of my dress and run down the stairs as fast as my feet can move. "Ana!" I pull the front door open.

But it's not Ana.

"I was wondering if you'd do me the honor." Dean is standing on my front porch, wearing a classic tuxedo with a black vest and shiny black shoes. He holds out an elegant white wrist corsage, and I just stand there with my mouth gaping open.

"Where's Ana?"

Dean smiles and pops open the plastic container. He holds the white orchid up to my dress and smiles. "I wanted to surprise you, so it was hard to choose the right one."

Ed pops his head out of the house and adjusts the lens on the camera. Dean gives him a thumbs-up and a cheesy smile, and Ed snaps a picture.

"Oh!" Ed pops his head back in. "Dreamy? Where's the video camera?" He disappears back inside.

"Ed . . ." I whine, my head still spinning. Dean hates prom. I never thought he'd want to come. How will I explain this to the girls? I don't want to hurt him or them.

"You know, it's really weird how you call your parents by their first names." Dean slips the corsage on my wrist, and my stomach warms when his warm hand lingers on mine. "Has anyone ever told you that?"

I shake my head, trying to make sense of what's going on. Okay, Zoe, use your mouth. "What are you doing here?"

"I'm taking you to the prom." Dean rolls his eyes and gestures at his monkey suit. "You think I dress like this all the time?"

"I'm going with the Miracle Girls." I cross my arms over my chest even while I'm trying to figure out exactly how much trouble I'd be in if I ditched them now. A lot, I decide.

"We'll see about that." Dean leans in and plants a kiss on my cheek, and despite myself, I feel my stomach flip. This is so like him to waltz in at the last minute and sweep me off my feet. And yet, as romantic as it is, it's a tad inconvenient.

"Now, if you'd asked me like a normal person would, maybe I'd have considered it."

"Zoe, up until a few nights ago, I thought you hated my guts." Dean scratches his chin and lets a slow smile spread across his face.

I smile at the mention of that night in the rain. "Right." I guess I was mad at him. Well, I did give him that impression at least. "Maybe I still hate your guts." I raise an eyebrow.

Instead of answering, Dean leans in and wraps his arms around me. "I don't believe you," he whispers into my ear, sending chills down my spine. I let myself lean in against him and forget what we were even talking about. I run my hands down his arms and then pull him in tighter. I hear a noise behind Dean, but he's pulling my face toward him, and I can't be bothered to pull away to see what it is. A horn blasts right behind us.

"Woo-woo!" I turn in time to see Ana yelling out the open window of the RealMobile. Riley is sticking her head out the driver's side window making kissing noises. "Zoe and Dean, sittin' in a tree."

Ana sings out the other window. "K-I-S-S-I-N-G."

I feel my cheeks burn. Oh my gosh.

"I thought you guys were coming in Ana's car." It's lame, but it's the only thing I can make my mouth say. Dean laughs and takes my hand in his in a comfortable way, like we've been together for ages.

"Not enough seats," Ana calls. "And they wouldn't go for a limo, so here we are, arriving in style."

"Um . . ." I can't exactly not go with Dean after all that, but I can't ditch the girls either. Why does he do this to me?

"Come on, lovebirds." Ana jerks her thumb toward the back door of the van. "Get in."

Dean pulls my arm gently and leads me off the porch.

"Dean." I pull back. "We don't . . . do you want to go with them?"

"Yeah, how awesome is this ride?" He motions at the side of the RealMobile.

I throw back my head and laugh. Someone—Christine, I'm sure—has replaced Riley's mom's real estate ads with new magnets. They say:

🅟🅡🅞🅜 🅦🅞🅞

Dreamy and Ed come running out of the house with our ancient video camera and begin to film everything. Dean is a great sport, showing them how to get a decent shot.

But I stand back and absorb the perfection of the moment. My parents acting like they love each other. Dean bonding with the most important people in my life and doing something for me, just because it will make me happy. And all my best friends in one place, looking like a million bucks.

"Ready?" Dean puts out a hand, and I take it. We smile for the video camera one last time.

"You guys get the middle row," Riley says, pressing the button to open the back door. The door slides open, and I gasp.

"Hey, Tyler."

"Yo." He waves from the backseat, where he and Christine are squished together, holding hands. His shaggy blond hair is sun-kissed and styled with the slightest hint of gel.

"Do you guys have anyone else stashed away in here?"

"That's it." Ana laughs. She looks stunning in a lemon-colored silk gown that sets off her caramel-colored skin beautifully.

"So I guess you changed your mind?" I cock my eyebrow at Christine, who shrugs.

"He's pushy." Christine is wearing a gorgeous silk kimono-style dress in a pale, minty green. Tyler keeps pulling at the collar of his dress shirt. "Besides, once we knew you were bringing a date, we decided it would be okay to let one other guy come along with us tonight."

"Why didn't anyone bother to tell *me* I was bringing a date?" I climb into the middle row of the minivan as gracefully as possible while trying not to let go of Dean's hand.

"Where's the fun in that?" Riley pushes the button to close the door. She's got her hair piled on top of her head, and her simple black dress is elegant without being showy. She puts the car in drive and makes a U-turn, pointing the car back down the driveway, and Dreamy and Ed fade into the distance.

"Party-mix time," Ana says and pushes a button on the dashboard. "Girls Just Wanna Have Fun" comes blaring out of the speakers. She and Riley start bouncing around in the front seats.

"Oh boy." Dean lifts his eyebrows and lets out an exaggerated sigh. He turns back to face Tyler, who rolls his eyes and leans forward and asks Dean about amps.

"Come on, Zo," Riley says, watching me in the rearview mirror.

And, okay, it's cheesy, but somehow it feels right. After all the crazy things that have happened this year, all I really want to do right now is forget about the world and have fun with my friends. I put my hands up in the air and bounce around a little bit, and even Christine gets in on the action in the backseat. We sing along to the CD all the way to school. We're dancing to "Hit Me with Your Best Shot" when we pull into the parking lot, and somehow it seems kind of fitting. Life has taken some swings at us this year, but we're still standing.

Riley parks in our normal spot, and we pile out of the minivan and start walking toward the gym. It's the same old boring parking lot we see every day, and the same stupid gym, but somehow, tonight, with our classmates pouring in dressed to the nines, it seems different somehow. For tonight, anyway, we're here because we want to be. For this one evening, we're part of something special.

"Hold up, guys." Riley stops before the entrance to the gym and glances around.

"Oh no, do you have a secret date too?" Ana pretends to be exasperated, but she's loving every moment of this.

Riley laughs. "Here she comes."

I know who Riley's pointing at before I turn my head. Of course. Ashley.

Ashley is arriving with a group of cheerleaders and jocks, but she smiles when she sees us and lets the rest of her group go ahead without her. She's a part of this mixed-up group of misfits as much as any of us.

Ashley leans in and gives me a hug, her blue satin dress rustling. She looks at Dean and winks at me. Dean squeezes my hand.

"Can you guys believe we're really here? It's prom!" Ashley laughs and skips a little bit.

Part of me *can't* believe it. A year ago, I never would have envisioned being here. That shy, overweight band geek never would have wanted any of this, which is what makes me so sure God must have had it in mind all along. If I've learned anything this year, it's that God is in the business of taking our expectations and shaking them up, turning them around, and rearranging the pieces in a way we never could have thought possible.

I look around at the faces of my best friends, lit up with excitement. This year hasn't turned out anything like we thought it would, but we're here, the four of us, and we're stronger for it. We've fought together, and we've cried together, and we've grown. And, I realize with a start, it's not really just the four of us anymore.

Maybe it never really was.

All along I've thought of the Miracle Girls as this closed circle, this special group called for some big task. But maybe the miracle isn't that the four of us found each other that lonely day in detention. Maybe it's always been much bigger than that. What I haven't noticed, what I didn't see all this time, is that God has brought others into our circle too, adding to our number, layering on experiences and memories and possibilities, in ways we never could have dreamed.

He has added, and he has taken away. I catch Ana's eye. We've grown, but we've also said some painful good-byes to people we never thought we would have to live without. I still hold out hope that some of these relationships will be restored—that Dreamy and Ed will be able to work things out, that Ms. Moore will be back next year—but either way, we're going to make it.

"Are you guys ready to go in?" Ashley says, bouncing from one foot to the other.

I look at Ana, Christine, and Riley, and I nod. Dean squeezes my hand, but I pull away and step forward and reach for Ana's arm. I slide my arm over her shoulder, and she grabs for Riley, who grabs Christine. Slowly, Christine reaches out and wraps her arm around Ashley.

Staring at the faces around me, I begin to understand miracles don't always look like you expect them to. Sometimes, they're even better.

Riley lets out a whoop, and we all laugh. It seems like we might make it through high school after all. I know next year, senior year, will be full of changes, but for tonight, we have each other, and that's all I need. We start moving forward, toward the door, and the music from inside the gym spills out into the warm night. I pull the Miracle Girls closer, and arm in arm, the five of us walk inside together.

about the authors

Anne Dayton graduated from Princeton and has her MA in Literature from New York University. She lives in New York City. May Vanderbilt graduated from Baylor University and has an MA in Fiction from Johns Hopkins. She lives in San Francisco. Together, they are the authors of *The Miracle Girls, Breaking Up Is Hard to Do,* and *A Little Help from My Friends.* Find out more at www.anneandmay.com.